VINLAND

THE BEGINNING

vinLand

the Beginning

R.G. Johnston

Vinland: The Beginning
Copyright © 2007, R.G. Johnston
CIPO Registration # 1044355

This is a work of fiction based loosely on the Vinland Sagas.
Names, characters, and places are products of the author's
imagination or are used fictitiously. Any resemblance to actual
events or locales or persons, living or dead, is entirely
coincidental.

Robert Johnston, P.O. Box 1713, Belleville, Ontario. K8N 5J2

www.vinlandthebeginning.com

First Paperback Edition

National Library of Canada Cataloguing In Publication
Johnston, Robert

Vinland: The Beginning / Robert Johnston
ISBN: 978-0-9782978-0-0

1. Fiction. 2. Viking. 3. Vinland

Printed in Canada

Mom
I love you very much.

Damien
Thank you for making me laugh and reminding me everyday that I can visit Never-never land.

In Memory of Eileen Piper
I miss our conversations about writing.

Mr. Loveridge
For sparking my love of English Literature.

Gary
Thank you for your support and companionship.

R.G. JOHNSTON

ᚠ

Cattle die,
kindred die,
every man is mortal;
but the good name
never dies,
of one who has done well.

Cattle die,
kindred die,
every man is mortal;
but I know one thing
that never dies:
the glory of the great deed.

Hávamál (The speech of the high one)

Thorfinn, the son of Thord Horse-Head, the son of Snorri, the son of Thord of Hofdi, looked beyond the mast of his ship, over the endless sea. Its surface heaved and dipped in the never-ending motion that only calmed at the end of the sky. He looked up the mast and could almost see the invisible touch of the wind, pushing them closer and closer to their destination. They sailed on the cold and lonely North Atlantic Ocean, owned by his people for the last one hundred years.

Thorfinn looked around. There was so much ice; white, mountainous blocks of it, like floating islands, some large enough for habitation, if it were possible for humans to survive in the desolation and the cold Atlantic temperatures. They were the colour of silver, as hard as marble and clear as cold crystal, blinding in the sun of midday and ghostly assassins in the dark of night.

He turned to the large full moon hanging off the port side. A wistful cloud gently veiled her. Every day, in ragna rökkr twilight, Thorfinn could swear by all the Valkyries in the heavens that he saw the flat, featureless coast of Vinland splitting the horizon in half. But as the sun rose, his hope changed to frustration. The morning light revealed only floating ice, glimpsed through a seemingly ever-present ocean haze with eyes blurred by yet another restless night. Now, though, the *Mimir*'s voyage was almost at an end.

It was a voyage of dreams — dreams of wealth and commerce, but even more important, exploration. With it came the unbridled adventure of fighting the numbing cold and riding the tumultuous whitecaps, the risk of capsizing always in the forefront of the adventurers' minds. Thorfinn did not have nearly the experience of many of his crew. His knowledge lay in commerce and business. But just as his crew sought acknowledgement of their brave deeds from the great families of Valhalla, Thorfinn hoped that Thor would reward his devotion.

The sleepless nights, the biting cold, baking in the scorching sun while riding the World Serpent's back — it all took its toll on the crew. At times Thorfinn felt, just as his crew did, Óðin's voice within him. It began as a whisper but soon built to a shout, its wild unpredictability threatening the crew and the voyage. *Praise to Vanir,* he thought, *for coming just in time to intervene and calm the brain.* And as Gudrid always said, it kept them reliable, civilized, and down to earth. Thor had to be faced, not feared; that was how he judged the worthy from the rest.

Gudrid is right. Thorfinn smiled. He had picked well when he asked her father-in-law, Eirik the Red, his respected and great friend, for his daughter's hand in marriage. And she had done well to agree to marry him. They were equals in marriage and equals on the ocean. Thorfinn didn't know what had first attracted him to Gudrid, but over the course of their twenty-one dægur voyage, Thorfinn had realized that Frey and Freyja had smiled upon them both. The house of Vanir had truly ordained their relationship and their love.

The deck of the *Mimir* was almost empty; most of the oarsmen had taken shelter below for a meagre few hours of restless sleep before being called back to the oars. About a dozen men remained on deck, some huddled in small groups in the full glow of the moon, backs against the chests of personal effects that doubled as seats when they rowed. Others stood looking off into the moonlit night, letting their thoughts drift with the motion of the ocean to the homes where wives and children waited, or wondering what awaited them in the new and alien land they approached. Would it be like Grœnlandia, or was it indeed the land of wine?

Thorfinn decided to take a walk around the knarr. Making himself visible was good for morale, and now was a good time. He moved between his men, exchanging words with some, nodding to others, gripping a shoulder here, slapping a back there.

He stopped when he saw Adam of Bremen standing by the steerboard, talking to Harald, the *Mimir's* helmsman. Thorfinn wasn't too sure what Adam was doing on this trip, and he didn't question a direct request from his king, but to him, the monk was as unwelcome as the religion he represented.

"I relieve you, Harald," Thorfinn commanded, ignoring the monk as he approached the steerboard side of the boat.

"Yes, Thorfinn."

Harald rose and moved away, Adam at his elbow. Thorfinn took Harald's place, relieved that the monk had opted to continue his conversation with the steersman. He turned the tiller and headed away from the moon.

The sea seemed calm and unimposing tonight. He heard the growlers just below the surface of the water thudding against the hull of the knarr and scraping along its length. They were not large, but over time, they could weaken the integrity of the hull. Their size made them easily missed by the two outlooks, Arne and Othere, at the front of the boat.

A mountainous white iceberg floated through the dark blue ether of the night. It was too far away to be a threat, but warranted a watchful eye. The air was changing. Even though Thorfinn's sea experience was confined to short distances between Norway and his home of Iceland, he knew that they were heading into unsettled weather.

* * *

Below deck, in the small corner of the storage compartment she shared with Thorfinn at the stern of the *Mimir*, Gudrid opened her eyes with a gasp. The constant rocking of the ship frequently woke her, but not this time. This time, as before, she'd been pulled from untroubled sleep and shown terrible things, terrible things to come.

Disoriented for a moment, she looked around at the barrels and crates full of supplies that formed the makeshift walls of this, the home of their first year of marriage. The small movements of the few cattle they'd brought with them pulled her back to the reality of the *Mimir* and anchored her there. Thorvald had seemed so real; what he had shown her had seemed so real-—would be real, she knew, if they did not succeed.

It will be well, she told herself. The seven men who had taken her first husband, Thorvald, to Kjalarness were men whose allegiance to the Eiriksson family was legendary. They had all fought together and Leif had, on a number of occasions, saved each of their lives, including Thorvald's. She silently reconfirmed her oath to her dead husband, then rose and went in search of Thorfinn.

"What is it, Gudrid?" Thorfinn asked when she'd stepped out of the hatch to the lower deck and moved to stand next to him, silent as she sought how best to share her fears.

She needed counsel on these matters, though, and so could not keep them to herself. "Thorfinn, I had a disturbing dream," she began. "I dreamt that my first husband, Thorvald, came to me. He told me that after the first great celestial war, the Æsir broke their word to the giant rebuilding the celestial dwellings. His payment was supposed to be the goddess of peace and pleasure, Freyja."

Gudrid paused, again horrified by the graphic events in the dream she described. She hugged Thorfinn for comfort before continuing. "Then Thorvald showed me that at the moment of the deceit, all the treaties and agreements in the heavens and on the earth were broken or destroyed. Gods, giants, and humans plunged into a net of abhorrence and savagery. Warfare raged across the face of heaven and earth." She lowered her head so that she was speaking into his chest. "I fear that this was a dream of things to come."

Thorfinn's arms tightened around her and he said gently, "I fear that our dægurs at sea have taken hold of your sleeping mind, as well."

Gudrid looked up. "No, Thorfinn," she said firmly. "I was pulled from my sleep and shown these events. This has happened before. My second husband, Thorstein, returned from the dead to tell me of future events; the night he died, he returned to life to tell me that I would marry an Icelander and have a child. You are that Icelander."

Thorfinn rested his chin on the top of her head and again tightened his embrace. They stood so until stirred by a disembodied voice that asked from the shadows of the silent deck, "Thorfinn, can I talk to you?"

Gudrid and Thorfinn parted at the sound of approaching footsteps. They turned to see Adam standing next to them as if he'd materialized from the dark ocean itself.

"Adam, I thought that was you," Thorfinn said. "Yes, what would you like?"

"I will leave both of you alone to talk," Gudrid said.

"No, stay," Thorfinn said abruptly, and she saw his ill-concealed discomfort. Despite the respect that Thorfinn showed to the Christian monk, Gudrid knew that in her husband's eyes, Adam might as well have shattered the ancient rune stones and used them to build the towering steeples to honour his God. Thorfinn didn't like how his beliefs would live in the shadow of this new religion, just as the jelling stones were shadowed by the new churches.

"Thorfinn, you have treated me with much kindness and understanding and I would like to thank you for allowing me to accompany you on this voyage," Adam said. "I know that with your help, my mission for the present king will be a success."

"You give me honours that are not deserved. I do this for the love of my king and my land," Thorfinn replied.

"How about for the love of God, Thorfinn?" He asked, the stench of wine on Adam's breath as biting as the question.

"It is best not to bring up such subjects, Adam. Everyone has their own beliefs that best suit them to live in this unsure and sometimes dangerous world." He unconsciously lifted a hand to touch the hammer of Thor he wore under his tunic. Gudrid knew how painful it was for her husband to bear the *prima signatio*, the Christian symbol that allowed him to do business in this new world. Thorfinn had replaced it with the symbol he was most comfortable with, once they were underway.

The monk standing before Thorfinn represented the end of an era that had lasted for hundreds of years. Already, though Gudrid had reached only the middle of her life, she had witnessed the end of the old religion and now the slow conversion of her people to Christianity.

Thorfinn had once told her the reason for the conversion. The nobles of his country saw how rich the European countries became when trading with the Christian nations. Pillaging was expensive: it cost lives and resources. Peace meant wealth for the people and, for King Harald, or the Converted King, as he was known, it meant the strengthening of his power.

But however prosperous Christianity would make his country, Thorfinn felt that this was a mess of Odinic proportion. It threatened the ancient stories and the religion of his people with extinction, with only the runes and the jelling stones as reminders of their long and proud history. He'd often voiced his fears that one day, no one would be able to read the inscriptions on the stones and his race's rich heritage would be lost forever.

The monsters and gods of the old religion were real to him. This new god confused people, with its conflicting priorities and messages. "We are a strong people, with definite ideas of our world," he'd asserted. "Christianity weakens our people's resolve, makes us look at the world as not our own, with its new ethics and new morals. Our future is being slowly and excruciatingly ripped from the womb of our mother religion." As far as Thorfinn was concerned, Christianity was as unwelcome as the violent North Atlantic storms.

"I will not try to impose my beliefs on you, Thorfinn," Adam said with a slight smile. "I would like to reveal to you the nature of my mission."

"You're not required to explain why you are on this ship," Thorfinn interjected. "I have mentioned why I've allowed you passage. I don't want to get involved."

"Still," Adam insisted, "if I do not return, I need *you* to return with the knowledge that I am about to impart to you."

"Very well," Thorfinn relented. "Proceed."

"Have you ever heard about a group of monks called the

Celi Dei—the Servants of God? Or perhaps you've heard them referred to as the Culdees."

"No, I have not," Thorfinn replied gruffly, as if insulted that anyone would think him preoccupied with Christian matters.

Adam either ignored his tone, or didn't notice it. He continued as if Thorfinn had not answered. "We do not know much about them, but they are a breakaway sect from the Church. They were last heard from about two hundred years ago; they were headed for a land called Irland Mikkla, or Greater Ireland. But we do not know for sure."

Thorfinn now looked interested. Gudrid knew why: he'd been under the impression that it was his people who had first landed on the shores west of Grœnlandia.

"The next chapter in the story happened twenty years ago," Adam said. "A Viking trader named Rafn said that after touching on Greater Ireland, he met a man named Ari Marsson. A storm had blown the man off course from his destination of Reykjavik. Rafn took him to Greater Ireland where, it is said, he was taken prisoner and baptized."

"What does this story have to do with our voyage?" Thorfinn asked, his tone impatient.

Adam held up a hand, seeking Thorfinn's patience. "Greater Ireland is located adjacent to Vinland—at least, that is what Rafn said. If it were not for one other piece of information, the name Ari Marsson would be insignificant, lost in the history of the world." Adam paused. "He is related to Leif Eiriksson by marriage. You have a direct relation to Eirik on board your ship."

"You mean . . . Freydis?" Thorfinn said, glancing at Gudrid. "This Ari . . . was husband to Freydis?"

Adam nodded. "Exactly."

Thorfinn again looked at Gudrid. She kept her face blank.

Thorfinn turned back to Adam. "What possible effect could a man being imprisoned and baptized by monks have on anything?"

"Church relics were taken—either in one of Eirik the Red's raids or by Ari Marsson himself; the truth of the events is very unclear. It is possible that Ari was not imprisoned and in fact could be in league with the Culdees. Who knows what the people who possess them will do to retain them? It may put this voyage in jeopardy," he added at Thorfinn's indifferent expression. "Every life on this ship could be in danger—including yours and Gudrid's."

Thorfinn crossed his arms. "And what are these relics, Adam?" he asked with scorn in his voice.

"We are concerned about the lance with which our Lord was struck in the side, as related by the Apostle John: 'one of the soldiers stabbed his side with a lance, and at once there was a flow of blood and water,'" Adam quoted from memory. "Being given the slightest prick with the lance gives eternal life. Have you ever heard about the cup of Christ?"

"Yes, I have," Thorfinn admitted. "But that's nonsense."

"Perhaps to you, but to those who believe, the properties of the cup are very real. Whether the lance, just like the cup, gives eternal life is really not the point. If it is believed that the relic does possess this power, the owner of the lance is perceived as possessing the power to bestow eternal life, and could actually usurp power by the mere mention of possessing it." Adam paused for the weight of that information to sink in.

"We do not know if the Culdees are with us or against us," he said. "We do not know how their being away from civilization and the Church has changed them. They could be devotees of God, as is their charter, or, if they do possess the lance, it could have twisted their faith into something evil."

Adam finished with the reminder, "King Svend, in all his wisdom, sees the danger of this situation and has agreed to assist in returning the holy lance to the Church."

"How will you identify the holy lance? Have you seen it?" Gudrid asked.

"Not the actual relic, but I have seen detailed drawings of the weapon. I am confident that I can identify it," Adam answered.

"What do you need from me?" Thorfinn asked, revealing a willingness to cooperate.

"I need a few of your men to accompany me on an expedition to Markland."

"And how do you know that these Culdees are on Markland?"

"From an ancient sea chart," Adam replied. "I do not know where it came from or who drew it, but the map marks a route from Iceland to Grœnlandia to Helluland, then to Markland and finally to Vinland. On the back of this sea chart is an inscription that King Svend had me commit to memory: 'There lay a land on the other side, directly opposite Vinland, where the people went about in white clothes and shouted loudly, and went about with poles with patches of cloth attached: Hvitmannaland.' The only possible location of the colony is Markland. It lies directly opposite Vinland, on the map."

Adam's description of his plans had captured all of Gudrid's attention. This was a good turn of fate—or was it her dream revealing to her how she could get to Markland without involving Thorfinn or telling him her actual reasons for returning to that land? *I will tell him eventually,* she assured herself again. *Just not right now.*

Thorfinn remained silent. He turned away from Adam and looked up at the stars, as if hoping to find the answers from his gods while their powers and influence remained over the earth. *Soon the Christian god will change that,* Gudrid thought, watching him.

"There is one final possibility that is too horrific for me to imagine," Adam added carefully. "It is possible that Ari has used the lance on himself and the Culdees and all those who would follow him. If they so choose, they could build an army that would be invincible."

Gudrid watched Thorfinn, whose closed expression wavered with uncertainty. If Adam was telling the truth, this was a threat far greater than his fear of the Church. *He will ally himself with the monk until both our missions are complete,* Gudrid surmised. *Then their surfacing differences will part them once more.*

"I will give you a small scouting party," Thorfinn conceded. "They will take you to Furdustrandir. If, by the fifth dægur, you do not find these Culdees and this Ari, you will return to Vinland and await our return to Brattahlið."

"Thank you, Thorfinn," Adam said. "There is one other thing. We also discovered another of our artifacts missing . . . "

Gudrid didn't know why, but her mouth formed the words to the rest of Adam's sentence as he spoke them: "The Book of Kells."

"It's an eighth century document depicting the four gospels," Adam continued. "As a religious artifact, the book is irreplaceable. But there is another, more important reason why the book must be returned to us. In one year our prince will ascend the throne. The book must be returned for the coronation. Within the book's images and intricate designs is one part of a code key. The second part of the key is passed down in secrecy from king to successor. The heir apparent must prove his worthiness to ascend to the throne and rule the country by passing through the catacombs under the palace to a secret vault where the relics of his power are kept: his crown, sceptre, and cloak. The keys map out the location of the vault and reveal how to open its hidden door."

Adam paused and his voice grew sombre. "If the prince does not leave the catacombs with his royal vestments, the present court officials and clergy will deem him unworthy to rule his people. Brian Boru, a tribal leader's son, is recognized as the next king of Ireland. I hope you can appreciate the delicacy of this situation, Thorfinn. With the ascension of this king to the throne, the Church can hope to secure an ally. I fear that if the book is not found, it could plunge the country into civil war. And in view of the current situation, Ari or the Culdees would in all likelihood usurp power, offering their followers eternal life by using the power of the lance. Legend speaks of terrible events: stars plummeting from the heavens, plagues of unspeakable horror. Because of our commercial connections, all of Europe could be dragged into chaos."

Gudrid could almost feel the burden of Adam's responsibility. She saw it in his stance. Adam stood slightly hunched, his bowed shoulders tense. She'd heard of Boru's successes in battle with his brethren. Boru was a dangerous opponent.

"I will assist you in returning your religious relics, Adam. But I will not incur expenses for these tasks, nor willingly place my people in danger," Thorfinn said.

"In my bags below deck," Adam said, "you will find a hide-chest filled with gold and silver. There should be enough there to compensate you for your troubles and any loses that you might incur."

Thorfinn's expression lost its hard edge. The monetary gesture struck at Thorfinn's merchant heart, Gudrid knew. "We will assist you to recover your precious relics," Thorfinn grunted.

"Then I go to sleep knowing that you will honour your commitment," Adam said.

* * *

Thorfinn watched the holy man walk across the deck of the *Mimir* and disappear into the cargo hold. He felt himself a man trapped between duty toward his leader and his own religious convictions. If not for the command from his king, Thorfinn would have left Adam on shore and set sail without him. Adam's

church had taken so much from his family and his people—
their gods, their culture, the very things that made them who
they were. He wished for the day that their lands were rid of
them.

But hundreds of years ago, the Christian church had seized
the most powerful empire in the world. And now his Christian
king gave the belief some dignity. Thorfinn sighed. What chance
did Norsemen like him have to fight something unseen and so
powerful?

Gudrid touched his arm, drawing him from his thoughts.
"Thorfinn, I want to go with them," she said when he looked at
her.

"No, it is far too dangerous," he blurted.

"Thorfinn, I need to go on this mission," she insisted.

"And why is that?"

Gudrid hesitated, then plunged into an explanation. "One
of my other reasons for insisting that you make this voyage and
bring me along has to do with the death of my first husband,
Thorvald. Not long after he was taken and buried at Kjalarness,
I began having terror visions—voices screamed in my head and
beasts stalked me. Sometimes I saw these images during my
waking hours, as shapes in the sky, visions in the flames of a
fire pit, apparitions coming through the fog."

Thorfinn caught her hand and held it tightly. He was still
trying to come to grips with his wife's mystical side. "Did the
visions impart any message to you, Gudrid?"

"I must return to finish what I've begun, and return
Thorvald to Grœnlandia and his family. And . . . There was one
more vision that until now I didn't understand—we must find
and return a great book."

"The book the Christian Adam mentioned," Thorfinn said.
Gudrid nodded.

Thorfinn secured the steerboard with a rope and walked
over to lean one hand on the side of the boat, battling jealousy
and frustration. He couldn't fight the ghost that his wife carried
within her. He tried not to feel anger, but rather understanding
for her feelings. Just because her previous husband had died did
not mean that he was dead in her mind; Thorvald would probably
always live within some part of her.

"What is it, Thorfinn?"

"Nothing," he lied. "I will allow you to go with the party."
She touched his shoulder. "Come, let's go to bed."

He took Gudrid's hand and led the way back down to their small section of the cargo hold.

The *Mimir's* wind-filled sail tossed the knarr from starboard to port; it rippled as the storm winds blew across the red bands woven into the fabric and then it billowed wildly, caught by another wind that pushed the knarr forward. The same wind grabbed the waves and slapped them against the hull as their speed increased.

Some of the crew were still below deck, securing cargo and trying desperately to remain calm; focusing on their job did help a little. For the ones on deck, the crashing waves made it a dangerous and slippery place, and the high winds blew past them with such force that they felt as if they were facing the cold ocean current instead.

Thorfinn clutched the ship's railing, trusting the skill of his navigator to get them through this. He had chosen his navigator well; the dwarf Tostig stood barely as high as the top of the prow, but what he lacked in height, he made up for in intelligence and experience. Tostig's wind-scarred face mapped the voyages of his life. He had navigated these waters many times and on many different sizes of ships. He could near-accurately predict their heading and position based on time and speed; his knowledge of sea birds, wave formations, and the position of the sun and the stars was infamous. Tostig was drawing on all of that knowledge and experience now.

The storm, in just a short period of time, had carried an iceberg from a relatively safe distance onto a collision course with the *Mimir,* pushing the mountain of ice as easily as it pushed the small ship. If the wind and the waves didn't change, the floating wall of ice would definitely rip through the *Mimir's* hull, tearing her in two.

Suddenly, the ship tilted sharply to one side. A wave reaching almost as high as the mast rolled above the *Mimir* and crashed down on the creaking deck, spraying water from bow to stern.

Thorfinn lost his grip and slid down the steeply canted deck toward the other side of the ship, his hands scrabbling frantically for a handhold. His yells for help were lost in the thunder of wind and rain and roaring waves. He tumbled onto his stomach, the water flowing across the deck accelerating his slide as if he were sliding across the ice of a frozen lake.

Thorfinn checked his headlong skid as the ocean swelled up again, threatening to push the water to the heavens; the *Mimir's* prow dipped, caught in the forming slope, then plunged to the bottom of the swell. Its sharp prow sliced through the Serpent's arching back, ripped into the flesh of the ocean, then bobbed up to the exhaling surface as the trough lowered to the level of the *Mimir's* keel.

Another swell tipped *Mimir* to its port side. Harald managed to hold onto the steerboard. The rowers hugged their oars, some even managing to wrap their legs around them, too. Anything that could be gripped had someone clinging desperately to it: the edge of the hatch to the lower deck; the mast; the oar ports on either side of the ship.

As they fought against the rolling ocean and torrential wall of rain, Thorfinn felt, for the first time on the voyage, out of control. His navigator had all but taken over the task of keeping them alive. Tostig barked out orders to the victimized crew almost to the point of scolding them for taking stupid risks. Some obeyed him, but others slithered into the cargo hold or hugged the mast for fear of being swept overboard.

We are losing our brave men to the sea, Thorfinn thought. But the storm wouldn't allow him to think of anything else before he was pulled back by the tipping of the ship, or hit with a wave of frigid water that jolted his mind back to the present. Like an ignored child, the storm did everything in its power to scream for attention.

A huge wave was building up off their port side, growing larger and more threatening in its strength as it mercilessly stalked the ship. By the second, more and more water pushed into its crest, forcing the wave higher and higher. If the wave hit the *Mimir* from the side, the tipped ship would take on water and quickly sink.

"Harald, turn us into the wave!" Gudrid yelled.

Thorfinn watched as Harald desperately pushed on the steerboard and held it steady until the boat turned, putting the wave behind the craft. Then he pulled the steerboard as far as it would go, counteracting the tipping of the knarr. Thorfinn realized the steersman was hoping the preceding trough would push them beyond the wave's crashing crest. It was a desperate measure, but considering the size of the wave and the speed at which it was approaching, caution wasn't a luxury.

The *Mimir* raced along the Serpent's back as it rose and fell in never-ending undulations. It travelled just below the ocean surface, but it was always there. If they could see it, they could fight it and return the water to calm, Thorfinn thought; but how do you fight a foe that you can feel moving, but you cannot see?

Harald's desperation paid off; the rising trough lifted and pushed them beyond the range of the crashing crest. But another wave trough moved under the ship, followed by its rising crest. It lifted the *Mimir's* stern out of the water and slammed it down again. The knarr shuddered.

Gripping their oars, the rowers struggled to tame the wild ocean, to gain some control over the ship. But trying to row in the stormy seas without direction to coordinate their efforts was fruitless. At last they let Harald steer the ship and concentrated on keeping the ship from capsizing by compensating for the unpredictable and rapidly changing movement of the ocean.

"Here comes another one!" Gudrid yelled, pointing at a massive crest building up on their port side.

The wave roared toward them. Thorfinn looked up and knew that they couldn't outrun it. The wall of water crashed down onto the *Mimir's* stern. Bones cracked as bodies slammed against the hard oak deck and thudded into the side of the boat.

Thorfinn tasted salt water in his mouth and gagged as the pungent liquid hit the back of his throat; he coughed and sputtered, pushing as much as he could out of his mouth, then spit a surge of bile from his stomach. He peered desperately through the wall of rain at the open sea, scanning the horizon for that one glimpse of starry sky that would be their beacon through the storm, but the clouds still rolled and darkened . . . and spat out their blinding rain.

Being washed overboard or the boat capsizing were just two perils that the crew faced. Without warm, dry clothing, they faced the possibility of freezing to death as the temperature dropped.

Thorfinn saw no break in the storm, but he did note that it carried the mountainous island of ice along with the *Mimir*. It bobbed and tossed in the waves as easily as if it were a log being carried by a rushing river. Waves crashed over it, momentarily hiding it from view, but it quickly resurfaced as an ever-present threat. He prayed to Thor, asking for their deliverance from not only the storm's wrath, but the implacable approach of that mountain of ice. Thor did as he pleased, occasionally listening to those who prayed to him for guidance and assistance. Thorfinn hoped this was one of those times.

He sagged in relief when Tostig yelled moments later, "We're coming through the storm." The navigator pointed at the rising moon on their port side, ignoring the wet ropes of his long hair that the wind blew across his eyes and mouth.

Thorfinn silently thanked Thor for releasing them from the clutches of the storm. He knew that they still had some distance to travel, but up ahead the troughs weren't as low and the crests weren't as high; the wind was much calmer and the sheets of rain had lessened to a mere downpour. Only then did he notice how his head throbbed. He gingerly touched his forehead; the contact produced a stab of pain and his hand came away red with blood. Groaning, he let his head and shoulders sag to the wet oak deck and closed his eyes.

He didn't know how long he lay so, but when he opened his eyes, he saw the blurry form of Gudrid, her body swaying from side to side as she walked down the length of the yawing deck toward him.

"Thorfinn my darling, are you hurt badly?" she asked, pressing the hem of her wet skirt against his forehead to try to stop the bleeding.

"I'll be fine," he answered in a bleak tone, rolling over to sit up, both hands holding his head. He staggered to his feet, his head swimming in opposition to the moving deck. The throbbing rose in protest. He saw the rising moon. "Tostig," he yelled, clutching his forehead even tighter in response to another stab of pain, "can you find out where we are?"

"Once we're past the storm I can get us back in the right direction, but I'll have to wait until the sky clears before I can get us back on course," Tostig replied. He pointed to the heaving ocean surface. "The Serpent is calming."

"Thank you," Thorfinn said, turning away to steady himself with a hand on the *Mimir's* rail. He sensed Gudrid's quick movement away from his side and turned to follow her with his eyes.

She had gone to Harald. The steersman's face was an angry red from the freezing rain and battering winds, and he shivered violently in his wet clothes; worse, Thorfinn realized, his purple fingers could not let go of the wooden handle, and they seemed to be coated in a thin film of ice. As a mother would a hurt child, Gudrid wrapped her hands over his.

"I think-k-k my hands are f-frozen to the st-steerboard."

"I know," Gudrid gently said. "We'll get them off."

Thorfinn stumbled over to help. As he placed his wet hands over Gudrid's, he looked into Harald's eyes and said sincerely, "Harald, thank you for saving our lives. I am proud to have you as part of this family." The words melted the tension from the steersman's face just as the warmth of their hands melted the ice holding him to the steerboard.

They removed their hands from Harald's and slowly pried his purple fingers from the handle. Thorfinn felt Harald's muscles tense as the pain cascaded from his stiff fingers through his body. Harald slowly placed his hands in his armpits, as if he needed to further protect them.

"Gudrid," Thorfinn said, extending his hand, "I need to lie down. Could you help me into the hold?"

"Yes, of course." She put his arm around her neck and supported him as best she could.

She helped him through the hatch, and they splashed through ankle deep water. The movement of the ship had shuffled the chests they used as their bed around and a few of the furs lay in the water, but two pelts they used as bedding remained dry on top of the makeshift bed.

Thorfinn leaned against the crates while Gudrid pushed the chests back together, then spread the furs on top of them. She helped Thorfinn to sit down and undressed him, running her eyes over his powerful frame. His icy wet clothing had left red patches on his chest and arms. Gudrid laid the garments out to dry in the damp salt air and wrapped his body in the dry fur.

"You rest here. I will go back up top to see what I can do to help on deck," she said, picking up the fur throws from the wet floor and spreading them across some crates.

"All right," Thorfinn answered in a docile tone, and lay back. He tried to take his mind off the throbbing pain in his head, and let his thoughts wander to his predecessors.

He planned not to make the same mistakes they had. He didn't want to make enemies of the inhabitants of Vinland and Markland. This was not an *i*Viking expedition and Thorfinn had no intention of turning it into such. The word was terrible to his ears, just a euphemism for stealing, killing, and destroying. He would offer the natives the same respect as a delegation would offer a potential ally, regardless of their military or economic strength.

Thorfinn drifted off to sleep, dreaming of sunny days, fields of tall grass, and fresh summer air.

Oaken planks creaked as ghostly shapes moved across the deck of the ship in the morning mist engulfing *Mimir*, solidifying into human form only as they drew close. No one knew in which direction the knarr was heading.

Gudrid couldn't sleep following the storm the night before that had threatened to end their voyage. She'd stayed awake through the night, and saw the starry sky changing into the quiet whiteness now surrounding them. It was as dangerous as the darkness of the night—with one exception. The fog cloaked the white ice, making the bergs nearly impossible to see until they were right on top of them.

Gudrid swore that there were apparitions concealed in the mist. Swirling wisps of water vapour formed shapes that quickly reformed into other shapes, or disappeared altogether. She jumped when she thought she saw the ethereal outline of another knarr alongside of them; it appeared and disappeared, then appeared again, looking as if it would collide with them, and she clutched Thorfinn's arm tighter and pointed in the direction of the ship. But when Thorfinn looked, it had vanished, and didn't reappear again. Thorfinn told her that it was the sun shining through breaks in the fog and reflecting the *Mimir* off the vapour at strange and random angles. "Almost like a reflection in the facets of a crystal," he said. But Gudrid was convinced that they were the ghost ships of previous, doomed voyages.

She'd made it her personal assignment to keep a lookout for the floating ice through the night. While Thorfinn was incapacitated, it was her duty to protect the crew. She willingly took on this job, knowing that the crew would listen to her just as they would Thorfinn, well aware that she was every bit as capable of commanding the ship as he was.

She walked to the bow of the ship, where Othere and Arne also kept a lookout from the prow, and watched the ocean ahead of them. They nodded to her, but otherwise kept vigilant eyes on the ocean, watching for floating ice and praying to the gods that there was no subsurface ice large enough to do damage. The larger "islands" of ice weren't as dangerous, because they could be seen from far enough away to be avoided. But the ones that bobbed below the surface were virtually invisible unless Othere and Arne looked straight at them.

Just as dangerous was a rolling cliff of ice falling upon them. A block of ice toppling from that height would instantly splinter the ship, no matter where it hit. In minutes the crew would succumb to the icy water. Even if they did make it to a mountain of floating ice, they'd still die from exposure to the cold North Atlantic wind.

Icy apparitions floated through the mist with them, their wakes the only evidence of their presence. The haunting squeal of a porpoise and the eerie moans of whales filled the hollow air with sounds that provoked the mind into thinking about the supernatural.

In the distance of the white night, a grey image slowly solidified from the swirling mist. It seemed to duck in and out of the whiteness, not a part of the wall of fog, but not separate from it, either.

Othere nudged Arne, unsure if he was looking at an iceberg or an illusion. Gudrid saw Arne nod, and Othere bellowed to the rowers, "Hold water." They immediately stopped rowing and let the oars drag across the surface of the water, slowing down the knarr.

Gudrid could clearly see the mountain of ice now. Its right slope dropped down beneath the water, then levelled out below the surface to a ghostly-blue plateau; its left side presented only a wall of ice.

A large growler floated by the ship. Gudrid jumped back

and grabbed Othere's tunic. She felt his body tense, as if her touch transmitted her fear to him. A large eye stared back at them, frozen in the floating ice.

"By all that is in Hel, what is that?" Gudrid yelled. As the ice floated by, the disjointed pieces she'd glimpsed began to form into a whole.

"Argh, it's just a frozen whale," Othere grunted.

The separate sections of the whale became one whole animal in Gudrid's eye. Its lifeless body had frozen in an unnatural position, victim to the ocean currents. Finally the tail floated by, its outer fin chewed, barnacles growing on its fatty tissue.

Othere chuckled. "For a moment I too thought it was Hel herself, coming from the depths to take us—"

"Turn!" Gudrid screamed.

Othere looked at Gudrid, then instinctively followed her stare; the twisting mist had solidified into a large wall of ice that was being dragged by the current in the water before their prow.

Harald heaved the steerboard, using his body weight to try pulling it beyond its capacity. But Gudrid knew that his efforts were in vain, the *Mimir* could not clear the floating ice in time. The amount of damage that the impact would do to the knarr depended on the speed of the boat and where, on the floating ice, the knarr impacted. The *Mimir* was turning, so the impact would be on her port side. The dragging oars might help to slow them down, Gudrid thought, but not in enough time to completely miss the ice.

"We're going to hit," Arne yelled.

Gudrid could've sworn she heard the Valkyries screeching overhead. But it was the sound and the vibration of the *Mimir's* curved prow grounding on the subsurface ice as the keel scraped across the top of a submersed plateau. She grabbed Arne with one hand and held tightly onto the side of the ship with her other, just in time.

As the curved prow pried into the ice, crew toppled over like sticks in a heavy windstorm. Some were rendered unconscious, while others slammed against other crewmen, knocking them into the frigid water. Loud thuds and rumblings rose from the hold as the cargo shifted, hitting the side of the hull. The oxen and sheep below deck wailed loudly. The sound of rolling grain barrels ended in an explosive crash at the bow.

The *Mimir* finally stopped with one final, ear-piercing crunch; her front keel surfaced and grounded on the ice, leaving the *Mimir* beached precariously on the floating white island. With its ballast no longer in the water, the ship tipped to starboard. If not for the central crag of ice jutting up from below the surface, the *Mimir* would have tipped over and sank. As it happened, the mast and the port hull dug into the hard snow and ice.

Thorfinn appeared through the hatch. He looked like he had regained some of his strength, but he hadn't fully recovered; his steps were a little unbalanced and blood matted his hair to the side of his skull. He looked around the deck and saw Gudrid standing at the bow with Othere and Arne. The crew were slowly dragging themselves off the deck in shivering and painfully disjointed movements; the cold made their movements all the slower.

Othere lay on his back, blood trickling from a long gash in his head; Gudrid knelt and cradled his head, trying to stop the bleeding with the hem of her dress. Thorfinn came over, saw her efforts, and grabbed his cuff, ripping it off his sleeve. He quickly tied the thick cloth around Othere's forehead. With the help of Arne, he helped Othere to his feet.

Thorfinn turned to her. "Are you all right, Gudrid?"

She nodded, wringing out her dress.

"What happened?" Thorfinn yelled, looking around angrily. Gudrid did not know what made him angry, the fear of lost lives or that their journey had almost ended before they reached Vinland.

Ran's feast of fish will have to wait for us, Gudrid thought, also looking around.

"The ice came upon us without warning," Arne said, wincing in pain. "There was not enough time to turn the ship."

"We are truly fortunate that we're still breathing air," Gudrid said as she looked over the prow of the ship. The impact on the ice had split the oak keel; the hull appeared to be still intact, but the full weight of *Mimir's* hull rested against the mountain of ice. The oak mast had cracked when it hit the ice.

"Tostig, come up here," Thorfinn yelled.

In minutes Gudrid saw Tostig moving through the confusion of men picking themselves up off the deck and frantically looking around for missing mates. His stubby legs moved with great effort, first lifting the opposite side of his body up and then propelling it forward in an awkward, tottering gait. He occasionally lost the rhythm of his step and stumbled, but his disproportionately large arms flailed in circles, keeping him upright.

"Yes, Thorfinn."

"Assess the damage to the *Mimir*, and search the hold for materials to repair her."

"The ice is taking us off course," Gudrid said, feeling the ship drifting on her port side.

Thorfinn could only shrug; they were helpless to stop it. He leaned over the prow.

Further examination revealed that the impact had actually split the ice, and a third of the keel was now trapped inside. Tostig reported that the pine tar sealing the wood had eroded away during the stresses of the voyage, and water continually splashed into the crevice and froze, further trapping the prow in the ice mass. If they didn't free themselves quickly, they'd freeze irrevocably to the floating island.

The *Mimir* could not afford to spend any more time at sea. The autumn storms would start soon. With the change in season, sea storms were much more frequent, and there was less daylight; their voyage would take longer and be more dangerous. And there was always the real risk of the World Serpent taking them farther and farther off course.

"Warrior Captain, assemble your men on the ice floe with swords and axes," Thorfinn yelled to the mass of crew assembling on the deck.

"Warriors, arm yourselves," the captain barked to his men. "We fight the sea and the Serpent."

Freydis Eiriksdÿttir was the first to head to the ship's prow. Being the only daughter of Erik the Red, she knew more than most the image that she needed to maintain; Erik's family were strong and powerful leaders and warriors.

"Freydis, we have no need for an archer at this battle," the captain told her.

"That is why I have brought my sword," she answered, brandishing a double-edged blade. "I am fully skilled in hand-to-hand fighting."

"Arghhhhh!" The captain yelled his battle cry, displaying the few crooked and blackened teeth still left in his mouth.

Freydis led the other warriors in a stampede to the front of the ship, looking as fierce as if they were about to engage an enemy, their axes and blades raised high in the air. Twenty warriors in all vaulted over the prow of the ship and landed on the ice. Some hacked at the ice with their axes and swords; the others simultaneously rocked the twelve-ton *Mimir*.

Gudrid thought she felt the *Mimir* move—perhaps only a little, but it moved nonetheless.

"Keep going, warriors," the captain yelled. "I think we're winning this battle."

Gudrid said a silent prayer to Thor to aid in their escape. She knew that Thor's power was limited, but perhaps he could be their advocate. She hoped that her plea would be well received, but as with all gods, it was difficult to enter their minds and know what they wanted humans to do.

"Warriors, fight harder," the captain growled. "Time is our enemy."

With renewed conviction and purpose, those wielding their weapons hacked at the ice harder and harder, while the others threw their body weight against the knarr, first pushing, then heaving the hull back and forth on its keel. Suddenly there was a long creak and then a thunderous crack.

"We've broken free!" the captain hollered. "Get aboard."

The victorious warriors jumped back into the *Mimir,* landing on top of one another in their haste not to be trapped on the ice. Those already on deck helped others up, or pulled them aside, tossing them onto the deck as fishermen would do with a jigger full of fish. The last of the men and the woman Gudveig were pulled and dragged over the side of the ship as the wool sail caught the breath of the gods and the *Mimir* floated away from her icy shackle.

Thorfinn congratulated the warriors as they piled aboard. He looked at Gudrid, his face a mask of relief and joy. "Thank Thor for our deliverance! I will make a tribute to him as soon as opportunity allows."

Tostig returned from below deck and fiddled with his bearing dial. With a few quick mental calculations, he determined that they were not too far off course, but the oarsmen would have to row like a school of porpoises to get back to their previous heading. Once the fog cleared, he could take much more accurate readings, but for now, he said, he was satisfied with his intuition. Once he got them back into the útsuðr wind currents, they could all relax a little.

"Port oarsmen, give way," the dwarf shouted. "Starboard

oarsmen, hold water." As soon as the orders were out of his mouth, the *Mimir* turned. "Starboard oarsmen, give way."

Both sides of the boat exploded into activity as the pairs of men at the oars heaved their muscular bodies, fighting the swells and the cold Atlantic wind.

"You're doing a king's job!" Tostig shouted, trying to keep their spirits high. "We're in debt to you for your brave and valiant job."

"Tostig, what is our condition?" Thorfinn asked.

Gudrid read trouble on the dwarf's face.

Tostig dropped his voice. "Our hull has split in three places. Water is leaking into the hold. I've put two oarsmen down there to try to keep it under control, with orders to keep our situation a secret."

"Can it be repaired?" Gudrid asked, hoping that Tostig's answer would fix all the problems that her mind was creating.

Tostig's expression was grim. "On dry land, but not at sea. The *Mimir* is sinking."

Thorfinn climbed through the hatch and looked at the morning sky. He could not remember the sky looking so incredible. A light mist slowly cleared in front of the ship, almost as if the *Mimir* dispersed the vaporous fog as its prow touched it. Thorfinn couldn't quite put his finger on it, but something was different this morning. He didn't know if it was a feeling or if it existed in the physical world.

The sun shimmered off the calm ocean on the other side of the fog. He wondered if Ægir's hand was in this sight, enticing them to their destination; whatever it was, it was beautiful.

A breath of wind dispersed the veiling mist, and Thorfinn could see ahead of them; it was strong enough to move the mist, but not to disturb the *Mimir's* sail. He looked around for his navigator, and instantly, the dangerous reality of their situation crept back into his thoughts. They did not know where they were on the ocean, or how rapidly the *Mimir* was sinking. Disagreeable uncertainty drove all appreciation of the morning sky from his mind.

Thorfinn could estimate the amount of water they'd taken on just by how close the top of the hull was to the ocean surface, and the ocean was now closer to their floating piece of dry land than was comfortable to imagine.

"Tostig," Thorfinn yelled. "Do you know where we are?"

"Not yet, Thorfinn," Tostig replied, consulting the bearing dial. "But I soon will."

Suddenly there was a great crash, its source cloaked in the veil of the mist and so instantaneous that the violence was more instant shock than force of impact. But it was forceful enough that not one person above deck or below had time to prepare for it.

The crash was not really a crash at all, Thorfinn realized; it was more like a split. He immediately knew what had happened: a section of the hull below the waterline, weakened by the impact with the iceberg, had separated till it reached a joint holding two oak planks together. Once that happened, the ship could not stay afloat.

As if the first impact was not enough, the sideways movement that it caused pushed the *Mimir* into an underwater rock jutting sharply up from the sea floor. The already weakened side became a prime target for destruction. Its wood splintered and the momentous force chewed through the hull, driving the rock deeper and deeper into the cargo hold and widening the crack into a hole.

The *Mimir's* lower deck began filling with water. No longer able to float with the added weight, she plunged to the bottom of the sea. The crew fought to get through the single hatch, only wide enough to accommodate three people abreast at a time. Thorfinn pushed past them, seeking Gudrid.

She was pulling on a rope with an ox tied to the other end. "Othere, Arne—help me with the animals," she shouted.

Satisfied she was well, Thorfinn returned to the deck to ensure the urgency of the situation did not carry away anyone's sense. He was pleased to see that, despite the veil of panic, they all managed to stay ahead of the rapidly rising water and make it safely on deck.

Then, as if on cue, another miracle took place—the *Mimir* hit bedrock and tipped to starboard. Caught up in the chaos of the moment, no one but Thorfinn noticed the clearing mist had revealed a rocky land, sparsely wooded

They had finally made it to Vinland.

* * *

Thorfinn, with Harald, Frÿbjÿrn, Freydis, and Tostig, waded through the water. They could reach down into the clear, icy water and pull out handfuls of fish, they were that plentiful.

Thousands and thousands of fish swam through and around their legs.

Unlike the others in the party, Thorfinn's gaze was fixed on Vinland and the existing settlement. He squinted, trying to see the details of its buildings and other structures. Vinland's tall grass swayed in the offshore breeze.

Behind the advance party, crewmen and warriors were pulling the two oxen left onboard after the storm through the water by their horns, and carrying the goats and sheep to shore.

Our ocean voyage will be glorified in the sagas, Thorfinn thought, *written down by our people.* But the bare truth was that even strong Vikings had their limits; the stress of the voyage had worn them down. They needed to see land and know that in moments they would be stepping upon it. This moment was the cure for all ailments that had afflicted them during the voyage, whether physiological or psychological.

Thorfinn's pace picked up to a run; he splashed through the water with his men right behind him. As he got closer to shore, he noticed more and more detail in the settlement: a boat lying on its side, a tripod stand with a cauldron attached to the top, swaying and spinning in the wind. Thorfinn could not imagine such calmness after their long and precarious voyage. If Leif's description of Vinland was accurate, then this was truly "Vinland the Good."

The land is rightly named, he thought, gazing at the tall grass and heather that undulated away as far as his eye could see. This was indeed superior grazing for their livestock. The wind touched the tips of the purple wheat, capturing husks and seeds and blowing them across the meadow. After witnessing so much death, he craved the slightest hint of creation . . . and this was it.

His cold, wet feet stepped onto Vinland's rocky beach. All he could do was drop to his knees and hope the salt water masked the tears running down his cheeks. In that brief second, Thorfinn knew how Leif felt when he'd found this land and stepped onto it for the first time.

"By the grace of God, we made it," he heard Harald whisper.

Thorfinn allowed the reference; he was far too joyful to disallow another's belief at a stupendous moment such as this. Privately, he thanked the gods—Óðin for not making their trek more treacherous than it already was; Thor for allowing them to travel through the ocean storms that threatened their lives.

At times like these, he wondered if a one-god world would be better. Interpreting one mind might be far easier than interpreting the shifting priorities of many gods. He shook that thought off, and silently thanked his crew for their dedication and hard work.

But like the end of all journeys, stepping onto Vinland was a beginning: the beginning of discovery; the beginning of prosperity; the beginning of a new age for his people. As with all ages, it would begin with the efforts of a few adventurers who felt the need to leave the comfort of their homes and lands and venture out into the chaos of the unknown. To adapt to that chaos and order it into a workable framework . . . he had with him men capable of that.

Thorfinn stood and turned to his crew, gazing into one weary face after another. Their heads were bowed, their faces long. The only cheers he heard were inside his head, rising and falling in harmony with the surf hitting the rocks and gurgling over the beach of water-worn pebbles. It might be asking too much, he thought, for his crew to be jubilant after such a long time at sea. He hoped that his people would share in his joy in the days to come.

He turned to look at the verdant landscape, eager to explore more of Vinland, go deeper into the heart of the country. Across the expanse of meadow stood a forest, just waiting to have its mysteries exposed. And beyond that forest, Thorfinn saw mountains with more forests to explore. His thoughts shifted to those who already inhabited this place—those that his people called Skrælings. He wanted to get to know them, to co-exist with them and trade fairly with them for items either useful or unique—raw materials and items that could be resold back in Grœnlandia, Iceland, and Norway.

All the rest of that day, the crew pushed through water that lapped against their stomachs and chests, carrying leather-wrapped supplies and cargo above their heads. They moved through the water like ducklings after their mother, in single file, dropping their burden on the beach and returning to the knarr to collect the next load. Sealed barrels and small rafts of goods splashed into the water off the *Mimir's* side to be towed to the pebble beach.

Thorfinn stood at the tip of Vinland and studied the *Mimir*, helpless in the water. He didn't know if it could be repaired or not. He'd have to wait for Tostig's assessment of the damage. Thorfinn intended that they stay on Vinland, but they couldn't be totally cut off from home; for one thing, they needed to let the Norse at home know that they had made it. Otherwise, the crew and ship would be considered lost at sea.

His gaze moved from *Mimir* to slowly scan the ocean. He knew that he was standing at the end of a peninsula that must connect to a larger landmass. To his left, across the strait, he saw the misty shoreline of Markland, as Leif had described it to him, and where his beloved Gudrid, along with Adam of Bremen and a small group of Norsemen and Norsewomen, would travel. Thorfinn knew that Thorvald was buried on Markland, at Kjalarness, but he didn't know why Gudrid felt that she needed to go there. Thorfinn didn't ask any questions; he wasn't sure that he wanted to go exploring *there*, just yet.

For some unknown reason, Leif hadn't claimed Markland for himself. Again, he wondered if the burial of Thorvald at Kjalarness had something to do with it. Thorfinn thought of claiming it; perhaps a business opportunity awaited him on the other side of the water.

Movement caught his eye; he turned and saw Freydis walking in the general direction of the abandoned settlement's main building. "Freydis, have you seen Gudrid?" he called.

"Yes, she's in the longhouse."

Sure enough, as Thorfinn approached the main house, he noticed that the door stood ajar. He picked up a barrel of grain waiting outside, then balanced it in his arms while trying to pry the door open with his elbow. The weather-worn door jumped out of his hand and fell diagonally across the doorway, blocking his entrance. Thorfinn gave the wooden door an angry kick, knocking it completely off its hinge; it tumbled onto its side, then fell flat on the packed-earth floor inside.

Gudrid was waiting for him, hands on her hips. "Did you successfully slaughter the enemy door?" she taunted.

Thorfinn ignored her comment.

"You can put the barrel down by the door," she said, then turned back to a makeshift counter to continue washing what looked like purple berries.

"What are these?" he asked, taking a handful.

"They're sweet berries I found. They're growing throughout the meadow."

Thorfinn put the handful in his mouth. They burst on his tongue, releasing a pleasant juice. "They're very sweet. Can we make wine out of them?" he wondered.

Gudrid smiled. "I don't see why not. We make wine out of everything else."

Thorfinn popped another handful into his mouth and nodded in approval as he chewed them.

Gudrid looked at him, then hesitated. "Thorfinn, have you thought when we can make the trip to Markland?"

"As soon as we get settled, Gudrid. We are at the beginning of the cold season and we have a lot to do before the snow comes." He grimaced. "We have missed the end of the growing season. Soon we will have to fish, harvest the salt from the ocean to preserve the fish, and do a thousand other jobs to make this settlement liveable during the winter months."

Gudrid nodded, knowing that Thorfinn was right. "We have at least fourteen dœgr of work before we can think about doing anything else. The houses need to be repaired and cleaned to make them even semi-liveable again."

A goat walked in the open door. Thorfinn looked at it and then at Gudrid, smiling.

Gudrid met Thorfinn's smile. "I guess it's milking time."

Thorfinn laughed. "Maybe you can train the goat to bring in the milk bucket when it is milking time."

Chuckling, Gudrid shooed the goat back outside. "I'll be out checking the other houses," she said, and followed it out.

Thorfinn hung back to examine the longhouse constructed by Leif and his men. It was just like the houses back home. In fact, Thorfinn noticed few additions that modernized the ancient and traditional design. Three wooden poles rose at intervals from earthen benches running along the long sides of the structure; overhead, beams crossed the width of the house to connect with the vertical poles and support a third pole, running the length of the building and supporting the traditional pitched grass roof. The long benches running along the perimeter of the sod house not only supported the walls; during the day they functioned as seating, and at night, with the addition of furs, they were easily converted into beds.

The roof was a simple design; straight, tightly bound branches rested on the frame, with sod laid on these branches to absorb the rain and insulate against the cold winter wind. As long as there was a fire burning in the central pit—and the fire was rarely, if ever, allowed to go out in the winter—the house would remain dry and warm. A trap door in the roof allowed smoke from the hearth to escape.

The wood and sod walls, along with the howling wind and the sound of the ocean surf outside, made Thorfinn feel at home. But he had to agree with Gudrid—much work needed to be done on the longhouse and all the other houses to make them habitable. The fire pit and the ember pit needed to be cleaned before they could light a fire and begin cooking. Pots, both hanging on nails around the central room and piled on the benches, needed to be scrubbed. He noticed a bellows buried among the cookware, which reminded him that it was dægurs since the crew had had a hot meal. For their bravery on the back of the Serpent for dægurs on end, the crew deserved a hot feast. And for their safe deliverance to Vinland, the gods needed to be honoured.

The building had a feeling of abandonment—no, not abandonment, Thorfinn thought; rather, waiting. It was security for some future return, or frequent returns. He tried to imagine people inhabiting this building. He couldn't see their faces, but he imagined them sitting around the central hearth, talking, smoking pipes, drinking wine, and telling stories of their travels and the legends of the Vikings who never returned from the seas, but now feasted on fish in Ran's palace. He heard their belly laughs; these were his people—they grabbed hold of as much life as they possibly could and held onto it for as long as possible.

The flames dimmed in his mind and he was back in the darkened dwelling. The wind blew outside and whistled through small breaches in the walls.

Gudrid entered. "You look like you've had a vision," she observed.

"I imagined that I saw the inhabitants of this dwelling."

She nodded knowingly. "It sounds like you had a vision of those who came before us and died, but have not yet entered Valhalla. Were the people in your vision happy?"

"Yes; they were laughing and talking," Thorfinn replied sombrely.

"Do not look sad, my husband. Their cheer indicates they will be in Valhalla soon," Gudrid assured him.

M

As Elsu led his party of Wendats through the land of trees, he was both excited and scared, and knew this mingling of feelings was a good thing. This was the second time the Wendat had sent a party to greet visitors with white faces from across the great body of water.

However, the Wendat people did not all think this was a good thing. Some saw the new encounters as potential alliances; others did not like the radical differences in culture and beliefs and did not see any benefit to the Wendat people. The white faces had powerful weapons and their ways were confusing at times; those who disagreed feared that the Wendat people could not have a truly equal relationship with them.

Their last encounter with people like these had not been very successful. Mistakes were made on both sides, and both Wendats and white faces were killed. The white faces left the land and his people fled into the woods. Elsu's father had warned their ageing chief that these people would return again. The permanent settlement that the white faces constructed indicated their intention.

Elsu had been just a small child the first time, but he remembered what his father had told him: that someday when Elsu was older and took his father's place on the council of the tribe, he would have to confront the people with the white faces.

"They should not be feared," his father had said; "they can stay on the land where they settled, by the ocean. But the white faces must always realize that they are guests on the land and nothing more." Elsu needed to make this known to the new settlers.

He needed to prepare himself, his people, and the white face leaders for the future. He could not afford to be swept away by the adventure of the trek. His people relied on his experience for a successful first encounter, and unfortunately this involved many risks. But Elsu knew that if the Wendats could make an alliance with these powerful people, they could help the Wendats defeat their enemies. It was a hope fraught with risk, yes, but if it was carefully devised and maintained, he believed that the alliance could work.

At the edge of the trees, Elsu stopped and turned to look at his party. Taima carried furs for the strangers. Kiche carried the greeting staff. Traditionally, first encounters began with an exchange of gifts, with the hope that they would lead to a trading relationship in the future. The gifts tested the fairness of the other people. If they took too much, then they were too greedy and too unworthy of trade; if they offered too little, they were also not worthy, because they lacked the capacity to evaluate fairness. This meeting was more than a trade, Elsu thought. It was a chance to right wrongs of the past and to ensure that the future was a prosperous one for both peoples. If everything went well, a bartering relationship could develop that could lead to trade in other areas, to establish blood relations between them. But this was too far into the future and far too uncertain, Elsu reminded himself.

The full day's journey through the thick brush and over the rocky land had not been easy for Elsu and his small band. But now, as he looked above the trees and saw clouds of grey and black smoke rising from the settlement of the red-haired white man, his heart began pumping. He knew that the clouds came from their smithy, where they made their sharp weapons of hard metal. This was what made them powerful: their skill in changing the shiny rocks from bogs into weapons; it was a skill that his people lacked. His people had tried before to acquire the skill and the weapons, but the white faces refused to trade their weapons and their knowledge of how to create them.

As Elsu extended his hand and took the greeting staff offered by Kiche, he thought of the many times that he and his dead love, Yakima, had performed this ritual. Her natural charm and likability had always made the greetings easier. She effortlessly attracted people to her with her generosity and energy for life. At times he had felt overwhelmed by the light that was so much a part of her, like the light of the morning sun, emanating in its rainbow of gold and oranges through dawn's wispy clouds. But with Yakima by his side, Elsu had felt confident and safe. He wished that she was here with him now, in body as well as in spirit.

The group stepped out of the forest into the meadow. In the distance, Elsu saw the white faces working hard in their village, probably preparing for the winter months when food was scarce. The winters in this part of the country were long and sometimes harsh; everyone had to make sure that they had enough food to last, sometimes for up to six months of the year. There were times in the history of the Wendat people when the growing season was not plentiful enough, and when the herds of deer and caribou had migrated south to the warmer and more plentiful lands until the snow melted, they'd had to make the potion of the evergreen tree to survive through the winter months.

They were close enough now that the white faces could see them. Some of them stopped what they were doing and stared at Elsu's group. Elsu felt a nervous tension building inside of him. It was the same tension he felt when he hunted: a heightened sense of fear that raised his awareness and filled him with a mysterious energy that could only come from the Guardian Spirit.

Because they were a small group, he didn't think that the white faces would find them threatening. Three men carrying bundled furs hardly constituted a threat to a settlement full of armed men and women. They approached the main entrance to the settlement of grass buildings. The white faces also moved, taking up positions opposite them, but within the confines of the settlement. Elsu noticed what he interpreted as fearful curiosity on their faces; it mirrored what he felt inside.

He purposely slowed his gait. Elsu knew that from now on, any moves made by him or his group had to be conscious and thoughtful. The smallest wrong move could be again misinterpreted as aggressive, and start another war. His chief wanted allies, not more enemies; they needed help to push their existing enemies to a distance where they could no longer harm the Wendat people. He only hoped that the white faces weren't a bigger threat than the native enemies of the Wendat people.

More of the white faces appeared from behind the grass houses. They converged at the opening in the fence, blocking the entrance. Elsu could not understand their fear and prejudice. There were only three of them. That was not a threat big enough to justify a reaction of this scale. But he did realize that if the white faces showed up in his village, his people would probably take precautionary action to assure the safety of their community.

A man walked through the crowd of people, approaching Elsu's group. *These must be the leaders,* Elsu thought. He and those with him stopped. A female white face pushed through the crowd, her sword drawn. Was she the protector of the other one?

* * *

Thorfinn slowed as he sized up the small group of natives, looking at each in turn as he thought about his next move. Fascination warred with nervousness. These weren't like the natives of Grœnlandia; their skin was much darker. He didn't feel threatened by them. One of them balanced himself on one leg without the benefit of support. Thorfinn stared until the man looked away uncomfortably, then, his jaw hardening with pride, or determination, or perhaps a bit of both, he took the furs held by the other and hopped toward Thorfinn. The man held the furs out, offering them to him.

Thorfinn took the furs with a smile, then turned and yelled, "What food do we have to give?"

"We have cheese that has been curing during the ocean voyage," yelled one of the settlers—Thorfinn didn't recognize the voice. "As well as some butter."

"Bring some to me," Thorfinn ordered.

Moments later, butter and cheese were passed through the crowd of Norse and handed to Thorfinn. He handed the food to the native leader, then watched and waited as the natives examined the container of butter and a quarter-wheel of cheese. They each smelled the food, then looked back at Thorfinn, their expressions puzzled.

Thorfinn mimed eating by raising his hand to his mouth several times. The natives caught on; the wheel was passed around, and they broke off pieces and placed them in their mouths. They exchanged looks. By their expressions, Thorfinn guessed that they were enjoying the trade.

The leader's eyes roved over the gathered Norse, lingering

on the weapons clutched in their owners' hands or fastened to their belts. He stepped forward and pointed. Thorfinn followed the native's finger to the sword in Freydis's hand. He looked at the native and shook his head.

Thorfinn's experience had taught him that to secure their safety, they had to maintain military superiority. If the natives acquired weapons superior to what they currently had, with their numbers, they could become a formidable fighting force. Thorfinn didn't want to have any part in the creation of that force. As it was, their numbers using spears and arrows could easily overwhelm the Norse in the settlement. If Thorfinn's people wanted to permanently settle Vinland someday, they needed to know that their safety was assured. Besides, Thorfinn had seen through his decades of trading and commerce that some societies possessing the monetary wealth to buy whatever they wanted did not have the skill or the experience to wisely use their acquisitions. He had witnessed states and territories plunged into war.

"Our weapons are not for trade," Thorfinn said, hoping that his meaning was understood, if not the tone. Since he knew neither their language nor the intelligence of the natives, he couldn't be sure that he got his meaning across. But the disappointed expression on the native's face told Thorfinn that he had.

Thorfinn gestured, inviting the group into the settlement to look around, with the hope that the natives would see other things they wanted to trade for . . . taking their attention off the idea of trading for Norse weapons.

* * *

Even though Elsu enjoyed the taste of the food, he hadn't wanted to give up the furs for the food. He'd hoped the friendship gift would be one or two of the weapons, but he wasn't surprised at the white face's decision. If he correctly interpreted their leader's meaning, then Elsu knew that the white faces were not going to share how they made the metal for the weapons. It was an uncomfortable position to be in, knowing that his people's relationship to these people wouldn't be equal on every level. But Elsu also knew that what they lacked in might, they overwhelmingly made up for in numbers.

Elsu looked at his companions and gestured for them to follow him into the settlement. This was not a time to give in to his fears. The lack of communication between his people and the white faces could easily descend into fear and distrust and finally into armed aggression. Elsu wanted allies, not enemies. He needed to take a leap of faith and trust the white faces, just as they would have to trust him. It was a step toward ratifying their alliance, which at this point seemed a little bit premature. Elsu felt more comfortable calling it a relationship.

The first thing he noticed beyond the gate was the structures; they were constructed from the grass of the meadow. Like his people, the longhouses provided much more space on the interior. The grass buildings had doors and windows and a door in the roof where smoke exited from the interior. These were not the structures of a nomadic people, like the Wendat, but the design and use of the materials provided by the land was a similarity that both peoples shared. As he walked through the settlement, Elsu secretly hoped that the white faces and his people would find many more similarities, to help build a relationship.

A rhythmic clanging drew his eye. Almost hidden behind a building, two white faces were hitting what looked like one of their weapons with a hammer. Its tip glowed red hot, and with each strike of the hammer, tiny flecks of fire jumped into the air like fireflies in the night sky. A kiln burned brightly beside them. The blows stopped, and one of the white faces put the tip of the weapon back into the kiln, presumably to heat the blade up again.

Elsu gravitated toward the men, hoping to learn how they were performing what he considered magic. When wood was put on a fire, the flame burned to glowing embers, but then turned to a grey dust. But when this hard, shiny substance burned red hot, it didn't fall to dust.

The white face leader cut in front of Elsu, preventing him from getting closer to the men at the kiln.

* * *

Thorfinn didn't think the native understood what he was seeing, but he couldn't be sure. Intelligence was not confined to a segment of the world. Thorfinn had noted several distinct types of what could be considered intelligence among his own people. The natives survived in a very different world than what he and the other Norse knew. His was a feudal society, where men and women worked the land for the landowners; there was a prosperous, currency-based economy. Eirik's stories of the new world revealed no evidence of this type of society; the people here were still tribal. But that only meant that they had a different kind of knowledge—not inferior or superior to the Norse knowledge, just different.

He smiled at the native leader and waved him forward, drawing the small group past the smithy.

* * *

Yakima had walked with Elsu, as she always had, though he could no longer see or sense her. Now, as the men moved on, she hesitated, more interested in what was inside the sod structures than what was going on outside. She noticed very few females in the settlement and wondered if the white faces would remain here, or if they would leave. If they were serious about staying, she found it odd that the men didn't bring more women with them.

She heard muffled voices; though she couldn't understand the words that were being spoken, she did recognize that they were female. *Maybe the women are in the grass structures,* she thought. As she walked past a partially open door, she timorously peered into the dark interior, and saw a woman pushing clothes down into a pot of hot water with a stick. The fire was low, to keep the water hot but not boiling.

Yakima stopped and watched the woman, not knowing what to do. She wanted to go in and talk to her, but she was afraid.

As if she'd sensed that she was being watched, the white face woman turned and looked directly at Yakima. They gazed at one another for a moment, and then the woman smiled and gestured for Yakima to enter the house.

Yakima squeezed through the opening afforded by the door that stood ajar and stepped into the dark interior. As she slowly approached the white face woman, she felt no fear; neither did she feel threatened. It was almost as if the woman she was approaching was her friend.

* * *

Gudrid had heard the commotion outside, but something inside her told her to remain where she was and to focus on her task. She sensed that natives were visiting the settlement. Leif had told stories, both humorous and otherwise, of his encounters with the natives. He'd said that they were a curious people who wanted to communicate with others, both natives of Vinland

and visitors.

The native woman peeking through the partially opened door seemed familiar. She sensed no threat. "Come in," Gudrid said, knowing that the native woman didn't understand her, but hoping that her body language would get her meaning across.

Gudrid read nervousness in the native's body language, but she didn't feel fear. Her skin was paler than Gudrid had expected. There was something so familiar about the woman; even though she was not a mirror image, Gudrid felt that she was looking at herself.

She gestured for the native woman to sit down next to her. "Gudrid," she said, putting her hand on her chest.

"Gudrid," the woman repeated, mimicking Gudrid's gesture.

"No," Gudrid said with a smile. "I am Gudrid." She pointed at the woman and shook her head. "No, Gudrid."

The woman looked blankly at her. Suddenly something over Gudrid's left shoulder caught her attention—her eyes widened. In an instant, she grabbed Gudrid's arm and pulled her closer. Gudrid didn't have enough time to feel fear—until the metal pot of hot water crashed into the fire, accompanied by a whoosh of steam that jetted in all directions.

As Gudrid rose from the woman's arms, the realization of the native's actions quickly overcame her. Steam filled the longhouse; Gudrid's saviour disappeared into whiteness. When the steam thinned, the native girl seemed to have evaporated along with it. Gudrid ran to the door and flung it open, hoping to catch up with the native girl, but she was gone.

She noticed a commotion over by the smithy; a crowd had gathered around the entrance to the building. Tostig held a bloodied axe; Thorfinn stood next to him, looking down at a dead native. Gudrid followed others moving toward the crowd and pushed her way to the front.

A one-legged native lay on the ground, his head completely severed from his body. Blood spurted from wildly dancing arteries in his neck and flowed into the sooty black earth.

"Thorfinn, he tried to take some weapons," Tostig was saying defensively. "He pulled out a dagger and pointed it at me."

Thorfinn's face was a mask, but Gudrid knew what he was thinking—the natives would look on the killing as a sign of aggression; they now risked war with the natives, and that was the last thing that Thorfinn wanted to provoke. But it was too late now. Gudrid wondered if he'd warned them to stay away from the weapons. *Probably.* She knew her husband's dreams, and the care he would put into fulfilling them.

"Bury the body beyond the settlement," Thorfinn said.

"What happened?" Gudrid asked.

"Natives came to the settlement, looking to trade. This one," he said, indicating the corpse, "attacked Tostig while trying to steal weapons. Tostig killed him in self-defence. The others were scared off by our bull."

"Where did the woman go?" Gudrid asked.

"What woman?" Thorfinn asked, frowning his confusion. "There were only three men."

"But—" Gudrid stopped, realizing what had happened.

As she entered her grass house, the face of the native girl haunted Gudrid. It was as if she had been looking at a reflection of herself—not so much in physical appearance, but in the way she knew who that girl was.

The native woman was part of her waking dream.

The steam from the boiling water still hovered above the cold dirt floor, like fog clinging to the air above the ocean surface. Above it, a light, greyish white haze permeated the room. The heavy iron pot lay on its side, and the clothes had spilled out of it to lie in a puddle of mud.

She could still feel a presence in the longhouse—not of a single individual, but a group of people. The room disappeared in a swirl of vapours for a moment, then Gudrid found herself in the middle of the room, surrounded by the people that she had come to know and love. Older men talked and laughed in muted tones on the benches, discussing the day's work. She heard the crackling of the fire in the central hearth. Thorfinn lay sleeping on the bench seat, mumbling in his dreams from behind a curtain of his unwashed, whitish blonde hair.

Looking down, Gudrid found her hand on a cradle, rocking a baby that she hadn't seen before, though its face looked familiar; she felt she should know this child. Short blonde ringlets framed its face. *This baby was born in the new world,* she thought.

The child had many admirers, from the adopted grandmother overseeing the evening meal simmering in a pot in the centre of the pit to the iron smiths, the hunters, the warriors (who had named him the Little Leader), to the natives who visited periodically and marvelled over his golden blonde hair. They called him Rising Sun, after the dawn.

At his birth, they had brought him gifts from their tribe: small gold nuggets, symmetrical samples of translucent quartz, and bushels of small berries and nuts. Gudrid had accepted them all. The native girl had forged a spiritual link between her and the new world peoples.

There was a lingering aroma, a mixture of simmering soup, wet, matted fur from the hares tied to the rafters, and the pungent odour of sweat, drawn forth while forging a living in a new land; it was overpowering as well as invigorating. These men and women worked and lived in conditions where the cold numbed their fingers and toes and bullets of freezing rain pelted their rugged bodies for half the tvö misseri; it was an existence that they would not trade with any other nation they encountered.

Gudrid touched her stomach and realized that the baby in the cradle was hers.

"Karla," Gudrid asked the old woman stirring the cauldron, "have you ever had visions?"

The woman puckered her brows for a moment, trying to think back over more decades than she could possibly remember. She stared off to a period back in time as she spoke the thought that formed and lingered in her mind's eye. "Yes, once in my life. I remember predicting the death of our king. And I remember seeing the man who had committed the murder." Her gaze sharpened on Gudrid. "Gudrid, have you been witnessing sights in your mind? Sights that you are not a part of, but are nevertheless happening?"

"Yes," she answered. "But since the birth of Snorri, the visions have been confined to my dreams. I don't know if they are real or the imaginings of a slumbering mind."

Gudrid felt that she was a part of two worlds, a participant in the drama as well as an observer. Periods of unconscious knowing mingled with states of present being.

"All visions, whether they happen while you are awake or while you are asleep, are the visions of a blessed female. Do not doubt them," Karla told her.

"I feel that I have a role to play in this . . . saga that's unfolding before me. I'm a participant as well as an observer who sees it from the beginning to the end. I've participated in three voyages with three husbands. The first was Thorvald, the second was my husband Thorstein, and now Thorfinn. The first two men have died, and I now fear for my husband and my son."

"You cannot run from the fates of the gods," Karla said, looking into the soup she was stirring as if she were seeing her answers in the pot. "We are instruments for their purposes, but they have a purpose for us that we help them to realize. It is both a tragic and an honourable duty."

"I do not want to lose my husband, nor my son," Gudrid cried.

Karla left her pot and came to Gudrid. "Gudrid, you will not lose your son, nor will you lose your husband. These are blessed times for you." She took a deep breath, then continued. "You did not know me before this voyage. My sister was Grimhild. She told me of a vision of her death and about this voyage made to Vinland by your husband. She mentioned the child that wasn't conceived on land. This was all given to her in a vision, two tvö misseri before she met you and your second husband, Thorstein."

Gudrid knew of Grimhild; she had a reputation among her people as a seer. She had lived part of her vision. She was happy that the gods' plan for her and her family was in communion with the life they were living. Gudrid couldn't suffer another loss; she feared that she could not survive on her own with a child.

As Karla moved back to the soup pot, the room quieted. Those present turned and looked at Gudrid as if waiting for her to say something, or come to some sort of decision. Gudrid looked into each of their faces, and then her eyes fell to the baby in the cradle. Snorri stared back up at her with innocent eyes.

She knew what she had to do. She couldn't be a passive participant in her life; she needed to take action that would guarantee the safety of her husband and her child. They needed her as much as she needed them.

And with that, the vision dissipated.

Harald and Tostig were completing the repairs on the small boat abandoned by Leif's Vinland expedition. Years of exposure to the salt air, the wind, and the pelting rain had damaged the small, wooden, twelve-person craft, but at the hands of these master builders, the repairs went quickly and without much incident.

The small boat was supported on two struts, as it had been when they first arrived at the settlement, but what had looked like a dead relic was now returning to life. They'd tipped the boat on its side and replaced its rotted boards with planks fashioned from the trees surrounding the meadow. A resin made of pine sap bubbled in a pot resting over an open fire. Into this, Tostig dipped a piece of shaved wood, thin enough to be pliable but sturdy enough that he was able to spread the thick, tar-like mixture into the many breaches left by years of disuse and neglect.

"How are the repairs coming along?" Thorfinn asked as he approached them.

"Faster than we expected," the dwarf answered, wiping sweat from his face with a dirty rag.

The wind suddenly changed and Thorfinn smelled the pine tar warming on the open fire. The aroma caught in his throat. On a much smaller hearth, pine roots were heating to leach the tar out. The whole area smelled of burning wood, smoke, and long days spent outdoors. "Where did you get the resin?" Thorfinn asked.

"We brought the pine tar with us," Tostig answered proudly, "to make repairs to the *Mimir* at sea when necessary."

"Is that one of Gudrid's cooking pots?" Thorfinn eyed the pot suspiciously. "You better not let her catch you with it, or you'll never taste cooked food for as long as you are in this land."

Tostig and Harald exchanged a look. Neither gave any indication which one of them had pilfered Gudrid's cooking vessel. They both looked guilty.

Tostig walked over to the pot on the larger fire pit. He pulled the rag out of his pocket again and took hold of the pot to steady it while he gave the pine tar a slow stir.

Thorfinn watched as the two men dipped planed pieces of wood into the bubbling tar and coated the inside of the boat. The dry wood quickly soaked up the thick liquid, filling cracks and defects in the wooden planks as well as the seams along the length of the boat.

"Is the boat safe to transport the party to Markland and back?" Thorfinn asked.

"I can't guarantee her seaworthiness in open water," Harald answered. "As you can see, the wood is weathered and old."

"But we reinforced its structure," Tostig interrupted. "We've replaced several planks near the prow; it will take the party safely to the shore of Markland and back again."

Thorfinn's unease about his wife travelling without him to an unknown and potentially dangerous land had lifted a little, but even though he had come to fully trust Tostig, he still feared for Gudrid's safety. He suspected his feelings were laced with jealousy of a past that kept leaking into the present; a past over which he had no control. He felt foolish for being jealous of Gudrid's dead husbands. It had nothing to do with the existence of past husbands, he knew, but rather the capacity in which they still existed for Gudrid. He realized that these feelings he wrestled with couldn't be resolved within the confines of his imagination. He needed to look at them with respect to the love, trust, and respect that Gudrid and Thorfinn had for one another.

* * *

"Thorfinn, Gudrid!" Jarlabanke yelled. "Come quickly, the

Mimir is gone."

Thorfinn rolled over and opened his eyes to see Jarlabanke in the doorway, frantically yelling at them. He didn't register every word, but he did notice Jarlabanke's desperate tone. Before Thorfinn had a chance to question him further, Jarlabanke was out the door of the grass house, vanishing as quickly as he'd appeared.

Thorfinn dragged himself out of bed, muttering curses. Noises outside, beyond the perimeter of the community, silenced him. They were coming from the direction of the water. He pulled on his tunic and staggered to the door, still groggy from his abrupt awakening. "This better be important," he mumbled.

"What's wrong, hon?" Gudrid asked from the bed.

"I don't know; I'm going to find out." He tugged on his boots. As he opened the door, Gudrid rolled over to go back to sleep.

Thorfinn walked toward the beach, where the settlers had gathered, talking excitedly to each other and pointing. He couldn't understand what all the commotion was about—until he looked out at the water. For a second he noticed something odd, but couldn't figure out what. And then it hit him—the *Mimir* was gone.

Tostig saw Thorfinn approaching the group and met him.

"Tostig, how could this have happened?"

"The tide must've pushed the *Mimir* away from the rock and pulled her out to sea."

It took a second for Thorfinn to realize it, but they had no way of getting home again. No one in Grœnlandia or Iceland would know that they'd made it to Vinland, so no one would be searching for them. He wasn't upset because he felt trapped on Vinland—he had decided that this was going to be his new home and the home of his family and the future home of his people. But to be cut off from his homeland, to know that the possibility existed that he may never return there . . . that was what he found more upsetting than anything else.

Then he realized that they could always build another ship; Vinland and Markland had enough resources to build a fleet of ships. Still, the sense of loss lingered. The *Mimir* was almost a part of him; Thorfinn had even named it himself, just as a parent names a child. And even though his relationship with the ship had been for a shorter than expected period of time, Thorfinn had grown attached to it and had planned and fantasized about all the voyages that they'd take together. Thoughts of building another ship, a better ship that would take them to far-off places, didn't seem to help. Thorfinn knew that in time he'd forget the *Mimir*, but . . .

"Thorfinn, Harald and I will lead a team to design another ship that will take us back to Grœnlandia," Tostig said.

"How long will that take?" he asked.

"We could have it ready to sail two summers from now."

Two tvö misseri seemed like a very long time, Thorfinn thought. But they were on Vinland for the immediate future and he had no plans of returning to Grœnlandia or Iceland until they had enough goods to make the return trip profitable. He could wait two tvö misseri. "Assemble the senior settlers in the Great Hall," he ordered. He turned away and headed back to the house.

About fourteen senior members of the Vinlander expedition gathered in the Great Hall. They sat on the earthen benches built into the sides of the structure; a fire sparked and snapped in its central hearth.

Hours earlier, Gudrid had hung a shield bearing their family crest on the wall just above a large chair at the head of the room. The chair served as a pseudo throne; the participants had to look up in order to address the person sitting in that chair. This, combined with the shield, lent authority to the meeting. Thorfinn settled in the chair and spent a moment looking at the faces around the room. He was proud of their accomplishments. But he knew that there was much more that they needed to do to create a prosperous place for his people to grow.

Crops would have to be planted next year; it was far too late in the season to be planting now. They had brought seeds with them, and Gudrid was confident that once they worked the soil, the seeds could take root. But she had noticed that the same types of plants growing in Vinland's rocky soil were hardier and seemed to thrive in the harsher soil.

Vinland provided everything they needed. The wheat grew in wild abundance, and they'd found a grove of sweet red fruit trees that some said were apples, something that most of them hadn't tasted before. They only needed to collect the fruits and store them in barrels full of soil for the winter.

Noticing that the group had settled down, Thorfinn began the meeting.

"I've gathered you here to make an important and exciting announcement," he said, looking around. "But before I make my announcement, I would like to express my gratitude for your hard work, and say that I've decided to increase your share of the profits."

They responded with excited mumbling.

"As you know, it's always been my hope to remain in Vinland and to claim this land for our people. There is more wealth here than we could all spend in one lifetime. In the spring we will plant crops; until then, wheat doesn't seem to be a problem—it grows most everywhere. We've been able to find berries, and the animals are plentiful; fish are so abundant that we can fish with our bare hands in knee-deep water. My plan is to establish a permanent colony here on Vinland and later, one on the shores of Markland."

Thorfinn paused to gauge the reaction of the group, then continued. "Here on Vinland I will build a fort, the size and stability of which will rival Aggersborg and Fyrkat. It will stand one túnlengd from this place." All eyes followed Thorfinn's finger as he extended his hand and pointed in a landsuðr direction. "A fort will allow us to protect Leif's settlement as well as establish a strong and lasting presence in this land. It will be the first step for Grœnlanders to stretch their influence beyond their homeland."

The crowd's mumbling grew agitated; they seemed to be catching the excitement of Thorfinn's idea.

"With a fort in Vinland and later Markland, we can protect the resources that we harvest from this land and from Markland." Thorfinn paused again, letting the idea of profits congeal in their minds. He understood that these people were not merchants and therefore did not see this opportunity in that light. Most likely their thoughts were on family and home.

"Thorfinn, will some of us be able to return home if we do not want to remain here?" Tostig asked.

"Yes, of course. In fact, once we've established a transport route, knarrs carrying people and supplies will be a common thing between here and Grœnlandia. The loss of the *Mimir* could be considered a good thing. It will allow us to focus our efforts on staying here. The very act of surviving on this land will be a commitment to building a permanent home here."

"I must return to Europe," Adam said. "My clerical duties must take precedence over your plans of settlement on this land."

"I understand that, Adam. But as you can see, without a ship that is not a possibility for the immediate future. Once we've constructed our ship, you will make the first voyage back. For the rest of you, I hope that you'll stay to be a part of our future in this new country. It's my wish and intention to bring skilled craftspeople with their families to Vinland to assist us in building a community."

Thorfinn noticed that his speech did have some effect on the group; the buzz in the room rose in volume.

"Thorfinn, I will stay!" Tostig yelled. "I will be a part of the creation of the future of our people."

Other voices echoed his response. Gudrid looked at Thorfinn and smiled. She and Freydis were the only two women present at what she'd called the early stages of a council. Knowing she wanted to ensure that the future they were creating was for all Norse, including women and children, Thorfinn nodded for her to add her voice to his.

"This fort will not be an establishment of male military dominance," she said. "It is a place where a community will form, out of the need to maintain a strong and long-lasting presence on Vinland."

"That's right," Thorfinn said. "It is prudent to protect ourselves and our land, but we will not use the fort for aggressive acts, only defence."

The group's agreement to this was a little less unanimous. Some believed that the Skræling presence should be wiped out to ensure a dominant Norse future on Vinland; Thorfinn was diametrically against that. His experience as a merchant taught him that any fair trade market created communities and exploitation destroyed markets. They weren't *i*Viking. In order to create and maintain wealth, they had to maintain an evolving plan of commerce.

The natives had a wealth of knowledge of this land and its resources, and Thorfinn hoped to make use of that knowledge to the benefit of all. His people could bring vital skills to the natives and they in turn would lead the way to those resources. True, all knowledge was not equal, but that did not mean that Norse ingenuity was superior to the natives'. They had a skill that the natives lacked. And with time, Thorfinn believed that he'd find out that the natives had skills of their own, skills that the Norse lacked.

"Tostig and Harald have finished the repairs to the *Ragnarök*. The boat is ready to sail to Markland tomorrow morning. Gudrid will lead the expedition; Freydis will be at her side to assist. Tostig and Snorri Thorbrandsson will accompany them, as will Adam. Jarlabanke will go to serve and the two warrior escorts are Ingibjörg and Ásgeirr. Are there any questions?"

Thorfinn paused and looked around the room at their faces. Almost one by one, they didn't look back. Instead they looked at each other, one person waiting for the other to reply or comment on Thorfinn's announcement. Thorfinn didn't know what to think.

"For the short term we'll split our resources. Some will begin the work on the ship and others will begin working on the fort. If there are no objections, we should put off the actual construction projects till the group returns from Markland."

"What is the purpose of the Vinland expedition?" Karla asked.

* * *

Gudrid's vocal chords tightened. She immediately remembered her vision, that Karla was the primary character in it. She wondered about her role in their future on Vinland and Markland. Was Karla to have a hand in its unfolding? Even though Gudrid didn't have sight on this subject, it didn't mean that it wasn't going to happen.

Thorfinn looked at Gudrid. Fearing that he might hesitate and arouse suspicion with the elders of their young community, Gudrid said, "We are going over for supplies."

"Well then, why is Adam of Bremen going with you?" Karla asked.

"Because . . . uh, he is searching for the Culdees, a small colony of Irish monks," Thorfinn cut in. It was a hasty answer to an unexpected question. Gudrid didn't know if the answer satisfied Karla, but it would have to do.

"If no one has any more questions, then I suggest that we adjourn so the Markland group can prepare for their trip," Thorfinn said.

People stood one by one and formed their own small discussion groups. Thorfinn and Gudrid left the meeting hall, preferring to spend their last evening together for a long while away from the rest of the community.

N

Gudrid took the brooch in her quivering hand. She grasped it lightly, as if it were a sliver of the most delicate glass. Its beauty made her entire body quiver with unnamed feelings that she'd not felt since her second husband was alive. She recognized the weight of the gold, but the sparkling frontal design looked as if a weaver's hand, and not a skilled jewelry maker, had intricately sewn its face. The light hit the ornament at different angles, and it radiated yellow and silver light that skipped across the brooch as if the craftsman had intentionally set in motion a flat stone across the still surface of a pond.

On closer inspection, she thought she saw the trinity symbol of the powerful European church. In the three-pronged centre of the brooch lay a raised, clover-shaped design accented with a silver outline. She suspected that Thorfinn had not noticed this. His allegiance to the Norse gods would not allow him to spend any amount of money on something with the slightest hint of a Christian symbol.

In the presence of this precious gift, Gudrid's beliefs remained in the middle. She could not quickly dismiss the cultural and religious beliefs she'd grown up with—they were too well ingrained in her heart and mind. However, she welcomed the wealth and prosperity that the monotheistic religion brought. It was moving across her lands like the locust swarms that descended almost every ten to twelve years on her country. Her people would no longer need to plunder foreign lands. Grœnlandia could trade under the prosperous banner of "the faith."

"It's stunning, Thorfinn. Thank you. I shall wear it with my cape," she said, pinning it on the neck of her cape. "My neighbours will think that I've found the treasure room at Uppsala."

"All the treasure rooms of Uppsala could not outweigh the treasure of your beauty," Thorfinn said. "It transcends anything from that sacred place."

Gudrid felt herself blushing. She could like the tone of a merchant's voice rather than the gruff and unfeeling sound of an explorer like Thorvald. At least Thorfinn would be at home more often and for longer periods than her second husband. Merchants dealt in commerce and so could understand the importance of negotiation. She had lived alone long enough. And by the spectacular gift she had just received, she knew that, at least for now, he loved her. "You are too kind, Thorfinn," Gudrid said as she allowed a pleasant shiver to pass through her body.

"Would you like to take a walk with me, Gudrid?" Thorfinn asked gently, extending his large hand.

"Yes, I would."

They walked out into the chilly Grœnlandia night and stood in front of Brattahlið, the dwelling of Eirik the Red. They looked out over the tundra, at the mountains of ice drifting on the shiny blackness of the Grœnlandia Sea. The crescent moon nestled in the sky. The still evening mirrored the peaceful silence she felt in her heart. It was as if the entire land had stopped for them.

Gudrid touched her brooch and smiled at Thorfinn. He smiled back.

"You're welcome," he said, knowing what was on her mind. "The brooch looks stunning on you — or should I say, your beauty makes the brooch look stunning."

"How did you know what I was thinking?" she asked, surprised at his accuracy.

"I don't know. I suppose right now our hearts are saying the same thing."

She intertwined her fingers with his and grasped his hand tighter as they walked out onto the grassy tundra, heading for the water.

"Too bad the moon isn't full," Thorfinn commented.

"We don't really need the moon, Thorfinn. We're the ones who give the moon its mystique."

"You're a poet!" He laughed.

Again she felt her cheeks heat. "Honestly, Thorfinn, I don't know where these words are coming from. I think you're bringing them out of me."

"The only thing I know is commerce and negotiation," he said. "I don't think it's me. It's probably Freydis." He laughed.

Frey and Freyja could not be happier than the two of them were tonight, she thought, while honouring the two gods for their blessings.

"Leif told me that the Eiriksson family adopted you into their family when your husbands died," Thorfinn said.

"Yes, I married two brothers in the Eiriksson family. My first husband was Thorvald, who died from a native attack on Markland; they buried him there at a place he named Kjalarness. Soon after that I married his brother, Thorstein. He died of a strange illness that struck his crew after they returned home from another voyage to Vinland."

They were silent for a moment. Then Thorfinn asked, "Gudrid, what would you like to see yourself doing in two tvö misseri from now?"

Gudrid stared at the white mountains floating by. "I think I'd like to travel, then start a family. I was unable to do these things with Thorvald. We married at a very young age and he was too eager to follow his family and to make a name for himself. I like living in Grœnlandia," she said, hearing her voice in harmony with the sound of the surf.

"Where would you like to travel?" Thorfinn asked.

"I think I would like to see Vinland and Markland again . . . someday."

"It is as though you are looking into my thoughts. Earlier, I was talking with Eirik and Leif about using their settlement at Vinland. I plan to make a trip there later in the year," Thorfinn said. He found Gudrid's hand without taking his eyes off the water. "Let's just stand here and quietly watch the world together."

It was Gudrid's turn to smile. She knew in her heart that she had found the man she would marry; his touch told her. Her heart and mind were devoid of every other emotion but love for him. "Tell me more about you, Thorfinn," she said.

"There isn't much to tell," he replied. " Most of my time I

spend scouting the oceans for raw materials for trade and
business opportunities. I have never been married, for no reason
other than being so busy travelling."

"Yes, you are young," Gudrid said, nodding.

"My life has been so full, I feel middle-aged, but I am only
in my early thirties," he agreed. "If I were to die tomorrow, I
think I could say that I'm fulfilled. I've been blessed with the
ability to make money."

"I think I can see in you the potential to fulfil a great many
things."

He looked at her. "Do you have the sight?"

Gudrid hesitated. "I . . . I have been told that. I sometimes
see things that come to pass, and I have had visions that no one
else sees." Up to this moment, she had only told her family; no
one else knew about these powers of seeing. She didn't know
why, but she felt that Thorfinn needed to know, and that she
could trust him.

They walked in silence, then stopped a foot away from
where the stony shore met the water. They just stood there,
looking out at the cold, windy night, and Gudrid had wrapped
her arms around Thorfinn's arm and moved close against him
for warmth . . .

With a smile, Gudrid again wrapped the brooch in its square
of leather and tucked it into her pack. *To remind me, while we're
apart,* she thought. She lifted the small bag of her belongings
and exited the longhouse, her mind turning to events even further
in her past than her and Thorfinn's courtship.

* * *

Thorfinn stood in the knee-high wisps of grass blowing in
the breeze. He watched Jarlabanke and the other men loading
supplies into the *Ragnarök* as it bobbed on the lapping waves.
The boat that Eirik's last expedition had left at the Vinland
settlement was aptly named for its short excursion capability.
Crossing the misty water to Markland was as far as it could
safely go.

This was not a good day for him. He feared for Gudrid's
safety. Thorfinn didn't consider himself a fighter except in
necessary and desperate situations. He thought himself a brave
man, but when love was concerned, fear turned every person
into a coward. Gudrid was a strong woman, but the sheer number
of Skrælings and the dubious relationship that his people had

with them scared Thorfinn. He wanted to promote good relations with the natives of this land, but their first encounter with the native delegation had been a failure. If they were to coexist successfully, then his people and the Skrælings needed to discuss and agree upon rules.

In his peripheral vision, Thorfinn saw another member of the team approaching the boat. He turned his head to see Adam tramping through the grass. "Adam!" Thorfinn yelled, and moved to intercept him. "I have one final question for you. Do you have a problem with taking orders from Gudrid?" he challenged.

"No," Adam blurted. "Our virgin—"

"Good." Thorfinn interrupted. "Other than myself, she is the only member of this crew that I trust."

Without another word, Thorfinn walked to the boat. By this time Tostig and the three warrior escorts for the expedition had loaded their belongings onto the craft. "I hold the four of you responsible for the safe return of my wife."

Tostig glanced at the men next to him, then spoke for all of them. "We'll bring her back safely, Thorfinn. You have my word."

Thorfinn placed his hand on Tostig's shoulder, knowing the importance of his wife's safety was now Tostig's priority.

Tostig and the warrior escorts turned as Freydis joined them. She slung her own pack into the boat, then stepped aside to allow Jarlabanke access. Thorfinn eyed the knarr. Even though the *Ragnarök* had enough places for six rowers and six passengers, with the supplies piled up at either end of the boat, it would barely accommodate everyone.

"Be careful with that," Adam growled from behind Jarlabanke as the servant clumsily dropped a wooden case into the boat. " It's delicate-—important!"

Thorfinn caught a whiff of yeasty breath; that and his slurred speech told Thorfinn that the monk was either drunk or hungover. No wonder Jarlabanke scrambled to comply; he didn't want to give the monk an opportunity for any alcohol-induced aggression.

Jarlabanke was working for his freedom. His grandfather had been captured at Walcheron, after seeing a great, heavenly fireball streaking through the night sky—a bad omen. Soon after Jarlabanke's grandfather spotted the object, he was captured and sold into slavery. Thorfinn hadn't told Jarlabanke when he would release him, but he figured that in six more full moons,

Jarlabanke would have paid him off in full.

Thorfinn looked into Jarlabanke's face, too weathered for a man of his young age, and wondered what he would do once free. What line of work would suit him best? *A farmer,* Thorfinn guessed. Here in this new world, any freedman with ambition might even surpass the wealth of his master. Jarlabanke's land holdings would increase; his offspring would own a district and would divide and lease out the land, and his family name would go on for a thousand years.

Gudrid exited the longhouse. She carried a small bag, probably containing some personal effects. Thorfinn moved forward and stood between her and the boat, waiting to spend a moment alone with her to say good-bye. He started missing her already; their life together up until now seemed all too short.

It was really not that long ago, he thought with a smile, *that I was sleepless with the terror of asking her to share my life . . .*

Thorfinn's chest had heaved and the cold morning air felt as if it held two pounding hearts as he knocked on Eirik's door. The sun had just peeked over the horizon. His focus was not on the time of day, but on Gudrid. He'd tossed and turned on his bed for most of the night, only to finally drift off from exhaustion, three hours earlier. The morning chill penetrated his thinly layered tunics; in the rush to dress before he lost his nerve, he'd not paid attention to what he threw on.

The wooden door rattled with Thorfinn's second pounding. He had half a mind to open the door and let himself in, but he knew such behaviour would be unforgivable. Perhaps Eirik was in his field, or perhaps not awake yet.

Thorfinn's answer came with the sound of a latch being tripped on the other side of the door. It creaked open.

"Thorfinn," Gudrid said, sounding surprised to see him.

"Hello Gudrid," he answered. The fear of what he was about to do tugged at the tether that tied his courage to his heart and to Gudrid. "Is Eirik at home?"

"Yes; he went out to the field just—"

Thorfinn didn't wait for the rest of her sentence. He feared that if he stayed and talked to her any longer, he would run in the opposite direction from Eirik and never see either one of them again.

He started up the hill where he saw Eirik talking to one of his bondsmen. Eirik was known as a fair and lenient landowner.

His tenants praised him, as they once did his father Leif, as an honest man. Both lived by and taught a strong code of ethics.

Eirik stared past his man when he saw Thorfinn running up the grassy hill. He put his hand on the bondsman's shoulder, indicating that the meeting was over, and they parted. He met Thorfinn halfway down the hill. Thorfinn stumbled to a halt, wheezing heavily.

"Catch your breath, my friend," Eirik said, and smiled knowingly.

"Eirik, I must speak with you."

Eirik remained silent.

"I cannot tell you how, for the past several viknatal, I've been overjoyed and tortured," Thorfinn said, unable to look his friend in the face. "I am . . . " Thorfinn gasped, "I-I'm in love . . . with Gudrid." He felt as if he was the first man to ever say those words. "This is very hard to say, and embarrassing for a man of my stature and place in society."

Eirik laughed. "I know, Thorfinn, I know. We have all been shamed to think that our feelings are weaknesses. But believe me when I tell you that it makes us warriors."

Eirik moved to grab Thorfinn's shoulders, but stopped as Thorfinn's hand went up, signalling that he was not finished. "I . . . would like your permission to marry her."

Eirik laughed out loud. "Nothing could make me happier. But the decision to marry you . . . is Gudrid's."

Fear crept back into Thorfinn. The last thing he wanted to do was confront Gudrid in this condition. "I understand."

There was a moment when the two men didn't speak; the chaotic thoughts in Thorfinn's head amounted to a silence of an unusual kind. The sound of his name broke the silence.

"Thorfinn," a female voice called from behind him.

"I will leave you two alone," Eirik said.

"No! Wait—please," Thorfinn blurted, but Eirik ignored his friend's words and ambled away, chuckling.

Gudrid walked across the field to him, her dress swaying in time with the short tundra grass. She looked so happy to see him.

"Hello, Gudrid," he managed before his vocal chords clenched, and further words were mired by a pasty tongue.

"You ran away from the house so quickly that I didn't get a chance to ask you, what brings you to Brattahlið so early in the day?"

"I . . . I needed to ask Eirik something."

"Oh," she said, sounding a little disappointed.

"No . . . I . . . ah . . . you," he stammered, noticing her disappointment. "I . . . um . . . uhh . . . Gudrid, will you marry me!" Thorfinn blurted loudly. From the corner of his eye he saw Eirik pause, though he didn't turn around.

Gudrid's expression changed to horror. She stared at him a moment, then covered her face with her hands and ran screaming back to the house.

Thorfinn whirled toward Eirik, about to call him back, but saw that he was already running back to him. Their shocked eyes met; for a moment both men were speechless.

"Gudrid!" Eirik yelled across the meadow. He started after her, leaving Thorfinn in his confusion and chagrin.

Thorfinn slowly followed, his disappointment becoming a heavier and heavier burden to carry. He could not understand what in Óðin's name could provoke such a response from her. Their relationship had been proceeding wonderfully—or perhaps it was only he who felt that way.

Eirik and Thorfinn burst into the house without so much as a knock on the door. Gudrid lifted puffy, reddened eyes to stare at Thorfinn, then she leaned into Eirik's waiting arms and buried her face against his chest.

"Gudrid, my love. What did I say that was so wrong?" Thorfinn begged.

Her crying subsided momentarily. Through her sniffles she managed to say, "Oh, it's nothing you said or did, Thorfinn. It's . . . it's just that Thorvald and Thorstein died in Markland and Vinland and I am afraid that the same will happen to you. I fear this is some ancient curse on my family playing itself out."

"Oh, Gudrid, I promise you that nothing will happen to me," he said, opening his arms and beckoning her to enter them. Gudrid moved to Thorfinn and hugged him.

"It's not a curse that brought you to me, Gudrid. It is a blessing," he said.

Eirik left the house, leaving them alone in their embrace.

* * *

Gudrid stopped before him. Her eyes fixed on Thorfinn's, her gaze the sun that lit up the darkest regions of his soul. "So you're all set," he said, hoping she would say no so that they could spend a little more time together.

"Yes." She hesitated. "Well, I have to go . . . they're waiting."

"I know. Here. Take this." He untied Thor's hammer from around his neck and put it around Gudrid's. "Thor will watch over you and the people with you."

She smiled. "What about Adam's god?"

"Adam can take his chances with his own god," he said, half joking.

Gudrid laughed and quickly kissed him, as if fearing that she'd change her mind and stay on Vinland with him. Thorfinn's hand barely brushed Gudrid's shoulder as she turned away. "See you in ten dœgr," she said over her shoulder. "I love you, Thorfinn."

The crew pushed the knarr off the stony beach. A wave captured the *Ragnarök* and pulled it away from the land. The crew looked back at Thorfinn and the few others who had paused in their work to silently watch the parting or wave a good-bye, but Thorfinn was not looking at them; his focus remained on his beloved.

Gudrid hugged a fur throw closer to her body. The cold Atlantic wind tugged at her long, curly hair just as it teased at the long grass in the meadow; its rustling blanketed every other sound. Thorfinn used all of his willpower not to let a tear drip from his eye, but the cold North Atlantic wind blew in his face and managed to force one out of him. He remained there till he could only imagine her sitting in that boat.

"Damn wind," he whispered, wiping the tear from his cheek.

The rowers lifted their oars into the air and let the small craft coast to the pebbled shore. Tostig tried to coax the *Ragnarök* as close to Markland as the depth of the water would let him. Once the keel grounded on the smooth pebbles, he jumped overboard and steadied the boat. One by one the group stepped into the frigid surf separating Markland from Vinland and waded through the water to the beach. They patiently waited there while Jarlabanke, Tostig, and the two warrior escorts carried the boat into some bushes. They tore branches from trees to place along the side of the boat, concealing it from any passersby.

An unusual inland wind chased the salt from the air with the smell of damp leaves and mud as Gudrid, the two warriors Ingibjörg and Ásgeirr, Snorri Thorbrandsson, Tostig, Jarlabanke, Adam, and Freydis Eiriksdÿttir entered the dense forest. Swarms of mosquitoes and blackflies hungry for warm blood immediately attacked the group. The rustling of underbrush and the buzzing of insects quickly replaced the lapping waves. Soon they were out of sight of the beach and swatting the air or slapping voracious insects from their exposed skin.

Unlike the flat, plateau-like landing site of Vinland, Markland was a place of high shoreline cliffs and towering pine trees. No one in the party had ever seen trees of this enormous size: forty cubits high and six cubits in diameter—three adults could easily fit into one tree trunk. There were enough raw materials just in the short walk from the edge of the forest to their present position to build a small fleet of ships: wood for the hulls, the keels, the oars, and the masts, and pine tar for the sealant. Gudrid wondered if they would come across a flock of sheep that could provide wool for the sail.

She now understood why this land was so magical. And with the death of Thorvald, the land seemed necromantic, as well.

They followed the afternoon path of the sun. Tostig used the same principles that he used to navigate at sea to traverse this wooded land. Unlike the sea, the land did not require that he consider wind direction or ocean current. Compared to the skill required to navigate the oceans, this was as easy as a child pushing a toy boat in his morning bath.

* * *

Once the sun had set and the stars dotted the sky, the wind calmed and the biting mosquitoes and blackflies abated. The burning fire was the centre of focus as they lay back and relaxed after their meal.

Adam stared into the flames. He didn't know what he was looking for, only hoped for a clue or a sign from God that would help him find the Culdees. He wasn't even positive that Markland was in fact the land he sought. The story of Ari's whereabouts could have been exaggerated, or the gaps in the narrative could've been filled in by the human mind, as the mind generally does. They could be thousands of dægur away on another part of the continent, or another island entirely.

He had prayed that he would find some sign that civilized travellers trekked along this route, had hoped to pick up some sort of trail that would indicate that they were getting close. He knew that it would be like finding a needle in a haystack. But he also knew that whoever they came across, native or otherwise, would know of the Culdees if they were here. In this wilderness, they would stand out like a group of heathens in the Church of Rome.

Firelight glinted in Snorri Thorbrandsson's golden-blonde hair as he shifted broad shoulders to look at Adam. "They call you Adam of Bremen," Snorri said, more as a statement than a question.

"Yes," Adam replied, knowing that the young man's

brashness had more to do with his age than anything that Adam had done.

"Why are you here?"

"I am on a mission for my church."

"And would this mission benefit only your people, or would it benefit our country as well?" Freydis interrupted.

"It was by the order of your—"

"Enough," Gudrid snapped. "The separate reasons for our journey do not have to be told. We are here and that is enough."

"But Gudrid," Snorri begged, "I would like to know if Adam's journey is for the same reason."

Gudrid started to retort, but Adam interrupted. "It is fine, Gudrid; I am happy to answer. If our missions are to be successful, there must be honesty among us. I will not have you swear to secrecy because I trust that you all will abide by the unwritten code of a warrior and will therefore keep your own counsel in this matter."

"Very well, Adam, but I hold you responsible," Gudrid warned.

Everyone watched intently as Adam opened up his wooden box of Christian vestments. There were three impressions in the silk interior, each holding a particular item: a silver chalice, a container of holy water, and a bottle of wine. He picked up the chalice with one hand and the bottle of wine with the other. Before anyone in the group could blink, the cork was off the bottle of wine and he was filling the chalice.

He took a gulp, then began. "I am on a mission to return some important items stolen from the church and to apprehend the criminal responsible. If I cannot find the criminal, then my orders are to find and return the items at all cost. I have reason to believe that he is hiding on Markland, perhaps with a religious order known as the Culdees."

The group continued staring at Adam as he took another gulp from the chalice. He still held the wine bottle in his other hand; he poured himself another drink and continued the story. "I have been chasing this man for the last ten years of my life, and I finally believe that this will be the end of my journey— God has shown it to me in a vision. I am looking forward to going home to Meissen, in Saxony."

"What makes you think he is in this land?" Snorri questioned.

Adam quickly explained about the Culdees. "An old trader

named Rafn said that the man I seek was captured by the monks of this colony and baptized by them. But . . . I do not know for sure if I will find him here. I will have to trust my instincts, and have faith."

"If he doesn't want to be found, finding him will be very difficult," Tostig interjected.

"Yes, that is true, Tostig. But I have several advantages in my favour. He doesn't know he's being hunted. And being in possession of these stolen items gives him security that may lie on a false premise."

"And what false premise would that be?" Freydis asked.

"That he's gotten away with his crimes."

Tostig's eyes fell to the holes in the front of Adam's habit, then travelled to the torn sleeves and down to the tattered hem. "Adam, are those blood stains on your robe?" he asked.

"Yes, they are. I've been in many dangerous situations in my travels. There have been instances when I've had to fight my way out."

* * *

Gudrid began to consciously distance herself from the conversation. A strange, intermittent sensation that the group was being watched distracted her. It was an unsettling feeling, even permeating the shield of security that the group represented.

As the fire slowly burned down to embers, so did the conversation and the energy of the group. They found staying awake harder and harder as the toils of the day took hold of them. Gudrid had assigned Freydis to the first watch. Adam had volunteered, but she couldn't trust him just yet; she suspected that his allegiance to his fellow clerics outweighed his allegiance to the group. And that presented a danger that she could not ignore.

The next morning Gudrid watched the sun rising, but was unable to enjoy it. Her head jerked and twitched toward every sound. Even the morning birds squawking at the rising of the sun and fluttering through the branches stole her attention from the peace of the morning. As the group gathered up their gear, Gudrid's feelings didn't change; she felt the eyes of the forest staring at them. She didn't know how she knew this, nor did she see anyone other than the members of the small party.

Gudrid felt sick; her upset stomach had changed into nausea during the night. She thought she might have eaten some bad meat or berries, but no one else in the group was feeling ill and they all had eaten the same meal. As the other members of the party finished their morning meal, Gudrid had to walk out of range of the food smells.

"Gudrid, you do not look well," Freydis observed, coming up beside her.

"I was awake for much of the night with sickness," she admitted.

"I have something that may help," Freydis said, bending to root through her pack. She unrolled a leather pouch, pulled out a few twigs of green leaves. "Chew only on the green leaves. It should settle your stomach," she said, handing Gudrid a twig.

"Thank you," Gudrid whispered. She picked off a few leaves and put them in her mouth. Expecting the worst, she began chewing. The leaves had a slightly bitter taste, but it was not unbearable, and she could keep them down.

"When we make camp again, I will brew you some tea," Freydis said. "That should settle your stomach."

She stared at Gudrid a moment, as if debating whether to say more. Gudrid could almost sense what Freydis would say; she had been wondering about it herself.

"Gudrid, I think you have the look of a woman who is bearing a child," Freydis said with a smile.

"I suspected that myself."

"I have some experience as a midwife. If you like, I can take a look later," Freydis offered.

"Yes please, Freydis," Gudrid answered, relieved.

Freydis picked up Gudrid's pack and without a word, slung it over her shoulder. Gudrid looked at her thankfully. Her headache and queasy stomach made balancing a little difficult even without carrying extra weight.

* * *

Tostig proved that his talents weren't confined to the ocean. He found evidence of a used trail—broken branches, torn up moss, and footprints that suggested repeated use and the possibility of a settlement close by, now or in the recent past. The band followed the well-marked trail for one dægur, and Tostig's conclusion was confirmed. They heard voices, coming from a clearing in the distance.

Whether the travellers were the Culdees was another story. It could be a group of natives, and an unfriendly group, at that. Eirik had warned of attacking natives and his decision not to remain in Vinland for fear of native reprisal, a tale still talked about by Grœnlanders. For Norsemen to run, these people would have to be very powerful in numbers, if nothing else.

As the group ducked and gently pushed branches out of their path, the same question was on all of their minds—were these people peaceful? They approached slowly, their steps careful and consciously placed, so not to startle the owners of the unknown voices into attack. If a larger group of armed Norsemen could not fight off a tribe whose only advantage were their superior numbers, what hope did this small group have?

As they were about to step into the clearing, Jarlabanke, in the vanguard, signalled quickly for them to stop. They heard approaching voices, then four natives clothed in tanned pants, shirts, and footwear passed by several feet in front of them.

"Your theory about the location of these monks may have been wrong," Gudrid whispered to Adam.

"Perhaps we could use this as an opportunity," Adam said. "We could attempt to communicate with these natives and take advantage of their knowledge of this land."

"We don't know how our presence will be construed," Freydis said. "The monks would have to make allies in order to survive in this land. We may be seen as a threat if we just appear from the bushes."

All eyes looked to Gudrid, waiting. She knew that the decision was hers alone to make. Her authority over the group was the same burden she had felt when she realized that she was now responsible for the human growing inside her womb.

Suddenly the group heard words they understood. They turned and looked into the clearing, where an old man leaned on what looked like a spear with an almost ornamental spearhead at its tip; he was using it as a walking cane.

"Maumturk, has Calliope returned?" the elderly man asked, approaching the younger men they'd seen earlier.

"I have not seen him, Father," one of them replied with a heavy accent.

"If you see him, could you please send him to Aidan's tent."

"Yes, Abba."

Adam pushed his way to the front of the group to get a better view. "I know that monk," he said. "He is Father Wicklow. He must be in his nineties by now."

Freydis looked at Gudrid. Gudrid understood the question

on Freydis's mind. Even she marvelled at the age of the Christian. Was this what the Irish god gave to all those who pledged their devotion to him? Extended life?

"I'd like to walk over and introduce myself," Adam insisted. "It would be less startling if we talked to one of the monks than to an entire group."

"No," Gudrid ordered. "We need to investigate more before we make our presence known. I'm not going to risk the safety of the group until we find out if we'll be looked upon as friends or enemies."

"I agree," Freydis said.

Just then a Caucasian child ran to the monk and tugged on his robe.

"Cartule, go find your sister," the old man scolded.

Adam's jaw dropped. "I cannot believe this," he murmured.

"How can you explain the children?" Freydis asked. "I may not know much about your order, but I do know that monks and priests are not supposed to procreate."

Adam looked at Gudrid. "Gudrid, these are my brethren. Once they see my robes, they will recognize that I am one of them and welcome me."

Before Gudrid could answer, a flash erupted in front of her eyes, as if lightning had struck. The forest around her disappeared. She found herself seated on a dirt floor in what appeared to be a cave. A hole in a high rock ceiling provided her only light. She was unable to move her arms; it felt as though they were in restraints. She looked down. Her stomach was larger and yes, her arms were in chains. They felt weak and sore.

Another flash brought her back in the Markland forest. Freydis was shaking her.

"Gudrid. Gudrid, can you hear me?"

"Yes, I . . . I can," she said, slowly regaining her senses, and surprised to see the group staring down at her. She lowered her arms, confused—why were they raised in the air? "What happened? I was somewhere else—in my mind, I mean."

"Do you know where you were?" Adam asked.

"I was in a cave, chained to a wall . . . I think I had a vision." Gudrid lowered her head and rubbed her forehead as if trying to rub the memory away.

"Do not worry about me," she said, looking around at their concerned faces. "I am not a stranger to these visions. I will be fine once my strength returns."

She looked at Adam. "Even you said that the monks could be accomplices in the theft of your religious artifacts. That would make them thieves, and potentially dangerous. No, we remain concealed until we find out more."

Adam looked about to protest, then clamped his mouth shut.

For the rest of the day they travelled over rocky and mossy terrain, not stopping to rest. The sun forced the clouds apart and the damp ground began heating up, changing the cool forest air to a humid ground mist thick with clouds of blackflies and mosquitoes. The close air tempted them to remove layers of clothing, but that would only expose more flesh to insect bites. The gentle aroma of the spruce and the cedar trees stimulated their appetites, and before long they were searching for a place to sit and eat.

* * *

Adam slowly and deliberately fell back to the end of the line of travellers. The group travelled in pairs, talking to one another in moderate tones, rarely looking behind them, so when Adam decided to jump into the thick brush, he was able to do it without being noticed.

He was unhappy in his decision to defy Thorfinn and Gudrid, but he was adamant in accomplishing his mission; the importance of it outweighed the needs of the few that would be affected by his decision. As Gudrid said, even though these were men of the cross, their integrity was in question. Without further investigation, he couldn't determine the morality of these men, and he knew that he could find out more within than without.

Adam needed to find out what happened to Ari. The answer to that question would reveal what had happened to the book and the lance. If the Culdees were in possession of the relics, would they return them to the Church? The answer to this would answer the question of their honesty. Or maybe the riddle would be solved by a religious truth that he'd know only by revelation.

Adam's intention was not to engage the Culdees initially, though he was prepared to confront them if need be. He planned to look around the site to see what he could find out, gather information that would bring him closer to finding Ari, the book, but most importantly, the lance.

He waited in the brush until the low murmur of the group's

conversation became the silence of the wind and the chirping birds. By the time Tostig picked up his scent, so to speak, Adam hoped to be back with the group at the campsite, and it wouldn't make a difference. To accomplish that, he needed to move quickly. It would most likely take him the rest of the day to backtrack to the camp. He didn't want to get caught out in the woods after nightfall; if he was attacked or injured, there would be no assistance for him.

Adam concentrated on the task at hand. He'd have to develop his strategy for infiltrating the Culdee site en route. He was used to lying when necessary—he'd done many questionable things that in retrospect conflicted with the tenets of his faith, but he'd felt at the time that they had to be done.

He remembered being part of a caravan in the deserts of Arabia when a group of bandits threatened them. The caravan was relatively unarmed, except for the few soldiers charged with protecting its contents and members. When the bandits attacked and nearly overwhelmed the soldiers, Adam found himself picking up a sword and using it against the heathens, as he later referred to them when he reported back to the bishop. It wasn't that he'd wanted to use the sword or that he was skilled at using it; he saw himself as protector of the faith against the "godless heathens" of the deserts.

When questioned by the bishop, Adam noted that David slaying Goliath was considered an act of faith, and cited many other incidents in the Bible that justified destroying evil. The bishop agreed, and ordered all records from the inquisition destroyed. The cardinal secretly commended Adam for his selfless service to the Church; there were even undercurrents of canonization for his heroic deeds.

These and similar thoughts roamed through his mind. They intermixed and conflicted with his teachings from the Church. But then, when Adam returned from Arabia, he thought that he'd be excommunicated from the Church. Perhaps there were exceptions to the celestial rules. It was not for him to say whether he or the Church was right or wrong.

"I need to stop," Gudrid announced to her companions. "I don't think I can continue any farther until I've rested."

The sun had dropped below the horizon and stars dotted the darkening grey sky. They'd planned to stop hours earlier, but several near encounters with natives pushed them further into the late afternoon and finally into the early evening.

Since her vision, an uneasy feeling had pervaded Gudrid's consciousness. Preoccupied with her thoughts and the random images that infiltrated her mind, she'd barely talked to anyone whenever the group had taken short rest periods. The feeling of being stalked did not leave her for a moment. It pushed her onward until exhaustion forced her to stop.

Seven hours of walking had taken its toll on her—and the others, she noted as she looked around at the weary faces. They dropped to the ground, letting their packs carelessly fall. The accompanying exhalations and groans were almost as loud as the constant drone of the blackflies in their ears.

Something was not right. Gudrid refocused and looked around the group, unsure whether she was having another vision or not. Then she noticed that Adam was missing. "By all the gods in Valhalla!" she yelled. "Has anyone seen Adam?"

"He fell behind this morning," Jarlabanke said. "I have not seen him since."

The bushes shook and rustled farther up the path. Gudrid turned, preparing to comment on Adam's slowness, but it was Snorri who entered the small clearing next. "Snorri, did you see Adam?" she asked.

"No, but I did notice him falling behind," he replied.

"Curses on his god!" she yelled. "Allowing Adam to come along was a favour to the king and his church, but they seem to see it as something that we must do. I fear that they will soon enslave our hearts and minds."

Uneasiness returned to Gudrid, but her feelings of being stalked were momentarily masked by her anger. They would all suffer for Adam's stupidity. And then her queasiness returned, momentarily distracting her from her anger.

It quickly returned. "We wait until morning and then we find Adam and bring him back in chains," she growled. "If we don't find him, then we leave him and let the Culdees do what they want with him."

The group prepared their beds for the night. Gudrid ordered that a fire was not to be lit until Baldur, the god of light, had lain to rest. She feared that native travellers might happen upon them and report back to their tribe, or mass the native tribes against them.

She hadn't had a chance to discuss it with Freydis, but their primary reason for returning to Markland was now being pushed back further and further. Gudrid and Freydis had orchestrated that they, Snorri, Tostig, and Jarlabanke were included in the excursion to Vinland. All had participated in the previous voyages to Vinland, and all had a stake in the outcome of this voyage. Adam had been a smear on her plans ever since Thorfinn had announced that he was coming with them. It was too annoying to fathom at first, but Gudrid came to believe that Adam would serve a purpose. He'd get the group closer to the Culdees and pull back the veil, so to speak, for her to initiate her plans. He would be a distraction to the Culdees while Gudrid and her companions accomplished their objective.

She had hoped that when the planned time arrived, Adam would infiltrate the Culdee camp so she could get closer to Ari; now, Adam's disappearance threatened her plans. She partly blamed herself for not watching him closely after he insisted on revealing himself to the old Culdee; she should've seen it as a warning. She had stupidly let her guard down and this was the result.

He was going to pay for his betrayal.

Gudrid desperately needed to consult with Freydis.

Tostig loosely piled brownish-yellow moss and some dry grass together while Jarlabanke searched for dry twigs to start the fire. These he left next to Tostig, and left to gather larger branches to use for fuel once the fire caught. Tostig struck two pieces of flint together; sparks jumped, and in moments the pile started to smoulder. With a few gentle breaths from Tostig, the wisps of smoke ignited into a flame. He gently added broken twigs and then larger branches till the small fire slowly grew into a small but comfortable hearth.

The group sat silent, transfixed by the flame that grew in front of them as if it were a dancing minstrel entertaining the weary travellers on this, their second evening. Slowly, a conversation began to take shape. Just as the sparks ignited the pile of moss and grass, ideas and words ignited thoughts that ignited more words, the sparks of ideas jumping from person to person. Soon the mood changed from tired silence to comforting stories of deeds from long ago, all controversial in their believability, but which nevertheless possessed some element of truth. But in the end the truth of the stories didn't matter; it was the gathering that mattered.

Freydis carried a cup of steaming liquid over to Gudrid. "How is your stomach?" she asked.

"I'm trying to ignore it," Gudrid said. She was tired and grumpy and had begun to feel that the mission was turning into a useless farce.

"I've brewed you some twig tea to help your stomach." Freydis sat down beside her and held out the cup.

"Thank you," Gudrid said, accepting the tea. It felt like the only relief she'd have today. She glanced around at the others, then dropped her voice to a whisper. "Freydis, we have not discussed our purpose for coming here. I think we need to discuss some things in light of Adam's disappearance."

"Do you think his absence may not be voluntary?"

"I have considered that. But this throws our plans up in the air to be carried away by the winds."

Freydis sighed. "Yes, I've been thinking of that as well."

"Do you remember the location of the grave?" Gudrid asked, again scanning the others. They were still wrapped up in the stories.

"Yes."

Gudrid lifted a brow. "You were not foolish enough to have it drawn on paper to be carried in your pack."

Freydis chuckled. "No, I was not. I had it tattooed over my heart."

Gudrid laughed with Freydis, partly at her wit and partly as a release for the tension of the last few days.

She and Thorvald had ventured onto this land so long ago; they'd explored Markland, not because of anything Leif had said, but because they were told by a group of natives who occupied the land before the Culdees arrived about an underground city. No one in their group could find out how long the inhabitants had occupied that city, or if they'd inherited the city from a previous culture. Thorvald could not communicate with them in any great detail, nor were they able to negotiate a trade agreement with them. The secret that the natives were hiding would later be the reason for their hostility.

The underground city had been built on a mine — a gold mine so abundant, it was said, the buildings in the city were chiselled out of entire rock faces of gold, gold of such purity that a torchbearer walking by the large veins of the precious metal could look next to her and see a golden companion walking along with her.

They'd located the city, but the find was marred by disaster: the only tunnel they had found leading down to its entrance had mysteriously collapsed, burying Thorvald and four of his men. When his brother and the other men finally dug the victims out, a subterranean dike collapsed and the rock cavern containing the tunnel flooded, permanently sealing that entrance. They later found out that the city's builders had created false entrances and booby traps to scare off unwanted adventurers.

The four men with Thorvald had not survived the collapse, and Thorvald died of his injuries soon after. His men buried him at Kjalarness, according to his wishes upon his deathbed. His brother Thorstein took command of the mission and continued the search for another entrance into the city. For two years they searched, but they didn't find one. They left Markland disappointed and empty-handed.

They returned to Markland the following year, and unearthed Thorvald's body. Initially, Gudrid had been confused by her husband's instructions that he be buried at Kjalarness and then later retrieved. But she quickly realized that death by a cave-in would leave different markings than death by a native arrow, as those at home had been told. In order to cover up the true cause of death and prevent the questions it might raise, he would have to be returned once the body had sufficiently decomposed to eradicate the bruising and the crushed bones.

And more: working secretly, Thorstein had drawn a partial map on a piece of Thorvald's death shroud before the body was buried. It was for this, as well as his brother's body, that Thorstein had returned. The drawing was meant to serve as one part of a key to the location of the cave entrance, for Thorstein had omitted obvious landmarks that would have made it easy to find. Above the drawing he'd written *Valhalla*. No one, including Freydis and Gudrid, recognized the features of the land. Another part was required to complete the map to the city.

However, the plan didn't go the way he'd intended. Under continuous attack from the natives, Thorstein decided to leave his dead brother—and the map—safely at Kjalarness and return some other time to retrieve it. But Thorstein, too, had died.

" . . . and the riches," Freydis was whispering when Gudrid returned from her memories.

She nodded, hoping she hadn't missed Freydis giving some important information. "Are you sure of the group's allegiance to our cause?"

"No," Freydis said. "But I am sure of their allegiance to the riches. They will follow us and do what we say."

Gudrid felt much better. Adam's disappearance did not seem as tragic as she'd originally thought. Soon they would find the entrance and find Adam and all would come together, as it should.

* * *

The sun peeked over the horizon, as it had every day since the first ape walked upright. It infiltrated the branches of the oak tree and landed on Adam's forehead. He wrinkled his brow and slowly opened his eyes, then threw up his hands to block the intensity of the light striking them.

As the memory of where he was came back to him, he moved slowly, his body stiff and sore. It felt as if he were peeling his body off the bark on the tree. He grunted with pain and paused, balancing himself on the large branch that he'd chosen to rest upon while he waited for a moment of dizziness, or perhaps a mild case of vertigo from his height up in the tree, to pass.

Many of the surrounding trees were coniferous; their prickly needles did not make them good candidates for a place to sleep. The oak tree's branches were not massive but as he'd looked up the evening before, Adam saw one branch jutting out from the main trunk with a second one jutting out about a foot above it and a quarter turn around the trunk. The position of the second branch made it an ideal backrest, and perhaps a place where he could lie down.

The dizziness passed, and he was able to plan his descent to the ground and his morning goblet of wine. Before he stepped on the next branch down, he squinted at the base of the tree and was happy to see his case where he had left it the night before. As he carefully descended, his anticipation of the dry, tart taste of the wine was so strong, he thought he could taste it in his mouth.

Adam stepped onto the dewy moss and immediately knelt to unclasp his wine box. Before one robin's morning call was answered by another, the cork was off the bottle and the wine was swishing and gurgling into the goblet. He quickly recorked the bottle and put it away to remove the temptation for more.

His first large gulp of the day felt similar to breaking the surface of the water after a long dive. Its acidic flavour flowed over his taste buds and burned down his throat and into his stomach. It was a morning ritual that he had grown all too used to; he even at times looked forward to it . . . and missed it when he could not experience it.

Adam looked around to get his bearings. The nocturnal forest looked far different in the light of dawn, alive with swaying branches, rustling leaves, and the distant roar of the ocean sounding as if it were a den of awakening lions. He looked along what appeared to be a natural gap in the foliage—the forest trail he needed to return to the site of the small Culdee camp. In his search for a resting place, he'd lost track of it the night before.

He picked up his case and resumed his trek to find Ari, the Book of Kells, and the holy lance. But first he needed to find his brethren. They represented to Adam a secret desire that he'd had since his early days in the clergy, when he had heard of the Irish monks travelling across the ocean to other lands, and for some reason it had ignited his adventurous spirit. Adam realized that the Culdees lived a harsh existence, with the risk of death always in the forefront of their lives. But it was an exciting existence. The isolation was not something that he feared. In fact, at times, Adam yearned to be isolated from the rest of the world. His periods of solace were all too brief and far between.

He'd searched his heart to find the real reason why he remained in a community where at times he didn't want to be. Was it for the security? He knew that part of his reason for remaining close to where the power lay was for his own advancement. He didn't know why, but he couldn't fully abandon his reason and live on faith alone.

Adam wondered what he would do when he encountered the Culdees. He didn't want to believe that the power of the artifacts could turn his brethren away from a holy and monastic life. For all Adam knew, there was a reasonable explanation for all of this. He had to admit that his evidence was circumstantial. He didn't have proof that Ari was with the Culdees, or that he had indeed stolen the book and the lance. Adam was going only on the words of Rafn.

He wondered if, put in the same position, he would succumb to the power of the lance—eternal life with just one jab. He was not convinced that was true and if it was, against the opinion and belief of the Church, Adam saw the power of the lance as evil. Its power was born out of an evil and aggressive act, after all—the Roman soldier Longinus used it to pierce the side of Jesus on the cross. Adam couldn't see how a weapon of destruction could be transformed into one so holy.

As Adam saw it, a person was put on this earth for a finite amount of time, and a person's actions in that fixed period of time determined whether his or her existence beyond death was assured. Any barrier to completing that cycle was sinful.

Adam stopped at a small patch of blue berries. They looked similar to berries in his country. A loud growl from his ample belly reminded him that he'd not eaten since yesterday and he didn't know when he'd eat next. He put one of the berries in his mouth and cautiously began chewing, prepared to spit it out. It was sweet, like the berries at home. He sat down next to the patch and began pulling the berries off the plants, popping each into his mouth faster than he could pick the next one and the next one. He didn't stop till the bush was empty of fruit. His fingers and lips stained with berry juice, he sat back and finished his second glass of wine, scratching at the growing welts on the back of his neck. Adam's meal had stirred up a swarm of blackflies.

Adam rolled onto his belly, about to get up, and paused on his knees. He remembered that he hadn't done his morning prayers. He would have to find a place to stop. He rose and resumed his search for the camp and the answer to his questions.

His tracking skills were not as advanced as Tostig's, but he had picked up one or two of the dwarf's techniques. He reasoned that the Culdees' trail should be easier to find simply because of the number of people trampling the ground in the last day. And since last night had been clear, the trail should be relatively undisturbed.

In time, Adam did indeed find the trail. As with most found things, he had not been looking for it when he noticed it, as he was looking at an unusually beautiful flower growing at the base of a tree. Faint impressions were noticeable in the mossy carpet. As he looked around the area, he saw broken branches. This was, without a doubt, the path they'd taken.

Just like the forest path, his life seemed all too clear now. Everything led up to this point. He felt ready to encounter the Culdees.

* * *

Gudrid couldn't get up; her stomach churned and her head spun. She felt as if she'd stayed up late last night, drinking. If this was what her life was going to be like for the next few months, she didn't want to have a baby.

She blindly rooted through the pack under her head for the wrapped package that Freydis had given her the previous morning. She found it and put another leaf in her mouth, letting her tongue slide over its smooth upper surface, then the raised veins on its underside. Then she chewed it, hoping its bitterness would provide quick relief.

She could no longer contain her stomach. Pushing up on all fours, Gudrid threw up. By the time she wretched again, Freydis was by her side. Gudrid heaved one last time, then coughed and sputtered. She knelt back on her haunches, breathing heavily. "I think it has passed," she said. "I don't know if I can take three more months of this."

Freydis smiled. "I don't have your sight, but I think you'll be fine."

It was easy for Freydis to say, Gudrid thought; she was not the one throwing up. Each churn of her stomach and each dry heave took away a little more of the joy and excitement at the prospect of being a mother. She now looked upon those months of being the "expectant mother" with dread.

"Perhaps a little bit of food in your stomach will help. Jarlabanke has returned with some berries," Freydis said.

The team was packing up their bedding when Gudrid decided to get busy, hoping to take her mind off of how terrible she felt. She moved slowly, her next thought always to lie down. But she had a day of decisions ahead of her.

The thought crossed her mind that Adam's disappearance was a security threat to the group and the Vinland community as a whole. There was no way of knowing what the Culdees would do when he found them. He could be imprisoned or held captive till he told them what they wanted to hear. And in that confession he could reveal the location and the strength of all of the Norse. From what Gudrid had observed the previous day, the Culdees had a certain amount of influence over the natives. One order from the Fathers, and the natives would be on them en masse. There was no point in thinking about the battle that would ensue, because all in the expedition would be dead.

Such thoughts upset Gudrid. After experiencing the vision of her native self, Gudrid knew that Thorfinn needed to create an alliance with the Skrælings. It was the only way to secure a place for the Norse people in Vinland. She trusted in the intelligence of her husband and knew that Thorfinn's merchant skills would serve him well here, but now it seemed that to secure that future, they might have to ally themselves with the Culdees, as well.

That could be a much easier task with Adam on their side, if his actions didn't jeopardize their success in that, too. She had no way to know for sure what was on that drunken monk's mind. Why in Hel's name had he run off like that?

Tostig walked over. "The group would like to know what we are going to be doing today, Gudrid," he whispered, as if everyone in the group had not already openly discussed the topic before he approached her. He hesitated, then added, "I know you are with child. When my wife was with child, we were told that a good remedy for the sickness it brings was to rub mud all over her. It seemed to take the nausea away."

"Thank you, Tostig," Gudrid said. She paused and looked up at the sky, hoping for the gods' help with her decision. She finally spoke. "We will go to Kjalarness, then return to collect Adam, if that is at all possible now."

A silence fell; everyone knew what awaited them at Kjalarness, and their obligation to fulfill their sacred promise to Thorvald. Its burden was a heavy one, yet they couldn't ignore their duty.

Tostig put his back to them and pulled the faded map out of his bag. It had taken him months to interpret its cryptic symbols and its writings, Gudrid knew. He'd studied its faded markings far into the dark northern nights, till confusion and the blurriness of fatigue took over, and he fell asleep where he sat. With the help of natives who had briefly allied themselves with the first expedition, he'd managed to break its code and to successfully interpret its instructions.

"Can you find the stone again?" Gudrid asked, leaning over the dwarf as he unfolded the map.

"I believe so." He didn't sound as confident as Gudrid would have liked.

"Tostig, you must be certain. We have no time for errors. We get one chance at this and if we fail, we must wait three tvö misseri; my child will be two."

"Don't worry, Gudrid. In two nights we will be down in that cave with more treasure than we will know what to do with."

"Are you sure about the night of the eclipse?"

"Yes, I took the readings from Stonehenge myself. I clearly saw the reflection of the half-moon in the útsuðr quadrant of its central reflecting pool. We are here at the right time; in four dœgr the lunar eclipse will take place."

Gudrid released a hopeful sigh. After so many decades, she was now so close to what she and Thorvald had discovered with Freydis. Now she and Thorfinn would have the riches for which the search had begun shortly after the discovery of Vinland and Markland.

"On the dœgr of the red moon," Tostig said, "the light will shine on the carvings on the stone, illuminating the map and revealing the location of the cave entrance. Then it will only be a matter of walking to the entrance and waiting for the red moon to unlock the door to the catacombs."

The ingenuity of the treasure's original owners fascinated Gudrid. They were able to both conceal and reveal the map by using reflected light. She'd been told that the sun was at different places in the sky at certain times of the year. So in fact the sun lit the map up every year at the same time, but it was the red moon that actually revealed the doorway and opened it. She had no idea how they could use light as a trigger for a door lock. Knowledge of this type was beyond her people's abilities.

Freydis kicked dirt on the smouldering fire, tormenting swarms of blackflies. Her flailing arms and dirt-shuffling feet created a strange, rhythmless dance.

"Freydis," Gudrid called.

Freydis's arms froze in mid-swing and she looked at Gudrid, then quickly began swinging again.

"I need to talk to you."

Freydis left the choking fire and joined Gudrid beyond the hearing of the others.

"We're all set," Gudrid told her. "Tostig has the day and time of the red moon in the sky, and we now head to the carved stone."

"What would you like me to do, Gudrid?"

"Keep the rest of the group away from the stone. By Óðin, the last thing we need is one of them going off on their own, knowing the location of the cave entrance."

"The entrance is difficult to find even when the location is known. We are the only two in this group who were present when Thorvald discovered it," Freydis reminded her.

"Yes, and one more who is not here."

"Do not refer to him again. He is dead to me!" Freydis exclaimed, loud enough that the others glanced over, looking confused. "Return to your duties," she snapped at them.

"And to me as well. He is no longer my kinsman," Gudrid said.

Freydis's huffing quieted and with one last exhale, she had calmed herself. "Are you worried that he may have returned for the treasure?" she asked in a low voice.

"The thought had crossed my mind. The doorway would not have opened, but Ari may have found another way."

"Yes, my husband was a very resourceful man," Freydis said sardonically. "If there were another way to get into that cave, he would've found it. But we turned every rock on that cliff and found nothing. In all the years of searching for another entrance, we found none. He is as hopeless as we are."

"Yes, you're right. Unless he has all the map keys and the instructions, Ari won't be able to locate the entrance or the map stone."

Freydis nodded, grinning. "Once we retrieve the other map, we will have the entire key to enter the caves."

Gudrid gave Freydis a suspicious look. "Freydis, Markland will be the cause of no more deaths. I have lost two husbands; I do not wish that on any of our sisters. Is that clear?"

Freydis knew better than to argue, especially after giving her loyalty to Gudrid. She would be a rich woman. "Yes, that's clear to me. I will take no aggressive action, only defensive."

"Good, then we are agreed. My late husband chose each person for a reason. Each possesses a necessary talent. We must remain together or we are all doomed. We can all be in agreement and be extremely wealthy, or we can disagree and fail. There is no halfway."

It took the group another hour to eat and ready themselves for the day's travelling. The circumstances surrounding Adam's disappearance slowly faded into the back of their minds; even Gudrid's mind was on the challenge at hand. The threat of Adam's disappearance occasionally occupied her thoughts, but she decided that she would deal with it in the moment, if something were to come of it, rather than worrying about possibilities.

Adam heard voices — not distinct words or phrases, but several voices tumbling together like the water in a trickling brook, the sounds as inseparable as myriad rustling leaves, or a multitude of deer crossing the tundra. He could make out giggles and the pattern of individual words, but their meaning was lost in the consortium of sounds.

His ears focused on a thunderous rush. At this distance he could only guess what it could be — a stampeding herd? Then, as he searched for the cause, he saw a mist rising above the trees; it was a waterfall.

What luck, Adam thought. Settlements were generally near a water source. He would just have to follow the river downstream to find a settlement, and go from there to the Culdees.

He began climbing a grassy embankment. Twigs cracked and snapped under his feet, the sound lost in that of the crashing water. Crouching to peek over the crest, Adam let his eyes follow the stick-like tree trunks to the ground and from the ground to the edge of the rushing river.

The water bubbled and frothed, rushing and dipping between jutting rocks before whirling dizzily into the relative calmness of the open river, only to be captured and pushed over a submersed embankment and flushed farther down the waterway, which eventually disappeared around a wooded bend.

Adam's eyes moved slowly and methodically up and down the river, seeking the source of the voices. Just below him and a little to his left was a massive tree log, suspended above the water. The base of its mammoth trunk had splintered and the top of the tree rested on the far bank. Just beyond it, he glimpsed two figures before they disappeared into the brush on the other side of the river.

Adam feared that he'd have to traverse the tree-bridge. The thought of the furious river below made him giddy. He looked skyward, hoping to be given a sign, yet he already knew what he had to do. He had to walk across that felled tree.

He opened his case and pulled out the bottle. Foregoing the red-stained chalice, he uncorked the bottle and raised it to his mouth. The recorked bottle went into one of his pockets, the chalice in the other pocket. Then, before his fear resurfaced, he half climbed, half slid down the gravel and rock slope to a rock embankment above the river.

Adam removed his shoes and climbed on top of the log bridge in his bare feet. He mustered up his faith, prayed with the zealous vigour he'd possessed as a young monk, and crept across the log. His focus wavered from the large trunk only once, his eyes involuntarily sliding past the bark underfoot to the blur of rushing water below him. Adam dropped to his knees, not in prayer, but in fear of falling into the swirling whitewater below. But since he was already kneeling, he did decide to pray for forgiveness of his actual and imagined sins, and request the strength to continue safely to the other side.

A miracle happened—or so Adam thought. He no longer heard the rushing river, no longer felt the rough bark scraping his knee or his callused feet. He felt only the peace that came with surrendering his will, and the serenity of relinquishing all responsibility and fear for the consequences of success or failure.

Then the Creator returned him to the present with a thud. Adam's foot caught on the hem of his habit and he fell off the log onto the mossy embankment. He didn't know why, but in those seconds of the fall, he realized his deceit.

Adam opened an eye and gazed at a rock that his head had missed by inches. It was actually no larger than an apple, but his perspective enlarged the rock, and the rounded edges took on a more sinister and sharper quality.

He slowly dragged himself to his feet and looked behind

him, at his route to this side. He had very little recollection of traversing the rest of the bridge and the fall, which he'd mistakenly interpreted as his prayer being answered. Still a little shaken, he put on his shoes and limped into the pine and spruce forest. The aroma of the sap quickly surrounded him and the fear and shakiness he'd experienced during the episode began to dissipate.

Adam trekked through clumps of trees and stumbled over bent and snapped tree branches. He stepped through pitch-coloured mud and sloshed through ankle-deep water. His hair and beard collected dead and moss-laden twigs, crawling blackflies, and curled, dry leaves. He swatted back at branches that slapped his face and neck. When it became too much for him, he covered his head with his arms and plowed through the forest, remembering that his faith had got him past the danger of the log bridge and that what he currently experienced was nothing more than an inconvenience.

When his route was relatively clear of trees and overhanging branches, Adam brushed the forest debris from his beard and his habit and emptied his hood of accumulated kindling, only to push through another patch of brush that filled his hood once again and clung to his habit once more.

And then the worst possible thing happened. Two native children spotted Adam pushing through the forest and without hesitation, thinking that he was an animal or even worse, one of the many monsters that inhabited the deep woods, ran back to their tribe for help.

As he heard the youngsters' screams, Adam roared and ran in the opposite direction, reinforcing the belief that he was a monster out to eat them. He hoped that their elders would not take their young imaginations seriously. Adam didn't relish the idea of being hunted down like an animal.

At last he stopped and leaned against a tree to catch his breath. He wheezed with each inhalation and coughed on each exhale. In his younger days he was quick to fight to defend his faith, but as the years enlarged his waist and his heart and diminished his lung capacity, he only picked the battles that he knew he could win.

Adam was comfortable with his self-image as the hard hand of faith. It was clerics like him to whom the Church owed the increase in their flocks. He had studied the martial arts of the Buddhists and had used the skill to fight for his faith. His church didn't sanction fighting unless instructed by the holy padre and in defence of the holy faith, of course, but Adam felt that physical violence was not totally incompatible with the holy scriptures. After all, was not Satan's expulsion from heaven an act of violence? And was not David striking Goliath violent, as well? These were prime examples of the choice that both clerics and practitioners must make.

Everything about his surroundings begun to look the same and Adam feared that he would lose his way. The longer he stayed out in the woods, the greater the risk that he'd run across some unsuspecting native whose impulsive reaction would get Adam injured or killed. He wasn't ready to die alone on this unknown continent.

Adam came upon a clearing peppered with moss-covered rocks. Unable to shake the feeling that some unknown assailant was pursuing him, he neither paused nor stopped. He wasn't paying attention to where he was going, and almost fell off a wall of rock. At the last second he noticed that the mossy ground that he'd been walking across and which he had mistaken for the forest floor was actually the top of a rock cliff. He immediately backed away from the edge.

Peering over the cliff, Adam saw that he was standing over a cave opening. There were voices coming from inside the cavern. A moment later, three natives and someone that Adam presumed to be a Culdee exited the cave. The Father was not dressed like the other Culdee monk that he'd seen days earlier.

"Father, what can we do for you?" the natives asked in Latin.

"Return to the camp. I will meet you there shortly."

Adam snuck closer to the ledge and watched the natives walk down a trail and disappear into the bush, leaving the monk by himself. He was a large, imposing figure, even from Adam's vantage. The monk just stood there, looking out across the forest.

Adam got up on all fours. His fat belly brushed along the ground as he slowly backed away from the ledge, knocking a fine curtain of dirt and rocks over the edge.

The Father whirled around and looked up. "Who's there?"

Adam's body hugged the ground. He didn't move; he hardly even breathed. Like a child avoiding scolding elders, he remained hidden.

"Show yourself!"

In a split second of realization, Adam decided that staying

hidden was foolish. This was his chance to reveal himself in a calm and non-threatening manner. He stood and walked back over to the edge. "I am Adam of Bremen," he unintentionally bellowed as he looked down.

"You are not from this colony."

"No. I've travelled across the ocean."

The monk's expression changed from scowling suspicion to one of almost elated trust. "Adam of Bremen, I am happy to meet you. My prayers have been answered."

Adam hid in the bushes, waiting, targeting the monk as a hunter would his prey. The Father carried the same spear that Father Wicklow had; the piece of cloth at its tip fluttered in the wind. His desire to know the story of Ari and the whereabouts of the artifacts had overwhelmed him with zeal. His mission for the Church and the king had now become a personal quest of faith. He knew that if God led him to the book, he would truly be blessed and worthy of his robes and the accolades that the king and the holy Fathers would bestow upon him.

His patience and faith paid off; the Father left the cave entrance, unaware of Adam's scrutiny.

Adam didn't know what he'd find in the subterranean dwelling, but he suspected that the lance and the book were either in there or he'd stumble across a clue to their whereabouts. The only person he'd seen enter and exit the cave during his vigil was the monk.

Many clerics chose the simple and solitary space of a cave for meditation and prayer. But in Adam's experience, the higher the position in the Church, the more luxurious were the clergy's lodgings. He'd always assumed that it was the well-deserved reward for a life of devotion and a vow of poverty.

Adam left the security of the underbrush and walked toward the cave. Dry leaves and dead needles crunched under his feet, with an occasional loud snap from a twig. He continuously scanned his surroundings for signs of approaching natives or Culdees. As he approached, he felt a cold, damp breeze blowing from the opening, accompanied by a mouldy odour. He entered with trepidation, but trusted that since his faith had led him this far, it would safely lead him farther.

Inside the cave he paused, temporarily blinded until his eyes adjusted to the dark interior. Finally he saw the outline of what looked like prayer books and some writing instruments. In the far corner was a bed and beside it a cold hearth. There were books piled up in nooks and crannies in the rock walls, but without light he didn't know how anything written in them would be of any help to his search.

The Book of Kells could not be among these books, Adam thought. *It is too important to be left in the open, where someone could look at it or even take it.* No, the book was probably hidden, protected by ingenious anti-theft devices in an underground reliquary.

He noticed an opening that was cleverly concealed behind an outcropping of rock. The entranceway was angled away from the cave entrance and therefore was not illuminated by light from without. Each side of the rock wall appeared uniform when seen from the angle of the cave entrance, but once he got closer and stared at it from a forty-five degree angle, the pattern broke up and a narrow but passable break in the wall was visible. A human body could fit through it; Adam wasn't sure if his could, though. He put his head through the opening; beyond was a narrow passage and beyond that, blackness.

He sucked his gut in as much as possible and tried to squeeze himself through the opening. He pushed and tugged, gave up and tried another angle, then another angle, and finally returned to his first position. This time he wiggled his bum, first side to side, then by thrusting his pelvis forward. With each movement, Adam made a little progress. He straightened his back and lay the back of his head against the rock and rested for a moment. His squished stomach oozed out on either side of the opening.

With one final exhalation and a simultaneous push, Adam fell through the other side of the opening. He remained on the ground and pulled the bottle from his pocket. With out sitting up, Adam tipped his head forward, raised the bottle in a thankful fashion toward the cave ceiling, then took a gulp. He rolled over with a groan and stood, mildly disoriented and swaying. There seemed nothing around him but grey space and the hard interior wall.

Adam's hands were his only guides; his left hand felt along the jagged rock wall while his right hand groped in front of him as if trying to push the darkness away. He blindly navigated farther into the tunnel. He heard noises around him and he could've sworn that something was either buzzing or hanging in front of him, crawling or slithering along the floor. The thought of being bitten by a snake and tempted into contradicting God's authority or worse, taking knowledge that was forbidden to him to use against his belief, mortally scared Adam. His shoulders tensed with the possibility of unknown creatures to which his psyche could assign evil thoughts and purposes.

In spite of his nervousness, the tunnel could not stop Adam. No other assignment was this important; no other cause he participated in had the same immediacy. Its difficulty was reminiscent of his faith. Failure was not permissible.

Without a torch, his trip was slow and arduous. This was the other side of his faith, traversing dark tunnels, stepping into the unknown. Faith was easy when everything was going well, but when the darkness of doubt shadowed the light, faith became a slow journey down a dark tunnel, with only a dim grey light at the end of it.

Though Adam experienced almost paralyzing fear, the importance of the book and the lance refocused his intent. He decided that one life was worth the ascension of a king and the stability of a kingdom. If it was God's will, he'd be willing to be a martyr for his faith.

He felt in his pocket for his bottle and took the last swig of the tart wine. The moment Adam stepped into his fear, he was always shown that the actual outcome was never what he'd imagined it to be—but cowardliness never is.

As the wall curved in a sloping turn, a glow permeated the tunnel's darkness. Then a sliver of the faintest light shone on Adam's hand. He looked up to see rays of light shooting across the width of the tunnel, catching on the dust in the air. His outstretched hand grabbed for the light as if he were grabbing hold of a tether that would pull him to the end of the tunnel. His entire posture changed from hunched fear to energetic poise. His pace quickened and his strides lengthened. The sliver of light quickly grew into a shaft of light and then into flickering shadows jumping along the wall.

Recklessly, Adam burst into the chamber without regard for his safety. His beacon was a single torch attached to a sconce on the wall. Adam's entire body exhaled in relief that his error in judgement had not brought him face to face with another person.

A central hearth provided a glowing light source and kept the room dry and warm. The floor was not of dirt but rather sloping rock. The higher elevation of the rock floor would be much preferable to a dirt floor, not just for comfort but for the preservation of the books along the walls and the contents of the chests and sealed clay jars resting on the floor. The jars probably held scrolls (a form of archiving that dated back to ancient times). The chests, when he tried them, were locked. To the left of these were several niches holding stacks of books.

Adam felt that he was very close. That the monks took this much care to keep this chamber hidden and climate controlled indicated the importance of its contents. He quickly went to work, lifting the heavy volumes out of the niches one by one and opening their heavy wooden covers, then laying each on an easel and brushing dust off the cover so he could read the engraved title. He was looking for clues, something that would bring him closer, if only by small steps, to finding the artifacts and Ari.

Adam pulled down another volume and another. Most of the books were works of a scientific or scholarly nature. Some books were older than the colony itself. He put aside a copy of Aristotle's second book of poetics on comedy and pulled forward the book underneath. Chiselled into the cover was the name *Marsson*.

He grabbed the wall torch and slid it into a crevice just above his head. He opened the book to the title page. The laborious and shaky handwritten script read: *The Events of My Journey to Greater Ireland: A Truthful Account by Ari Marsson.*

A folded piece of translucent cloth dropped onto the floor. Adam picked it up and unfolded it to see a hand-drawn map. Various sections of the map were labelled: *Vinland, Helluland, Markland*. He folded it back up, thinking nothing of it.

From a pocket inside his robe, Adam pulled a parchment with a confirmed sample of Ari's handwriting on it. He laid the scrap next to the title; the handwriting matched. This book was without a doubt the writings of Ari Marsson. He hunched over the book, carefully turned the page, and began reading.

* * *

I am endeavouring to write down the events that led me to this land, which the Celi Dei name Greater Ireland. It was not my intention to land here and to find these pious monks. But I now understand that the events that led me here to His Holy Land were meant to be, so that I might be given atonement for my crimes through the sacrament of the baptism. I accept the fact that God has led me here to answer for and to seek absolution for my crimes. But I also know that he led me here to lead His people as Moses and Jesus did before me.

My journey began on a merchant ship of no great importance or distinction. I was hired as one of its rowers. It's only worth mentioning because from the very beginnings of the trip, there were strange happenings. Our destination was somewhere in the British Isles; some say it was Ireland, but no one was willing to confirm that. We were told to keep to our work and not to think or ask questions.

In actual fact, I was not hired. I took the place of another sailor whom I murdered. I stole his identity by speech so that I could take his place. If I am to tell the truth, then I believe that the lies are a good place to start.

King Harald's soldiers hunted me for crimes of rape and robbery. The only logical progression of this life was murder for personal gain.

Another strange occurrence was that we didn't load cargo onto the knarr, only supplies. Two men led the voyage, a Norse owner and an Irish abbot. They didn't share any instructions or details of what our duties would be when we reached our destination. Only that, under no circumstances were we to leave the ship. We suspected that the cargo was human rather than objects. But everyone had a duty and no one stood out from what I thought of as the crew.

During what was supposed to be a four-dægur voyage, unusual events continued to be the norm. The crew were, not surprisingly, suspicious about why we were ordered not to go down into the fore cargo hold. We were permitted only in the aft hold, where our supplies were stored. Guards, which comprised half of the crew, took turns guarding the hold. Otherwise they wandered around the ship with very little to do but watch us. These men were not experienced sailors, but were quick with a sword and the edge of a shield, for those who didn't follow instructions.

Rumours abounded as to why guards protected an apparently empty hold. Some said that the hold was not empty and that the cargo was secretly stored before the crew arrived. Others were of the opinion that the cargo hold was empty and that we were to pick up secret cargo and return it to Iceland. There was mention of a meeting with high officials in the Irish Church, which would explain why the hold was off limits to us. Rumours of revolution to overthrow the kings of Europe kept us awake and thinking during the long, cold North Atlantic nights.

But the most unusual thing was how late in the season the voyage commenced. It was dangerous for prolonged voyages at this time of year. It was as if the planners felt that they didn't have a choice, or the purpose outweighed the risks.

At the end of the first day, the rowers and the steerboard man were told to rest in the supply hold. The waters had calmed and we were told that our strength was needed for the following day. One lookout man remained on deck, scouting the waters.

We had just finished eating some dried meat when I heard a roar that I had heard once before, and prayed that I would never hear again in my lifetime. I crawled to the hold's opening and looked up through the darkness to the shaft of light entering the hold from the lamps on deck. It was like the sun shining through the fog at dusk. I could see the fear in the eyes of my shipmate, Tory. Just as I had, he recognized that horrendous sound for what it was.

It had started out as an almost unnoticeable rumbling, lost in the background noise that an experienced sailor filtered out. Then it rapidly grew into a thunderous roar, so loud that we had to cover our ears. Tory and I jumped through the hole and onto the deck. Even in the darkness of the ocean night, I saw the starry sky veiled by a wall of water rapidly coming toward us.

"Turn us into it," I heard. The voice sounded distant, but I turned to see the order coming from the Norseman standing next to me.

I didn't know if it was my panic or if the deadly wave had surrounded us, but I no longer saw the heavens. It was as if the Norse gods had abandoned us and we were left alone to the wrath of the Christian One.

I felt the ship tipping, then flowing water pushed me back into the hold. The last thing I remembered was the sound of my head hitting the edge of the open hold.

I awoke with dim light all around me. At the time I didn't know it, but I was looking out of the hold entrance above me. The light blinded me and I thought that I was resting in Valhalla, that I'd finally reached the end of my life's journey to begin a new life as a warrior. The creaking yawing of the ship chased away that thought. I returned to the knarr and remembered the events that brought me to this instance.

I slowly lifted my head and felt a sharp pain, like that of a drunkard waking up the morning after a night of heavy drinking. I tenderly touched the right side of my head and felt dried blood matted in my hair and beard. I rolled over and felt the pain of a second injury on my left side, where I'd obviously landed when washed onto the lower deck.

I had survived the storm, but how damaged the ship was, I did not yet know. We were still afloat, so perhaps Óðin in league with the Christian God had deemed me worthy and had spared my life. I forced myself up to search for other crewmembers and to find out what had happened.

My shock had momentarily subsided and I realized how cold the hold was. I was shivering uncontrollably. My wet toes were numb inside my stiff boots. I could still move them, so they were not yet damaged by the cold. My body ached with each movement; I tried to ignore the jabbing pain in my side, the pounding pain on the side of my head, and the burning pain in my lower back.

The deck was at a precarious angle. Water had leaked into the hold and kept the keel just above the waterline. The wool sail was still intact, but the mast was broken in three places. All that remained of the thirty crew and passengers were eight bodies strewn across the deck in haphazard positions. The rest must've been washed overboard. The wooden debris served as headstones that marked the position of each body. I gazed at the cemetery in front of me and couldn't believe that this was all that remained of the crew.

The sky looked like it would explode again into another storm at any moment; black and grey clouds menaced me. They rolled and churned, mixing their deadly brew into another fatal concoction.

I struggled to the side and looked overboard. The boat was struggling to remain on the surface of the water. Even with the angle of the tilt, the waterline was almost to the edge of the deck. With its every movement, the ocean threatened to spill more and more water into the boat. *The supplies in the aft hold must've shifted in the storm,* I thought; *they're keeping the ship at this angle.* If I redistributed the cargo, the knarr would settle back on her keel again.

The norðr wind blew through me and I shivered more and more uncontrollably. My clothes were soaked and it felt as if I was standing naked in the wind. If I was to remain alive, I needed to find some dry clothes. I looked around. Most of the bodies on the deck had a thin sheet of ice over their skin and clothing that crunched with the slow bobbing of the ship.

The monk's limp body lay before me, clad in its heavy wool habit; it was the only body whose clothing was still relatively dry. Matted blood in his hair revealed the fatal blow to the side of the head that sent him from this world to the next. It seemed that in calling his servant to their heaven, the Christian god had saved my life. I quickly stripped the clothes from the body and changed into them.

Now that my immediate survival had been taken care of, I set to the task of examining my location and surroundings. My inexperience as a Viking made it difficult for me to read the currents and to know in which direction I was being taken. I did know that I was adrift and that a current was carrying me somewhere, but where? I had no means of navigating the waters.

I looked out beyond the keel, now that I had taken several steps back from death. A blanket of white draped the ocean, interrupted only by the rhythmic movement of the water. Growlers occasionally thudded against the bottom of the ship, followed by the lap of waves against the side of the knarr. The wind blew into my ears. Those were the only sounds I heard. If I stopped and closed my eyes, I imagined my body riding on the wind, drifting with the light-carrying touch of the Valkyries on my arms and feet. But as quickly as my thoughts travelled skyward, the images in my mind collapsed and I returned to the knarr, still adrift on the Serpent's back with the howling wind stinging my face.

Drowsiness began to overtake me, due to a combination of the cold and hunger. My inexperienced body and unskilled mind made my fear and frustration all the more palpable. At the time I didn't know it, but I later found out that this was a normal bodily reaction to my environment. I hunched my shoulders and wrapped the habit around me as I felt the numbing cold and the sting in the wind intensify. I looked out beyond the side of the boat and saw that the mist was clearing.

Suddenly I heard voices—not words, but the intonations of human speech. I squinted into the mist, trying to see the owners of the voices. I feared the worst, remembering stories of evil men and monsters on the water, ready to attack voyagers. But they were just stories, and I wasn't ready to lie down and die yet.

At the water's surface, the mist twisted and churned with activity. I saw two dark, ghostly objects gliding through the water toward me. As the objects moved closer and closer, I made out more and more of their detail, until I could see what they were: four men sitting in two small boats. They were wrapped in white furs and paddling boats of white, grey, and tan.

The moment they looked up and saw my waving hands, they stopped paddling; they were so still, it was as if the cold wind had instantly frozen them. No longer propelled by their passengers, the small boats flowed in the current with the knarr.

They gently placed their paddles inside the boat next to them and stood up in perfect balance, even though the boats bobbed up and down. And then they did something totally unexpected—they knelt down on the floor of their oblong crafts and bowed toward me in reverence.

I could not explain this odd behaviour. Seeing me in monk's robes could've provoked this response, but how could they know . . . unless they'd encountered monks or priests before seeing me. That had to be the answer; it was the only conclusion that made sense.

They rose and one of them, with a grin on his dark face as if he knew me, extended a welcoming hand. The others paddled the boats closer and kept them steady along the side of the knarr. Hesitantly, I extended my hand and gripped his arm, allowing myself to be taken aboard their boat. I knew that I couldn't survive out in the elements much longer. My only choice was to trust that my gods were guiding me in the right direction.

Now that I was almost face to face with one of them, I could see that their faces were unlike anyone's that I had encountered. Perhaps these people were what my people referred to as Skrælings. They had puffy red cheeks, and their eyes were frozen in a squint.

I was gently placed on luxurious white furs. The man behind

me draped another fur over my shoulder and wrapped it around my body. The fur tickled my chin and nose as the cold norðr wind blew through the nap; I settled into the warmth of the pelts.

My rescuer turned 180 degrees and paddled back into the mist. The other boat stayed behind, I assumed to check the ship for other survivors—something that I hadn't thought of doing while I was aboard. I was under such distress that it had not occurred to me.

I was happy to be off that death ship. I wish that I could honestly say my reason was just to be en route to dry land, but the truth of the matter was that I detested the thought of death near me. I didn't consider myself a violent man; I usually obtained what I wanted through more clandestine means, though I was not against murder—in fact, the strong should take from the weak, including life. It's how the natural world works.

My destination was as concealed as the ocean around me. I couldn't tell in which direction we were headed, but one thing did occur to me (now that the thought of my survival was no longer weighing heavily on my mind): I must've been drifting in a current that passed very close to a shoreline, or how else could the natives travel to meet me in such small boats?

I let my escorts worry about taking us to our destination. My eyes were very heavy and they were beginning to burn from the cold wind and the lack of sleep. The side of my head still ached from the earlier impact, though the pangs were slowly subsiding. My hours on the ship had been filled with such worry and preoccupation that I hadn't noticed the pain, but now that my mind was at rest, all of my discomforts resurfaced.

Strange that I never once thought of these men as my captors. I do not know why, but their demeanour and constitution were worthy of trust with my safety. If indeed these were the natives rumoured to be murderers and savages that I had heard much about, they were in my opinion labelled unfairly.

Their paddling seemed effortless in the choppy water. Small, rounded blocks of ice drifted past us. Some hit the side of the craft and harmlessly bounced off. The side of the boat was made of some material stretched taut across its wooden framework. My hand instinctively touched the side of the boat; it felt like animal hide.

I looked ahead as we were battered by another gust of norðr wind. The mist swirled and lifted as we passed through it and I could see the ghostly outline of what looked like a large landmass. The mist parted, and before us was a blinding field of ice. Cliffs of grey and pink seemed to levitate in the air beyond the ice field, like monolithic apparitions. Wisps of clouds clung to the mountaintops; in places they reached so low that it was sometimes difficult to tell the difference between cloud and ice.

The cold, barren landscape was like nothing I had seen before. It was as if I was staring into the beauty of heaven and the extremity of hell. I was in awe of what seemed to be my destination, but I feared the cold and the vastness of this land; it left me with an empty feeling in the centre of my stomach.

The snow-covered land reminded me of something Eirik had described to me: "We cast anchor and went ashore and we could see no grass there. The background was all great glaciers, and right up to the glaciers from the sea the land was like a flat stone. The land was barren and useless. I will call it Helluland."

The only sound was the ceaselessly blowing wind. I don't know how long I gazed at this barren and featureless land. I was so mesmerized by it that I hadn't noticed our craft beach on what looked to be a shelf of snow and ice. With perfect balance, one of the men stood, and created a sort of equilibrium between the motion of the waves hitting the shore and the bobbing boat. The other stood and grabbed my hand — not in a forceful manner, but to escort me off the boat.

Once on the shore, I noticed that I stood two full feet above the man. I was soon standing alone, as he walked to an unmarked place in the snow and began digging. He put his hand under the snow and pulled out a snow-covered bundle of animal skins tied together with twine. He opened the bundle and pulled out a pair of fur pants and a fur coat.

Kneeling down in front of me and holding the pants open, he gestured for me to step into them. I did so and found that they stopped the wind from blowing up my legs. The bottoms of the pants already had shoes sewn to the cuffs. The bottom of my habit fit nicely into the outfit. He reached around my torso and pulled twine sewn into the hide tightly around my waist. Next he pulled off the fur wrapping my shoulders and pulled the coat over me. Its design was as innovative as the pants — a hood was sewn onto it. Its pungent animal odour met my nostrils as the hood was pulled over my head, but I didn't mind the smell, considering the protection from the elements the outfit provided.

He returned to the bundle and pulled out a frozen pink object. He put it in his mouth and sucked and chewed until it softened, then he held it in front of my face. I instinctively recoiled. With his other mittened hand, he gestured to his mouth, and I understood that he wanted me to eat the object. I didn't know what to do; the thought of ingesting saliva-soaked raw meat made me queasy. But I was very hungry, and knew I needed to keep my strength up to traverse this ice field, so I gingerly took the meat from between his fingers. I tried to wipe off as much of his saliva as I could, then bit into it with my back teeth. I tasted blood and another taste that I wanted to ignore. I tried not to think of what I was eating. I kept telling myself that I was eating this for my own survival.

He took out a second piece and gave it to me to melt. I duplicated his actions exactly. I told myself that in time, the taste would grow on me.

I saw him kneel down and hit the snow and ice with his fist till he broke through the crusty surface. He scooped up a chunk of ice and bit off a piece. I grabbed the snow without further instruction and bit into it. It was cold on my teeth and gums but once it melted, I realized how thirsty I was.

The native returned to the pack and bundled it up again and buried it in the snow. I guessed that this cache remained here and that there were other caches of food spread around this land. I could see the strategy of having them, though I wondered how those who left them were able to find them again. It was an ingenious way to make use of the environment. Why expend valuable energy to create a manmade storage unit when the natural world provided such a convenience? The frozen land would keep food from spoiling and the snow would keep it hidden from predators.

I kept watch on my escort, realizing that without this man, I was as good as dead in this strange land. I had a much better chance of survival back on that death ship. Unless there were animals to hunt, here I'd only have the snow for sustenance. And I knew that I could not survive only on water for too long.

My escort waved for me to follow him across the white, glistening ground. The cold arctic wind carved repetitive patterns in the hardened snow, like ocean waves frozen in time. A vast white ocean separated us from the distant mountains, for the snow extended all across the land. I could not be sure of the distance to the mountains, but I knew that it would be a long trek, taking at least two dægur, maybe longer.

I didn't have any means of communicating with this native. I knew that we'd have to develop a way. Up until now we'd communicated through hand gestures; gestures that I deciphered correctly, but without a systematic way of communicating I wasn't sure that I was getting my full message across, or correctly interpreting his, either. I didn't know if his people communicated with words. What I had heard sounded like mumbling to me. I couldn't distinguish any familiar pattern from the murmur. I later learned that the native words began with a root sound and then other sounds were added as the suffix.

He turned and began walking toward the mountains, neither telling me he was going nor waiting for me. I quickly realized that he had no intention of assisting me on this leg of our journey. It appeared that I was to trek across the ice field under my own locomotion. I bundled my outer clothing around me and followed him across the barren land.

I was still weak from my ocean ordeal, but found that the meat and the snow banished my intermittent dizziness and helped to restore a little of my strength. My hunger had subsided for the moment, but my body was still craving water. During our trip, I always had a mitt full of snow, ready to bite into.

The day was waning; I didn't know how long we had walked. My mind drifted in and out of focus, sometimes dwelling on the last few dægurs, occasionally interrupted by a fear that if I didn't keep moving, this land would be my prison. There would be no need for chains and dark pits for my crimes—the ice and the ocean would keep me imprisoned here. I felt helpless, small, and insignificant.

The rapidly setting sun had turned the side of the mountain ahead a gentle rose hue. And the shadows created by the mammoth mountains were a calming blue. Strangely, this was very calming to me.

My guide was still in the lead; in fact, he stopped several times so I didn't fall too far behind. The continuous wind stole away my wheezing cries to stop and rest. The close of the day marked the limit of my strength. I was rapidly weakening; my headache and the ache in my side had returned. I didn't know how much farther I could travel.

Suddenly the land began to spin; it whirled into a sea of white and then I felt myself falling into a well of darkness.

I awoke in a small structure with a dome-shaped ceiling that glowed with what I guessed was outside light. This subdued light provided an evenly lit environment within. I peered through a square hole at the sky above me. A small fire blazed in the middle of the room. At first I thought I was back in the aft hold on the knarr. Then I remembered my rescue and the trek across the frozen land.

A wrinkle-faced female rubbed her rough palm across my face and forehead. She put her hand behind my head and simultaneously touched a steaming cup of broth to my lips. I hesitantly opened my mouth and she tipped the cup. A pungent taste and an astringent pine smell invaded my senses. The smell of the concoction made me queasy, but at my slightest hesitation, she scowled. I decided to submit to her treatment and drank the foul potion, but I had no sooner swallowed it before I vomited it up again. She used a piece of my robes to wipe my mouth and chin.

Undaunted by my protests, she fed me more of the drink, only moving the cup away when the hot liquid overflowed my mouth and ran down my cheeks. I finally raised my hand, hopefully signalling "no more." She hesitated, shook her head at me, then slowly lowered my head.

Within the next few moments, my escort entered the

structure through a snow-sheathed tunnel. The thought that this entire structure was made of ice and snow fascinated me. The domed ceiling was reminiscent of the domes of the great cathedrals in Europe and as I was later told, could withstand violent winter storms. More and more, these people impressed me; over and over again, they demonstrated creative intelligence that was on a par with the so-called civilized societies of the world.

He smiled at me and I managed a weak smile back. I instinctively put my hand to my chest and said, "Thank you." It was for saving my life. I didn't know whether he was capable of understanding my gesture, but I wanted to do it anyway.

"Quyanaghhalek tagilusi," he replied, directing the Thule words at me. I no longer felt like I was the third person. I took this as a version of "you're welcome," if not the actual words. It was as if the words were a charm or an incantation that improved my spirit as well as my vitality. I took this as a good sign; I knew that these people were wise and would help me to return to my previous state of health.

I slowly lifted my hand to the centre of my chest and said, "Ari . . . Ari."

"Qallunaat-Aaari," he said, pointing at me.

The female laughed, displaying a toothless smile.

I didn't understand the first part of the name he repeated back to me, but when I heard him include my name, I felt that we were making progress.

"Taliriktug," he said, hitting his chest with a closed hand.

I repeated his name several times to get the sound. Each time he nodded and smiled.

Taliriktug turned to the woman and said something to her. She nodded hesitantly and then looked at me. She pushed on my forehead, indicating that I should lie down. She ran her hand down over my face. I took this to mean that she thought I could do with more sleep. I did what I was told and went back to sleep, with the sound of activity receding further and further from my thoughts.

Some time later, I felt my body being shaken. I opened my eyes to see Taliriktug standing over me, smiling. He helped me to sit up on my fur covers and supported me while I balanced myself. I was a little dizzy, but I felt much better. Taliriktug put a cup in my hand containing the same pine-smelling broth that the old woman had given me. I trusted that these people knew what they were doing and drank the hot liquid regardless of its foul taste.

Taliriktug began talking, gesturing with his hands. He pointed at the current position of the sun and followed its future path across the sky. From what I could gather, he wanted us to continue our journey. This was how I interpreted him resting his elbow on the palm of his other hand and moving his arm in an arc from left to right. Then by walking his first and second fingers across his palm, I understood that we were to go to another place, perhaps a camp, and that he wanted to get there before nightfall. I nodded, indicating that I understood him. And I tried to mentally prepare myself for a day of travelling.

He sat next to me and we began eating. Taliriktug had a different kind of meat with him—it looked fresh. He tore a piece off with a bone knife and handed it to me. Rather than put it in my mouth, I placed it on the stone side of the hearth. Taliriktug watched with interest as the meat began to smoke. He followed my example and put his piece of meat on the stone edge of the hearth as well.

In about a minute or so, the bite-sized morsel looked like it was cooked most of the way through. I carefully picked it up and put it in my mouth. I relished the hot food, the flavour and the cooked texture of the meat. Whatever he'd given me had an unusual, fishy-beef taste.

Taliriktug picked up his meat and began chewing it. Immediately his eyes squinted and his lips twisted and puckered; he spit the morsel into the fire. He immediately put another piece of raw meat into his mouth, presumably to cover up the foul taste of the cooked meat.

We took turns eating our individually prepared meat until all that was left was the bone. To my surprise and shock, Taliriktug broke the bone in two and began sucking the inside of it. He picked up a rock and hit the bone, splintering the remaining halves. As before, he sucked the splinters of bone and discarded them when he'd drawn out all the marrow.

We dressed in our outer clothing and headed toward the exit. Taliriktug picked up a pack that was propped against the tunnelled entrance and led the way through it; the tunnel curved downward and then back up again. I felt and heard the blowing wind as I crawled upward. I fully realized the ingenuity behind the design of this structure. The living space was underground and somehow the ice and the cold snow insulated the occupants from the elements.

I crawled out and squinted at the sunny morning. The wind slapped my face and my nostrils felt like they were closing in on themselves as I took my first breath of frigid morning air. Hearing movement behind me, I turned around to see a pack of wolves watching us. I jumped and was about to run away when Taliriktug indicated to me that it was all right. It was then that I noticed that the animals were tied to a sled. I had heard of these beasts whose primary use was transportation, but this was the first time I had seen one, let alone a pack of them.

They sat staring back at me, some with their tongues hanging out, the steam of their breath visible in the sunshine as it dissipated in the cold air. Taliriktug indicated to me that we were to take his sled across the frozen land, and through the mountains. I didn't know where or if we were supposed to meet someone, so I abandoned myself to his will.

He picked up a whip and gestured for me to board the sled, while he stood on the two back skis. I sat down on top of some supply packs in a compartment at the front of the sled. The dogs stirred and formed a line in front of us.

I heard the spinning of the whip as it sheared through the air, then an echoing *crack* as it snapped in mid-air. The dogs bolted across the ice. I clutched the sled as it jerked and stuttered; I could feel the blood rushing from my knuckles. The sled's skis skimmed over the packed snow and we quickly picked up speed as we crossed the field.

From what I could interpret, our destination was on the coast of what I now understood to be an island. I didn't know whether he was taking me to an island across the ocean, or whether we were *on* an island. He was taking me to see people or a person . . . or perhaps it was on a mountain . . . or maybe both. His language was intimidating, unlike anything I had encountered before.

During our journey, Taliriktug taught me some other words using hand gestures. I didn't fully understand the meaning of some, but later when some of them were used in context, I was able to understand them, and combine them in a very rudimentary way.

His people are an ancient race. Several groups, he told me, had crossed a large body of water to arrive on this land; other groups of his people had separated and travelled to various other lands. Some unknown enemy had wiped out some, but enough survived to establish communities along the coasts of this land. Some went even deeper inland. But all remained linked by a complex, interconnected, trading relationship.

He told me about a man that I guessed was a leader, or someone of importance in the community. I didn't understand all the words he used to describe him, but I did know he was different from Taliriktug's people and eventually I figured out that I was being taken to him. Taliriktug compared the man to the walrus, an important animal to his people. I knew that they used this water creature for many things and depended upon it for survival.

I was fascinated to learn that Taliriktug's family was spread out across the land. Despite their movements, they all managed to meet, and stayed in contact with one another by passing messages from group to group; trading and information (and sometimes gossip) kept them linked and prosperous. If one Thule had two walruses, for example, and the other family's travels would not take them close to a pack of them, then a walrus would be traded for some other food, perhaps a caribou. And in extreme cases, they traded items on credit.

This was curious to me because I could not understand why they didn't fight amongst themselves for the limited resources of this frozen land. Taliriktug explained to me that his people had never fought with one another. At some time in their history they had escaped to this land from a place of warring peoples. He didn't know how long ago this happened but he did say that his father's father told of having to move several times to escape various aggressors. He explained that their experiences as a people favoured working as part of a larger family; they all benefited from this type of existence.

I looked at our route ahead and thought how deceptive this land was. Hidden beneath the surface was an abundance that I hadn't seen before. The waters underneath the frozen sheet teamed with life; on the land, caribou ran, wolves hunted, and the snow and ice camouflaged the white bears of the noðr. Where I once saw scarcity, I now witnessed life and resourcefulness; to me, scarcity had more to do with how the resources were used rather than the amount in existence—it only existed in the mind.

We rested for a while at the base of a dizzyingly colossal mountain. Taliriktug threw raw meat into the centre of the pack of dogs; the pack leader ate first while the other dogs watched.

Once he'd walked away from the food, the others in the pack ate what was left. Occasionally, growls and bared fangs threatened to erupt into fights, but more often than not, jaws snapped in the air and one beast backed down.

Taliriktug pointed up the mountain pass. "Angakkuq . . . Angakkuq," he yelled. I took this as the direction we would be going. I was to later find out that it meant "wise person." At the time, I thought he was speaking of his god.

Our route would take us up along a narrow path, compared to the openness of the ice field. I looked up and wondered how we were to ascend the mountain; the pass seemed to rise straight up. I couldn't imagine the dogs pulling the weight of two grown men, our supplies, and the sled up the path that lay before us.

Taliriktug indicated to me that our break was over; it was time to leave. He roused the dogs and directed me to climb aboard the sled. Rather than climbing back onto the sled himself, he walked ahead of the dogs, leading them and sometimes pulling them up the mountainside.

I could tell that the climb was laborious for the dogs. Not only did they have to deal with the weight of the sled and me, but the blowing snow settled, then froze on their snouts and over their eyes. The snow surface of the pass was firmly packed, indicating frequent travel, but when the dogs encountered drifts, they had to jump forward with each step, as they sank into the snow. And whenever they slowed, the sled snapped backward. We took frequent breaks to allow the dogs to rest.

I looked to my left. Rising over that side of the pass was another mountain, barren of snow. Its rock face was almost vertical, preventing snow from accumulating on it or at its pinnacle. On the lower two-thirds of the mountain, its flank remained in shadow, but on the last third, the sun reflected off the minerals veining the rock face.

I looked to the surface of the pass and saw indications that this place was alive with life. Deer and wolf tracks occupied the same path; even blood dotted the white trail, and if the eye followed far enough, it encountered a bloody, half-eaten carcass. The dogs sniffed the frozen carcass but didn't stop.

I lay back, resting my head on the stacked packs, and stared up at the sky. Swaths of clouds chased the light across the atmosphere, as if Frey had painted them with one stroke. I remained mesmerized despite the uncomfortable cold and discomfort of the journey.

After a dægur's travel up the mountain, we reached a summit. The wind blew harder and it was much colder, and it also had a different smell and feel to it. Something in the wind made me feel a little light-headed. I didn't know if it was my illness returning, or a spirit.

The snowfall had quickly become a storm, the higher we ascended. Up here the snow had tapered off somewhat, but the blowing snow had slowed us down considerably. I was now in front helping Taliriktug lead the dogs up the perilous mountain path. At times we had to literally pull the dogs through the snow for fear that they might lie down and fall asleep.

We stopped on a small plateau just large enough for the sled, the dogs, and us. The dog team lay down on a patch of grey rock where the wind had cleared the snow away. The animals huddled together for warmth, hiding their cold snouts under their curled up bodies.

I looked out over the escarpment; beyond our isolated plateau was a land of mountains, hanging mist, and blowing snow as far as I could see. A winding ribbon of turquoise water ran through the grey-black rock faces stealing the attention and the natural light. Gentle slopes rose up from the winding river and then jutted up dramatically to snow-dotted peaks.

I followed Taliriktug down a narrow, sloping ledge, and

into a cave just below the plateau; it faced out over the side of the mountain, hidden from anyone who didn't know it was there. But as Taliriktug led me through its entrance, I could understand how someone could choose to live in it, if they wanted to lead an autonomous life. I assumed that this was our final destination rather than another rest.

A damp, putrid smell struck my nostrils as I passed through the rock portal. Taliriktug didn't seem to mind it. Balancing himself on tumbled boulders, he was clambering down to a sloping rock floor.

All around us, tunnels branched off in different directions. The drip . . . drip . . . drip of water surrounded us. I noticed water running down the walls and suspected it was partly due to the warmer interior air meeting the frozen air; closer to the entrance, sheets of ice covered the walls. We passed several pools of water being fed by milky-white stalagmites along the ceiling.

An ever-present wind blew from deep within the catacombs. There had to be a source of underground heat because the wind was temperate enough to make the catacombs liveable. It made a strange sound that seemed to come not from one particular point, but all around us. It was similar to the sound made by blowing through a large, hollow pipe. A higher-pitched flute sound punctuated it at random intervals, and perfectly harmonized with the unending, low bass sound. I both feared and was enchanted by this haunting melody

Torches added a ghostly, iridescent glow along the ceiling of the deep cavern we traversed. They flickered but didn't go out as the wind passed over them. We walked past cave drawings, some beautifully painted; they depicted groups of people hunting antlered animals. They carried what looked like spears; some carried bows with nocked arrows, ready to fire at the animals. It seemed to me that these paintings depicted Taliriktug and his people in hunting parties.

Deeper, there was another depiction of a group of people, and then a much larger and more elaborate sketch, with a taller figure at the centre of the group. It was difficult to decipher the image, but I assumed this figure was a visitor to the community because of its prominence. As I looked at the two separate images, everything began falling into place—this was a history of the community; the cave served as a type of museum for their collective lives.

As Taliriktug grabbed a lit torch from the wall, it occurred to me that someone had to keep these torches lit. I suspected that he was taking me to see that someone—perhaps the large figure depicted in the cave painting.

The pictures continued as we moved farther into the cave. Ink line drawings were drawn over what looked like chiselled marks in the rock itself. Unlike the paintings, the etching and the line drawings were much more rudimentary; the trunks of animals were square rather than rounded like their painted counterparts. The marks had faded over time, but within those lines I could complete the shapes of people, a herd of animals and, on the opposite wall, a drawing of two groups of people; one group bore what looked like weapons and they chased an unarmed group. In the wake of the attackers, bodies lay strewn on the ground, depicting injuries or death.

"Ari," Taliriktug said, struggling with the word. He pointed to a fungus growing in an area on the floor and indicated by moving his head along with facial expressions that I was not to touch it or eat it or even inhale the air around it. I paid careful attention and acknowledged his warning.

We passed several cold hearths, a second sign of either recent or current habitation. Taliriktug led me into a tunnel, where a light source reflected off a pool of water, casting dark, randomly dancing patterns on the opposite wall.

I was now convinced that we were not alone. My body tensed and my senses remained alert; my steps were steady and slow. I jumped when Taliriktug unexpectedly called out a name: "Angakkuq . . . Angakkuq."

I heard a stirring farther down the tunnel, then a silhouetted figure stepped into a doorway that I hadn't really noticed. I could make out a few features—the face, although dimly lit, was the face of an older man. A grey and white beard rested on his chest. He wore a torn, tan-coloured habit with a rope tied around his waist and a crucifix depending from that.

"Taliriktug, maungarpok . . . please come in."

I followed Taliriktug nervously, staying close to my companion who, during the last several days, had shown nothing but concern for my well-being. I took some comfort in the trust that I felt toward Taliriktug; I considered him my protector and a friend.

The figure backed away from the doorway and shadows once again danced across the wall; I noted that their seemingly random patterns were synchronous with the cave harmonics carried by the constant breeze blowing through the tunnels.

He led us into a larger chamber. In the centre of the room lay a hearth, its embers glowing orange between dark cinders. On the right side of the room was a scribe's table containing the instruments used to take measurements and other strange mathematical devices. I glanced at one of the many opened parchments on its surface and recognized a liturgical calendar; I identified Lent and Easter.

The large figure sat down on a natural seat of flat rock. He still towered above both of us. "Please, be seated," he said to me. "I am Dionysius."

Taliriktug walked around the hearth and sat to the right of Dionysius. The shimmering heat and smoke from the hearth gave them an ethereal quality.

"And who are you?" he asked me.

"My name is Ari . . . Ari of Marsson," I said.

"Welcome, Ari," he said. "Welcome to my heaven on earth," he boomed, though his voice still maintained its welcoming tone.

I scanned the chamber. Although he had made a comfortable home in this rugged setting, it was hardly heaven. The walls dripped with moisture into pools of green and sapphire blue. The wind whistled through the tunnels at varying pitches, the worst being an occasional squeal. I failed to see how this environment could be confused with utopia. It was damp, dark, and lonely.

I couldn't quite place his accent. "How long have you been living here?" I asked, hoping to lead the conversation to his homeland.

"It's been so long that I can't remember," Dionysius replied. "My reason for coming here does not require me to keep track of time. I came here to find solace, so that I may be closer to God. For that, eternity does not seem like a long time."

"But you keep a calendar on your table."

"A relic from my past, nothing more."

"You are in this foreign land alone?" I asked in disbelief. How could someone relegate himself to such a place?

"Yes. I am a Culdee. My order is sworn to service through hardship and solitude."

I nodded without really knowing what he meant. I had never heard the name Culdee, but I guessed that the order was

Christian. All Norsemen had heard of Christians and I, with my Viking past, was no exception.

The hearth burned hot; I felt the tickle of perspiration trickling down my face. As I removed my outer clothing, I noticed a change in Dionysius's face. And then everything made sense to me: Taliriktug's rescue, the reverential treatment I received from his people. They all had mistaken the habit I wore for membership in a religious order. The fact that my habit was of a different colour from Dionysius's didn't seem to matter.

"Ari, you should have told me you are a monk," Dionysius said, putting his palms together.

"I . . . uh . . . I didn't think to," I stammered. "Of course — you would not have known because of my outer clothing." I didn't know why I lied; it was not out of contempt for Dionysius's belief, but the truth did not fit into my immediate needs. "Your order . . . the Culdees. I have heard of them but I do not know much about them," I said.

"We are an Irish order."

Irish! I thought. *That's what his accent is.*

"We believe that in order to find God, we must have faith in God. So to exercise our faith, we travel and endure hardship, hunger, and the elements. It is our suffering that gives meaning to our faith. There have been many such trips," he continued. "Saint Brendan was said to have held mass on the back of a whale during one of his journeys. I ended up here."

"By the grace of God, I've been provided for by Taliriktug and members of his tribe. They provide me with furs and help me with finding food. This allows me to pray and meditate. I am grateful to them and to God for granting this to me. I originally planned to join my brethren south of here, but I became settled here, and realized that I didn't want to be part of a community anymore, so I decided to stay.

"But I have questions to ask of you. Tootega, who was the other Thule, has provided me with some information about your ship. All aboard her — or at least the ones that we found — have perished."

"Yes." I hesitated, fearing that Dionysius would implicate me somehow as the cause of the disaster that killed the crew and set the knarr adrift.

"Angakkuq!" someone yelled from behind us.

Dionysius, along with Taliriktug, stood and ran out of the chamber. I could hear muffled voices in the other chamber, including Dionysius's, but I didn't understand what any of them were saying.

They returned with a limp human figure cradled in Taliriktug's and another Thule's arms. Dionysius led them into another part of the cave. I followed them to see who they had brought in, expecting it to be a Thule—either injured or suffering from being caught out in the snowstorm. It took all three men to lift the figure onto a fur-covered rock in the shape of a bed. Once they stepped away from the body, I saw the face within the fur-lined parka.

It was Tory.

My emotions were mixed. I was happy to see Tory alive— he'd been a good shipmate during the trip. But if he woke up and saw me, my assumed identity would be compromised.

"He seems to be suffering from exhaustion and exposure to the elements," Dionysius whispered. "He needs to rest, if he is to recover at all." He turned to Tootega and barked an order. Tootega disappeared into the tunnel.

Dionysius began inspecting Tory's fingers and toes—for frostbite, I assumed. Tory's fingertips around the nails looked purple and bruised.

"His name is Tory; he is a member of my crew," I said, fearing that at any moment he would open his eyes and expose me. "Do you think he will survive?"

"My knowledge of medicine is only as much as is required by my religious order," Dionysius said. "We will have to trust in the will of God."

It is the will of God that bothers me, I thought. For now I decided not to do anything, but I began devising a plan to rid myself of this new threat. I decided not to take my eyes off of Tory; the closer I was to him, the closer I could keep watch on him. "I will care for Tory as well," I said. "After all, he is my crewmate."

As I watched Tory lying helpless on the bed, I thought the best way to silence him was by killing him without leaving evidence of the murder. My options were limited. The only weapons at my disposal were rocks and heavy objects that would certainly leave marks on his body. Dionysius, with his knowledge of medicine, must be one hundred percent convinced that Tory had died because of his weakened state.

I volunteered to take the first watch, feeling too agitated to sleep anyway. As I sat next to his bed, various plans flashed through my mind; they branched off into other plans and if I reached a dead end, the course of my thinking brought me back to a previous idea. The same question arose over and over again in my mind: how could I silence Tory? I purposely didn't use the word murder; avoiding that made killing him so much easier.

However, I did find the actual act of silencing him difficult, because I didn't feel malice toward him; he hadn't harmed me in any way, nor had I felt threatened by him at any point. Nevertheless, he was now a threat to me. At this point I began rationalizing his death and transforming my fear and uncertainty into motivation. In this harsh land . . . it was the way of things. The weak must succumb to the will of the strong. As I sat there staring around at the rock room and the burning hearth and the flickering flame of the torch, my mind momentarily quieted. Then it began racing again. To take a human life was so simple an act, and yet it was the most difficult thing to do.

My eyes focused on the books inserted into every crevice and alcove in the walls. But I wasn't really looking at them. My mind was still on the present problem; the books only served as a focal point for my thoughts. And then the thought struck me — if Dionysius had knowledge of giving and keeping life, then perhaps his knowledge could be turned to cause death. I leapt to the first book my eyes fell on.

It's such a simple plan, I thought as I leafed through the pages and scanned the neatly written words and carefully drawn illustrations. The medicines that healed, in the proper hands, could also kill. *There must be some elixir or potion that I could mix up that would leave little evidence.*

I put the book down and picked up another book . . . and another, partly looking for either an image or words that struck me as familiar, and partly hoping Óðin would guide my murderous hand.

I reached high above my head, groping within the niche I'd been exploring; the tips of my fingers brushed the spine of a book, and I stood on tiptoe to wiggle it from its jagged rock shelf. I misjudged its weight; it fell from my hand and hit my head, then dropped to the floor. Pages fell out of the book and floated to the ground, whirling over and over of their own accord.

My eye fell on half of a familiar illustration as I reached for the loose sheets of paper. I picked up the book lying facedown on the floor and flipped it over, then slipped the loose page containing the partial illustration in next to its neighbour. I confirmed the image that I'd glimpsed—it was the fungus Taliriktug had warned me about at the cave entrance. Although I couldn't read Latin, the picture was unmistakably of the same fungus.

I felt a sense of calm that slowly changed to a macabre excitement. The beauty of this plan was that Dionysius would not be any the wiser, because the poison would be perceived as being naturally caused.

I didn't know how long it would take to affect Tory, but I thought the sooner I started with my plans, the better. Of course this didn't guarantee his demise, but in his weakened condition, my chances of success were good. And besides, I had very little choice—I didn't have time to study Dionysius's books and I couldn't risk Tory waking and recognizing me. This act had to be decisive and as immediate as possible.

I heard rustling on the fur-covered rock bed. Tory was moving as if he were in a dream state. His legs kicked off the fur covering his body. I walked over and found myself picking up the cover and placing it over him again. I found this act surprising, considering that moments earlier I'd decided to silence Tory to prevent him from exposing me. The thought did cross my mind to take the fur and bunch it up over his face.

Beads of sweat had sprouted all over his forehead and chest. As I lay the cover on top of him again, I touched his clammy skin. Perhaps I didn't have anything to worry about after all. Tory's death may be inevitable without my intervention.

"How is our patient doing?" Dionysius asked from somewhere behind me.

Still leaning over Tory, I answered, "This is the only time that he's stirred, Father."

"Please get some rest, Father Marsson. I can watch over your shipmate."

I watched as Dionysius placed a sack around Tory's neck. He looked up and smiled at me. "It is filled with herbs collected by the Thule every fall," he said as if reading my questioning thoughts.

I retreated and walked up the rock corridor to the entrance of the cave. The snow had stopped and the sky was clearer than I'd seen it since my arrival in this frozen wasteland. The stars were so bright that in some places, it was hard to distinguish one star from another.

The Norðr Star, which I recognized, shone brightly

overhead. Distant howls bit into my senses along with the stinging touch of the cold arctic breeze. For some strange reason I wasn't tired; my senses were fully alert, my head was clear, and my pulse was strong. The moment that Tory was carried through that door, I noticed a calm discomfort rising inside of me. I was forced to remain calm so I wouldn't alarm Dionysius and Taliriktug, and forced to conceal the discomfort that at any moment I may be found out.

I began to understand how Christianity worked. It wasn't so much the consequences of sinful thoughts and actions, but the guilt of those sinful thoughts and actions. It was about not being able to live with the self-torment of knowing that you had or planned to sin. Of course, this applied only if you were a believer.

I know that my reason was the fear of being revealed, fear of the repercussions of my actions. It certainly wasn't fear of the afterlife or punishment of any kind. If that were the case, then every Norseman who plundered the Christian churches for gold and gems would have need to worry.

I returned to the cave and immediately the warm breeze hugged me; I shivered with delight. I looked down at the approximate location of the mushroom-like fungus that Taliriktug had pointed out to be poisonous if inhaled. The white tops shone pale in the moonlight. I reached down and carefully picked the fungus from the ground, all the while turning my head so I didn't accidentally inhale its poison.

I planned how I could administer the poison to Tory as I returned to the inner caves. I'd mix it with the ingredients of the medicine sack around his neck. The fungus would have to be crushed and blended into the sack's other ingredients to conceal it from Dionysius's skilled eye. Of course, the more I handled the fungus, the more it increased my exposure to its vapours. I'd have to be quick and work on it in the tunnels, where the constant breeze would vent the vapours away from me.

The next few hours would unveil how successfully my plan would or would not unfold.

* * *

As I approached Tory's chamber, I heard Dionysius's deep and resonant snores over the howling cave winds. I looked in and found Dionysius slumped in a chair, his thick beard resting on his chest. He had wrapped an animal pelt around the length of his body. If I didn't know better, he could've been a sleeping bear sitting in that chair.

I thought it ironic that he sat there trying to protect Tory from an illness, and all the while there was a far worse sickness ready to strike. It was me that Dionysius would have to eradicate so that Tory could survive.

I moved cautiously, closer and closer to Tory. If Dionysius woke, I would be caught in mid-step with the task of explaining myself. I mentally formulated my answer: *I couldn't sleep and I was concerned about him. I wanted to see if Tory was sleeping comfortably.*

I had the ground-up fungus folded in a piece of animal hide. I slowly pulled the string holding the satchel around Tory's neck. I unfolded the hide into a trough shape, held my breath, and poured the fungus into the open satchel. I then stuck my finger into the sack and mixed the fungus into the herbs. Then I quickly tied the satchel up once again.

"Father Ari!"

"Dionysius, you startled me," I said, turning to the big monk behind me.

"I apologize," he said sincerely. "I seem to have drifted off. How is our patient?"

"He seems to be relaxing comfortably. I wanted to make sure there wasn't anything else I could do for him."

"You are a credit to your robe," Dionysius said, rising to check on Tory.

"Well," I said, "all will be returned in heaven."

Without touching my hands to my face or other parts of my body, I walked back into the front chamber of the cave and thoroughly washed them in a pool of water. I sat back, inhaling my first full lungful of air since I walked into Tory's chamber. I even welcomed the stuffy, earthy smell of the tunnel.

I returned to the small chamber Dionysius had given me and put a few more logs on the burning embers. I lay down on what I loosely refer to as my bed. Sleeping on it felt like I had not rested at all. The rock I lay on, although relatively flat, had depressions strewn across its surface that made it feel like a lumpy mattress. No amount of furs—for I had laid three on top of one another—disguised the bed as anything other than a cold, hard slab of rock.

Thoughts ran through my head concerning the events that

led me to this point and the lies that I told that got me here. I was not afraid of any repercussions of my lies—I lied because I was good at it. Lying is nothing more than a frame of mind, a way to believe in another perspective. I was good at it because I could convince others and myself that my lie was the truth.

My nerves popped and cracked in time with the sounds from the hearth. My thoughts drifted to Dionysius; this evening I'd had a narrow escape and there might come a time when I would have to defend myself, or at the very least fight my way out. Dionysius's large frame and the stamina that allowed him to live in this rugged and dangerous environment, that in turn toughened his body as well as his resolve, could make him a difficult opponent.

I needed to make alternate plans—plans of escape, plans to survive. But this land of Hel made that impossible. I had to get off of this rock. I needed to stay one step ahead of Dionysius—he had the Creator on his side; I had only myself.

I soon drifted off into that other world, and dreamt that I was drifting, lost in a snowstorm. Suddenly, a disembodied hand touched mine, then grabbed hold of it. It gently guided me as a father would his child, leading me back to the warmth and the safety of Dionysius's home.

* * *

Days and nights drifted by with Dionysius, Taliriktug, and I watching over Tory and caring for the dwelling in general. Mediocrity had replaced what I now defined as an adventure, rather than a hellish experience, as I'd considered it before.

I spent the days standing at the cave opening, staring into the distant sky. Thoughts materialized on the edge of my consciousness and then disappeared, not really taking any recognizable form. Others drifted into my dreams about the wealth and influence I expected to gain one day. At times the snow and ice and the frigid wind disappeared, replaced with the warmth and comfort of that imagined future time.

One morning I awoke from my first real sleep in eight dægur, lying on my slab of rock with a clouded head and stiff limbs. I glanced at the fire. Its high, crackling flames had been reduced to burning embers. I dragged myself off of the rock bed, grimacing through every stiff movement and muscle ache, and tossed another armful of driftwood and dry shrubbery on the hearth. Sparks and tiny embers jumped like thousands of fireflies flying to escape the heat of the renewed blaze.

Living and travelling in this harsh environment had finally caught up with me. Seemingly separate events metamorphosed into parts of my story; I was living a narrative. Whether they were fact or fiction was difficult to keep separate. I was no longer that responsive and energetic person who escaped from the Icelandic authorities and signed onto the ocean voyage. I felt twenty years older. The weight of the burden on my chest took my breath away. But . . . when I thought that the weight of my burden would soon crush me, I felt an infusion of energy. Always, the thought of wealth heated my body like a fever.

Loud groans travelled on the cave-wind, coming from the other chamber. They sounded like they could be coming from Tory, although I couldn't be sure. The sounds carried by the wind changed into sometimes-unrecognizable forms. I decided to investigate, hoping that today would be the day of my deliverance from this waiting.

I entered Tory's bedchamber to find Dionysius standing over him. The cloth satchel had been untied and placed at the foot of the bed. Tory was writhing and moaning in pain. I was secretly hoping that my corrupted medicine satchel had been the cause of it.

Dionysius grasped his head and opened his eyelids with his thumbs. Taliriktug stood next to him, holding a lamp that lit up Tory's face.

"Can I be of help?" I asked.

"His fever is worse and he has trouble breathing," Dionysius said as if he had not heard me. "I know that I mixed the correct herbs in the satchel."

"I'll check for you," I said, taking the bag from him and walking to the hearth.

I held my breath and opened the pouch. I turned my back to them and used my body to conceal the fact that I was pouring the fungus chunks and the herbs into the fire. The dried leaves instantly incinerated in the heat and the white chunks of fungus shrivelled up and disappeared among the ashes.

"Are you familiar with the herbs used by the natives of this land?" Dionysius asked.

"Ah . . . no. But I thought that perhaps I'd recognize what was in the bag."

I detected suspicion in Dionysius's voice; I felt trapped in his unbelieving stare. I felt my disguise and my lies begin to dissolve and I quickly ran through my behaviour in my mind, trying to locate anything that may have aroused his suspicions. I noted an air of avoidance in myself. Tory's sudden eruption had caused my mood to change, prompting questions in Dionysius. Our words irregularly danced around each other. I suspected questions he wanted to ask. But I also suspected that he either could not ask them or he felt that it wasn't the appropriate time to ask.

I saw Dionysius lean over Tory, hover there, examine and dissect his movements and physical condition. His ear moved over Tory's mouth as if Tory had whispered something.

And then in a moment of rapture, the events that I had set in motion came to fruition. Tory's body convulsed, paused, and then he exhaled his final breath. In a macabre sort of way, his passing saddened me. He hadn't done anything wrong except interfere with my plans; his passive aggression toward me was his only crime.

Dionysius gave him his last rites. I didn't know what else to do so I knelt down next to the rock that Tory lay upon and prayed. I had never prayed before. I began by thanking God for taking Tory's life so that I might live, and then I praised him for his wisdom, comparing my wisdom to his and all the while congratulating myself for my ingenuity and astuteness.

After several minutes of prayer, Dionysius opened his eyes. I had to congratulate him for his theatrics. I had not witnessed a Christian ritual before, but if this was anything like what the practitioners participated in, I could understand how they remained devotees.

"What would you like us to do with the body?" Dionysius asked.

I couldn't care less, but I had to say something that was in character for a member of the clergy. "The ground is frozen, but we need to bury him; is a burial at sea out of the question?"

"The ocean is a dægur's walk from here. Taliriktug can take the body," he said while pulling the fur over Tory's face.

Dionysius turned to Taliriktug and said something that may have been either an order or a request. Taliriktug disappeared into another part of the cavern. Dionysius looked back to me. "A hunting party brought me some things from your ship this morning while you slept."

Taliriktug returned from the adjoining chamber with two pieces of cargo: a chest that he dragged across the floor by one handle and a wrapped oblong object almost my height, which he cradled in his arm. I recognized the Iceland parliamentary seal embossed on the top of the chest. These must've been part of the secret cargo that was hidden from us on the voyage. I was eager to see what had been of such importance that it was kept hidden from the crew.

"Please assist me, Father Marsson," Dionysius asked. He pulled the furs from Tory's body and unfolded a large piece of translucent material that Taliriktug had brought to him. "Please roll his body toward you," Dionysius instructed me.

I placed Tory's arms at his sides and rolled his heavy body toward me. The body was still warm, so if I could imagine that he was still alive and sleeping it would alleviate any pangs of guilt that I might feel. I realized that fear had surreptitiously attacked me. It was strange; I was fearful of touching Tory's dead body. He was harmless. Why was I so afraid?

Dionysius wrapped the body in the white gauze, being meticulous about tucking in the head and the feet. "I was hoping to save this for my death, but I can find something else that will work just as well," he said as he worked.

Those were the only words Dionysius said to me.

He pointed at Tory and instructed Taliriktug to load the body on the dogsled outside. The freezing temperature would preserve his body until we were ready to give him a proper burial. The Thule picked up Tory and carried him out of the chamber, completing the strange ballet that Dionysius had been conducting for the last few minutes.

I dragged the chest closer to me. A lock protected the chest's contents but by the look of it, it was only there for official purposes and to keep out wandering eyes—it wasn't strong enough to keep out someone who was determined to get at the chest's contents. I picked up a rock and gave it a couple of swift blows and the lock broke in half and fell to the floor.

Dionysius sat close by and looked on with interest and anticipation. While he looked on with genuine curiosity, I looked on the chest as a pack of wolves would a caribou. My desires heightened as I imagined that this chest might contain tribute or some of Iceland's treasury.

Inside the box was a smaller chest. It had metal-reinforced corners and a metal hinge with a metal closure. I pulled the pin from the lock and lifted the latch. Carved into the lid was an inscription: *A generous gift from His Majesty King Harald*

Hårfagre of Norway to the Holy Irish Church, taken as the spoils of war during the Norse Campaigns.

I paused for a moment—that brief moment where the killer looks at his prey, knowing that what follows will change his life forever—then I lifted the chest lid. My heart sank in disappointment. What lay inside was not what I had hoped to see. It was a book. I stared at it, hoping it would somehow transform into what I wanted it to be.

I pulled the hide-bound book from the box that had protected it from the salt air. Springing the latch on the tome, I opened it to the title page and read *The Book of Kells*. I leafed through the book; it was a magnificent collection of illustrations and text, much of which I could not read. For all its beauty, the book didn't interest me. I was after valuable objects, not monks' drawings.

Out of the corner of my eye I saw Dionysius eyeing the book. His expression was slightly different from mine. I saw interest and love on his face. And wanting in his eyes. "Do you recognize the book, Father?" I asked.

"Yes, I do. It is a book written by the Irish monks of Columba."

I grudgingly handed the book to Dionysius, preferring to think till the last minute that the book contained some important information that I had missed.

I untied the leather ties and unwrapped the animal hide from the other item by rolling out the bundle. Doing so revealed a lance. On closer examination, it was a lance with what looked like a bloodstain on its tip. My heart sank further. My disappointment was turning to anger, anger toward Dionysius and his faith. I couldn't even value these artifacts for their religious significance because I wasn't a Christian.

I thought I could sell them to the first people I came across once I returned to Oslo. Dionysius probably didn't have any money. I'd have to sell them to a wealthy Christian like a banker or a merchant.

"May I examine it?" Dionysius asked, referring to the lance.

"Yes, by all means. Go right ahead," I replied, nearly choking on my disappointment and anger.

Dionysius slowly turned the spear and examined the head of it. He stood and compared the height of the spear to his height. "This is the holy lance," Dionysius said. He gently placed the lance on the dirt floor and opened the book once more.

Call it my heightened mistrust in people, but Dionysius's examination of the lance was too quick. If indeed it was religious in nature, he would not discard it so quickly but rather spend more time marvelling at it, turning it over and over in his hands, relishing the moment of touching something that acknowledged his faith.

When he looked at me, his eyes held a cutting sharpness that made me feel as if my chest were being pulled toward the tip of a knife. It was a look of suspicion, anger, and outrage. And if my instincts served me, there might've been greed in that stare as well.

Taliriktug returned. Dionysius spoke to him in abrupt tones, then Taliriktug left again. My suspicions quickly changed to a certainty that something was going on. I prepared myself for the worst.

"Where did you obtain this book?" Dionysius said, his tone interrogative.

"I didn't obtain it anywhere. The book was on our ship. As far as I knew, we were on our way to Ireland—at least that's the destination I was given. I was not privy to detailed information regarding our voyage. Until I opened these items from the cargo a few moments ago, I didn't know what we were transporting."

I began piecing together the parts of this puzzle: Dionysius's composed reaction to the artifacts, his inquiring looks at me over the last five or six dægurs, and how I'd reacted to Tory showing up—maybe not the reaction he'd expected from me. I also recognized that my feelings could've been caused by my own paranoia, as well.

Dionysius slowly turned the pages and remained silent. He scrutinized the pages, either purposely ignoring me or so enthralled in his examination of the book that he didn't hear me.

"That would explain the rumours surrounding our destination," I continued. "We were to return the book and the lance to its place of origin."

My thoughts spun in my head. The sound of a full purse clinked in my ears. I'd take the relics back and sell them for as much gold as I could possibly get. Christians would pay handsomely for such things; even wealthy (and greedy) clergy couldn't resist owning the artifacts.

"Then this must be the holy lance, the one that Longinus used to pierce Christ's side," Dionysius marvelled, running his finger over the speartip.

A relic that actually pierced the side of Jesus would fetch hundreds, even thousands times more than the book, I thought. "I must take these relics and complete our voyage," I said.

"Yes," Dionysius agreed. "The Book of Kells with the Book of John. I never thought that I'd touch this document . . . " His voice cracked and his hands trembled as his fingers lightly touched each page, as if he were caressing a sleeping lover's skin. "I've been truly blessed with this honour, that I may be the one to hold it."

Dionysius carefully closed the book and looked at me. "It is time for truth between us, Ari. And you notice that I no longer call you Father Marsson. Tory momentarily regained consciousness. Tory knew that you had survived; he witnessed you leaving the ship's hold before he collapsed into unconsciousness."

"I don't . . . what—" I could do nothing more than stumble over the beginning of an explanation, which Dionysius interrupted before I could finish.

"He told us the story of Ari, a fellow rower aboard the knarr, and the priest who accompanied the owner and the soldiers. You are not the priest, are you, Ari."

I picked up the lance and pointed the tip at Dionysius. "Stay away from me," I warned.

"Ari, I am not your judge. You have not done anything wrong, save claiming ownership of the book and the lance, artifacts meant for our holy church. I am here to help you." He extended his hand toward me in charity.

I replied by jabbing the lance in the air in front of him. "Step back," I warned, sidestepping to a rock where my fur clothes lay. I picked them up and grabbed the book.

Catching him off guard, I aimed the lance at his chest, intending to run him through; he sidestepped and I missed my intended target, but I did stab him in the arm. I didn't wait for his shock or pain to subside; I turned and ran out of the cave. I knew Dionysius's zealousness would compel him to prevent my escape. I didn't look behind me, but I knew that he was following close behind.

"Stop, Ari," Dionysius yelled. "There is no place for you to run. It's not too late; you can still be forgiven, if you truly repent your crimes."

His voice was lost to the howling winds of the norðr storm;

no longer protected by the warmth of the cave, I now felt the full impact of my nakedness. I quickly dressed in the fur outerwear and looked for Taliriktug, hoping he was still close by. He would not know what had transpired within the last few minutes—I could quickly dispose of Dionysius and catch up with him. I now realized that my survival didn't depend on outrunning Dionysius, but rather turning to face him . . . and so I did.

A wall of blowing snow partially obscured the cave entrance where Dionysius stood. He seemed to hang in front of me with the wind circling him and tugging at his crucifix and the ends of the rope belt around his waist. I thrust the spear toward him once again and missed—he deflected the tip and grabbed the upper part of the shaft. With a quick and decisive movement he twisted it out of my grip and threw it to the ground near the melted snow at the mouth of the cave. I immediately lunged at his shoulder, attacking where I'd previously seen the lance enter his upper arm.

He deflected my attack by stepping back, then grabbed me around my shoulders with one bear-like arm while his other hand twisted my head in the opposite direction. Rather than resisting the headlock, I used it to add force as I slammed the side of my head against his jaw. It took another couple of hits to momentarily stun him enough to twist myself out of the hold. But Dionysius retained his grip on my shoulder, and I spun around.

The wind hindered both of us. It blew around us in varying degrees of ferocity, and we tripped and stumbled as we sank into the deep snow. Neither one of us really had the upper hand for long; we traded the advantage back and forth as we fought the elements as well as each other.

Still clutching my shoulder, Dionysius lunged for the book that I cradled in my arms with his free hand. We wrestled for the book, wrapped our arms around it, both striving to deny the other sole possession. Dionysius maintained an iron grip on the cover. Struggling to counter that, I grabbed as many of the intricately coloured pages as I could, letting what I couldn't grip flap in the storm. Only the tightly bound spine held us together in our struggle.

The book was now the epicentre of our greed and rage. We spun around in the battle to own it, tried to kick each other in an attempt to loosen the other's hold on it. This struggle went far beyond the book; it was a struggle for power and our personal war for religious and monetary wealth. There was no letting go; our teeth were firmly in the book, two alpha wolves struggling for the bloodstained carcass of their kill.

"I will not give it up," burst from Dionysius. His voice resonated in the swirling wind. His feet slid closer and closer to the precipice. I used this advantage by reversing my struggling, trying to push him toward the mountain ledge.

My rage became as cold and as fierce as the blowing storm; I was caught in the frigid tempest. Dionysius's face remained calm and focused, a product of the peace that he sought on his mountaintop. I didn't think it was fear, although I suspected that both of us experienced that, as well. And yet his calm was also deceptive—his lust for the book could not be disguised; he held onto that book out of his greed for faith, just as I held onto it out of monetary greed.

"Then you will take death, the only end your greed deserves," I bellowed, and lashed out.

My foot landed just above his groin. It wasn't hard enough to make him release the book, but it did propel him closer to the ledge; drifted snow collapsed under his weight. Painted pages fluttered in our faces, and a final wrench tore away the binding, releasing them into the storm.

In an instant, Dionysius's expression changed from grief over the loss of the book to the terror of his own demise.

His weight pulled me toward the precipice. I anchored my foot against a rock that jutted out of the snow. Dionysius teetered on the edge, the lower half of his body dangling and the upper half still on the ledge, but his hold on the book forfeited his stability. I peered into his eyes. My cold, victorious stare crept into his peaceful soul and I saw a look of terror transform his face. I couldn't tell if he was in any immediate danger, but any sudden movement from me would cause his death.

And then the condition of the book came back to me as I heard the sewn binding tear once more, each tear a knell, its beautiful images crushed tighter and tighter in my grip.

I saw through the wind and the snow that Dionysius was crying. I couldn't tell whether his tears were for the slow disintegration of the holy book or the fear of his eventual death.

"You will die, Dionysius."

He spoke no words, only gasped for breath. My gaze strayed to his shoulder, where the point of the lance had ripped his habit.

The torn cloth flapped in the wind. I saw a healed scar on his arm where a gash should've been; the only blood was a stain on his habit.

And then the last fibres of the book and moments of his life tore from my grip. In silence he fell, his body disappearing into the white abyss of the storm.

I pushed myself away from the edge and hugged what was left of the Book of Kells. Its wrinkled pages were still crushed in my grip. My hands were stained with the ink leaching out of its pages. Dionysius had taken the cover with him, along with a few pages. I gathered the loose pages strewn across the snow-covered ledge, stacked them together, and stuffed them under the protection of my fur coat.

My body ached from the ferocity of the fight; Dionysius had strained my muscles to their limit. The stinging wind made my exposed skin sensitive. My arm felt like I'd wrestled Thor, and my hands, bitten and sore from struggling for the book in the cold, bitter wind, had surpassed numb and now were a persistent, throbbing ache.

I limped back to the cave entrance where the lance had fallen to the ground and searched around for it, but the weapon was no longer there. I kicked the newly fallen snow around, thinking that snow had blown over it, but I turned up nothing.

The longer I delayed, the farther and farther Taliriktug was getting away from me. I saw him as the key to this cell of ice and snow, my guide across this great white desert.

An unnatural howl overloaded my already heightened senses. I whirled around, stopping in an aggressive stance. Taliriktug stood in the cave entrance. He had the holy lance raised high above his head. He shook it in the air, threatening me with it.

I was ready for his attack. I didn't want to kill him—after all, he had saved my life several times since my arrival in this frozen land—but if provoked, I would protect myself.

Judging from the expertise of his people as hunters, if Taliriktug threw the lance from where he stood, no farther than twenty paces from me, I would not be able to move in time to avoid it—my reflexes were already compromised from my struggle with Dionysius. There was no place of refuge; if he hurled the lance into my chest, it would kill me. I composed myself to face my fate. My muscles tensed and my anxiety increased.

Taliriktug manoeuvred the weapon in his raised hand, tossing it in the air and twirling it so the head was aimed at me. His arm drew back, then recoiled like the torque on a catapult as he leapt forward and released the spear. I could see its tip spinning toward me.

It struck my chest.

I fell backward with the force of the impact. I lay in the snow, momentarily stunned, waiting for the pain. I thought that I had felt a piercing jab or a burning in my lungs, but once I opened my eyes I felt nothing; I only heard the wind and felt the cold snow under my body.

The lance was sticking out of my chest, wobbling in the wind. I could not see blood on my coat. I laughed out loud when I realized that the lance had pierced what was left of the Book of Kells that I'd concealed beneath my coat.

"I'm alive," I yelled.

I grasped the lance and with one pull, wrenched it out of the book. I stood, still hugging the book under my coat. I looked at Taliriktug, who stumbled backward in horror. To him my survival could only mean one thing: there was magic at work.

Taliriktug bowed down in submission.

I quickly checked to make sure that the tip of the lance had not entered my flesh. I was surprised to see that it had. The only mark was a small scar where the tip had entered my chest, but no blood and no pain.

I approached the shivering Taliriktug and told him as best I could that I would spare his life if he gave me transportation to the ocean and a boat; he agreed. I told him that I was going to enter the cave and warned him that if he left me, I would place a curse on him and his children. He quickly nodded, his eyes wide with fear.

I entered the cave. The whistling tunnel wind caught my attention once again. The harmonics had changed slightly. It was as if the wind was trying to speak to me, as if the cave were a mouth and the wind that created the sound, the breath. I understood why Dionysius chose this cave; there was definitely a spiritual quality within these rocks. I couldn't understand why I hadn't heard or felt it before.

I scavenged anything I could use in the way of food and weapons. I found a pack with a few supplies in it and room for some more, and stuffed into it some dried meat and berries, and nuts. I lit a twig in the hearth and took it over to Dionysius's worktable, where I examined the instruments and looked through the papers, hoping to find something of value. My eye stopped on a piece of papyrus. It was a map. I stuffed it into the bag, thinking that it could be useful; I'd examine it later.

I headed back into the storm. Taliriktug was waiting for me at the entrance; he ran over to the dogsled and roused the team when I emerged. I knelt on top of the packs piled on the dogsled, the spear upright in my hand, as the dogs leapt from the beds they had made in the snow. Taliriktug jumped on the back of the sled and snapped his whip.

The descent along the mountain path was nearly as arduous as the ascent had been. The sled picked up speed the farther we travelled down the side of the mountain. To keep ahead of the sled, the dogs had to run faster and faster or run the risk of being hit by the heavy wooden conveyance and killed, or at the very least, seriously injured. In an attempt to control the sled's speed, Taliriktug dragged his feet behind the sled. It seemed to work, because the dog harness went taut again.

If there was a colony of Culdees as Dionysius had said to the suðr of this land, then I had to head there. I took the map out of my bag and examined it. On first examination it looked like a map of the Norwegian realm, but with several additions. There was an interconnected landmass on the left-hand side of the page called Grœnlandia and below that Helluland, then Markland, and Vinlandia. Between Markland and Vinlandia was Skræling Land. On Dionysius's map there was an X drawn at a point on Markland, with a notation at a place called Kjalarness — King's Ransom.

I looked up from the map to scan the mountainous skyline. In the distant mountains I saw gold, rubies, and silver, glowing sapphires and emeralds. The clouds were made of the purest diamonds and opals I had ever seen.

We were approaching level ground. I raised my hand, instructing Taliriktug to stop the sled. He pulled the reins on the sled and used his foot for braking.

I crawled across to the back of the sled and showed him the map. He looked at it for a while, trying to make sense of it. I asked him if he knew where any of these lands were located. Pointing at Kjalarness, I asked him if he knew where this was. After a moment he nodded and said that it was a one dægur trip suðr from this land. Putting his finger on Helluland, Taliriktug indicated that this was where we were. To get to Markland, he said, I would have to travel by water.

I wondered if Taliriktug had helped create the map. His people would have an in-depth knowledge of the lands and the islands in this part of the world. I knew that I couldn't let Taliriktug go once he took me to the ocean; he would have to be my guide until we reached Markland and Kjalarness. I couldn't navigate the ocean by myself, anyway—I'd need at least one other person. But that detail would have to remain a secret until we reached the ocean.

My immediate future, which was all I ever had, did not look so grim anymore. I had the means for survival and I had a guide. Markland didn't seem that far away. I instructed Taliriktug to continue our journey. He quietly obeyed, probably fearing retribution if he dared to disobey me.

In retrospect, I highly regretted the death of Dionysius. I didn't see that it was my fault. He, as well as I, were both actors in this tragedy. Why I was allowed to live and he to die, I don't know; that decision was not up to me. In the biblical text, there were always sacrifices by some for the good of others. And I see now that Dionysius's death needed to take place for my rebirth and subsequent conversion. My only regret is not for the life that it took, but that our Heavenly Father did not allow my destiny to unfold without the killing of an otherwise innocent man.

Taliriktug and I travelled for most of that morning. Leaving the mountain pass, we travelled across a field of ice till we came to a river. Its blue-grey waters ran past ridges of black rock so fast that it didn't freeze. Taliriktug said that for as long as his people had inhabited this land, this particular river never turned to ice. This was so the gods had a route to travel back and forth between this world and the next. His people called it "the river of life" and they believed that their gods and his people had been created from its cold blue waters.

Farther downriver an umiak, the same type of boat Taliriktug had been in when he rescued me, was beached on the shore. We tipped the boat right side up and put it in the water. Taliriktug held it steady while I loaded the supplies into the back of the small vessel, leaving enough room for one other companion and me.

I turned to Taliriktug and told him that he must come to Markland with me. He shook his head and began backing away. When I insisted, he protested by pointing at his dogs and asking me what he would do with them.

"Leave them!" I replied. "You will only be gone for two dægurs. They will be here when you come back."

Taliriktug stared at me; he didn't move. I suspected that he was going to try to escape. His look changed to indignation, followed by sorrow, or fear—I couldn't tell which. He walked to the dogs and untied them from the sled and from each other. As I'd suspected, they didn't run off but stayed huddled together for warmth. I understood his concern—the storm was not as bad as it was on the mountaintop, but its rage could still kill.

Taliriktug went to the sled and lifted off the packs. He picked up Tory's body, wrapped in its death shroud, and walked over to the river. Without ceremony or prayer, he dropped the body into the grey water.

The body bobbed up and down, hitting rocks and turning in the eddies and spinning in the whirlpools, sinking and resurfacing again on its final route down the river. I watched it and thought of nothing—I didn't think of Tory's life, I didn't wonder if he was leaving a family behind who needed him for their survival. In my stomach there was a black void; I faced the feeling and accepted it.

I held the side of the boat and gestured to Taliriktug to get in. I was not going to let him out of my sight till we arrived at Kjalarness. My only guarantee of keeping him in line was fear.

As we cast off, the river quickly grabbed us and pulled us along. We dragged our oars in the water, hoping to slow down. I was surprised at Taliriktug's skill. Where I fought for control of the boat, he knew when and where to place his oar to keep the boat steadily on course. The frigid, muddy water splashed on my cheek and in my mouth; I tasted dirt and felt the sting of the cold water. My body jolted as the craft scraped and leaped over submerged rocks.

I quickly adjusted to the random movements of the boat and looked ahead, trying to anticipate the movements of the river by observing how the currents flowed around the rocks. It was much more challenging than rowing on the open ocean. The principle was the same, but my reaction time was too slow to keep up with the changing eddies and rapid current.

I lifted my eyes from our route to look ahead. The river widened to meet the vastness of an ocean filled with floating blocks of ice. I wasn't looking forward to casting myself onto that sea again, for an unknown period of time. But Dionysius's stories of a land one dægur útsuðr of this place pacified my fears. The map in my breast pocket was my talisman; I believed that my path was divine and righteous.

Soon the noise of rushing water faded and the sound of the ocean wind was a welcome change, like the sound of a baby falling asleep after crying all morning. We were safely away from the ravages of the currents, but the frigid ocean came with its own dangers. The ice threatened to take a section out of the side of the boat, or collide with the boat and tip us into the water to either drown or die from the cold.

The stinging wind of the open ocean escalated the storm to a blizzard; snowflakes whipped around my head and blew into my eyes. It became increasingly difficult to keep looking ahead. I closed the parka around my face, masking my mouth and nose from the wind, and only looked up occasionally to see in which direction we were headed.

We spent the rest of the afternoon in dull grey solitude. I had nothing to say to Taliriktug and I assumed that his fear of me kept him silent and distant. Gone was the caring and close relationship we'd shared on our trip to Dionysius. I liked this new relationship; it was comfortable for me.

My feet started to feel cold. I didn't think anything of it until they also started feeling wet. I looked down. The bottom of the umiak was filling with water. We must've sprung a leak somewhere. I turned and looked at Taliriktug, for a sign that he knew what to do. His eyes showed shock, but the rest of his body seemed submissive to our fate.

My fear quickly changed to panic as the waterline rose higher and higher. I tried to bail out the boat as fast as I could with my mittened hands, but that only resulted in my hands becoming heavier and colder as they soaked up more and more seawater. I finally gave up—the boat was now filling faster than I could empty it.

Once again, fate stared at me, toying with my life. But I wasn't about to give up. I wasn't ready to accept its terms. And it seemed that fate wasn't ready to fight me, either.

In the distance, I heard voices that I understood.

"Go slowly, men. We don't want to hit one of those mountains of floating ice." The words seemed to ride on the wind, giving them an almost ethereal quality; it was hard to know if the voice was from this world or beyond it.

"Hello!" I yelled, standing up in the sinking umiak. The

water was now past my ankles and halfway up my calves. The longer I stood there, the more the numbness overtook the feeling in my legs.

"Who said that?" a gruff voice answered.

"Ari Marsson!"

"Are you person or spirit?" he yelled, his words pelting my face with the snow and the wind.

"For the moment I am still a person, but if you don't rescue me, I could be spirit very soon," I replied through the veiling snow.

I thought I heard laughter, but it could've been the howling wind. A serpent's head peered through the storm, coming toward us. Its head was level with mine. At first I thought it was the World Serpent intervening in the rescue, but when I saw the keel, I knew it was a Viking ship.

"We are down here," I yelled, raising my arm, waiting to see human lookouts standing at the bow, looking for us.

I finally saw an outline of two men in the whirling snow, who in seconds materialized into two Vikings. The water was almost to my knees and the umiak was nearly totally submerged. I untied the cargo and supplies and threw them up to the two waiting men. Soon several more crewmembers were at the front of the ship with their arms extended, waiting to catch the case and the hide sacks. Taliriktug and I were the last from the boat to be taken to safety. As we stepped onto our rescue ship, the umiak disappeared under the ocean waves.

"It was fortunate that you arrived when you did," I said, addressing the group as a whole.

A large, authoritative figure approached us. I assumed he was the longboat's captain. "I am Rafn and you are aboard my boat," he said.

"Thank you, Rafn, for our rescue. I am Ari of Marsson, and this is Taliriktug."

"What are an Icelander and a Skræling doing out here?" he asked.

"I'm on my way to Irland Mikkla," I said.

"And what business do you have there?" Rafn asked, making no apologies for his inquiry.

"I am not at liberty to say. But you will receive a heavenly reward for your kindness," I replied, removing my wet pants and my fur overcoat, showing my habit.

"Oh, I wasn't aware of your position, Father," Rafn said,

sounding a little startled. "Return to your work," he ordered his men. He turned back to me. "I am a trader from Limerick, Father. A storm blew us off course two Wodnesdæg past and we haven't been able to get our bearings."

"Yes, it probably was the same storm that blew us toward a frozen land norðr of here," I said.

"Do you know the location of Irland Mikkla?" Rafn asked.

"I don't, but Taliriktug may." I looked for the Thule. He stood behind me, eyeing some of the Vikings with suspicion. I could tell from their looks at Taliriktug that they had violence on their minds. I distracted Taliriktug by asking him if Dionysius had ever told him the location of the Culdees.

He replied that he knew. The location was close to Kjalarness on the Markland map. It was another dægur journey from where we were, he added.

I understood. The pieces of the puzzle were falling into place. I didn't know the Culdees' reason for establishing a colony on Markland, nor did I know what was located at Kjalarness and the Culdee colony, but the two had to be connected in some way that would make this trip worthwhile. Perhaps the Culdees were protecting a secret.

Rafn called his navigator over to us. I pulled out the map that I had taken from Dionysius's cave and ordered Taliriktug to show the navigator where we were and in which direction to head. Taliriktug seemed to get the information across to the Viking.

"Rafn," the navigator said, "I know where we are. We passed a current a little farther back that I now know will take us past this Markland and then back home."

"It's fortunate that we saved you, Ari," Rafn said. "We would never have found our route home. We'll drink to celebrate, and not from frost-cups—no, we will drink from horns, given to me by the King of Sweden, Eirik Segersäll. To Markland we will sail, and to Markland we will drink."

Rafn started toward the hold, presumably to find his keg of beer, but he stopped and turned around. "The native doesn't drink beer, does he?"

"No," I replied.

"Good." He laughed. "There will be more for us! Come with me!"

I took the map back from Taliriktug and ordered him to remain with the cargo, then followed Rafn to the hold. He sorted through some cases and found his drinking horns. Then he ripped the lid off of a keg like a bear trying to get at food. The horns disappeared into the keg and then appeared with beer dripping from them.

"I can't live with my wife, which is why I chose the merchant life, but the woman can make a great ale. I suppose that's why I married her." He laughed again.

I examined the gilded horn and marvelled at the craftsmanship. I couldn't believe that my mouth would be touching so beautiful and magnificent a rim. It was a horn fit for kings.

We lifted our drinking vessels and took a swig. The drink was nicely chilled, thick and bitter-tasting. I couldn't remember how long it had been since I'd had good ale.

We talked of our travels and traded stories about our encounters. Rafn had barely escaped the same storm that we went through. His ship had encountered the worst of it. His destination was Reykjavik, but the storm had carried them so far off course, they didn't know where they were. The map Rafn had purchased was unreliable; he'd bought it from a questionable Viking while intoxicated at a drinking establishment in Stockholm.

"In payment for taking you to Irland Mikkla," he said, "I want a copy of your map."

"Agreed," I said. "Before Taliriktug and I depart from your vessel, I will outline the landmasses, but I will not copy the details within the lands."

We drank to our deal. I wasn't sure whether I could trust him because I knew that I couldn't trust myself to honour my part of the bargain. But I thought it was a small price to pay for saving my life and for stopping on their journey.

"I want to buy your native," he said. "Is he for sale?"

"No," I answered.

With that one question, Rafn revealed to me what an uncivilized and savage Viking he was. There were some lines that I was not willing to cross. I didn't know if my answer had to do with the fact that I felt responsible for Taliriktug, or whether I did consider him my property. Besides, I was not going to take the chance that Taliriktug would tell Rafn what was located at Kjalarness.

I felt a little tired from the events of the last few dægurs and a little light-headed from the beer. Its mild taste was deceptive; the brew was powerful. I wondered if Rafn's wife made such a potent drink so she would not have to deal with her husband. Women have the same feelings about men that men have about women; they just express them differently.

The beer was quickly loosening up my tongue. I wanted to brag to Rafn about my exploits, but for the moment, I remained silent—one disclosure would lead to another, then another. And then my secret would be out, all for the sake of my ego. No, Rafn must not know.

"Father, I'm curious, what do you have in those packages and that case? Is it something that you're willing to trade?" he asked, his words beginning to slur.

"Nothing but some religious artifacts."

"Silver religious artifacts and perhaps some gold ones, as well?" he asked.

"Why does it matter what I have? I asked defensively.

"Argh! Never mind," he said. "Old habits die hard. If my wife wasn't a Christian, I think I'd be tempted to rob you and throw you and your native overboard. Do not worry, Ari of Marsson, even though my wife is a constant dagger in my side, I still love and respect her. Her faith is important to her, so it goes without saying that it's important to me."

I was surprised. That was the first statement he made that I think I believed. I was very happy that I no longer had to worry about these Vikings; there were so many of them, if I didn't have their leader on my side, I might fall victim to the frustrations of his crew.

Rafn tried to carry on a sensible conversation, but his voice became more and more slurred with each gulp of his beer, to the point where I found it difficult to understand him. *Perhaps if I was as drunk as he was, I'd be able to understand him,* I thought. I quickly became bored with Rafn and his drunken ramblings, and the alcohol was making me sleepy, but any attempt to leave the table would be considered an insult. I wanted him to pass out so I could lay my head down and sleep, but Vikings were known for their beer-drinking as well as their bravery. In fact, the two often went together.

Rafn stood and walked to the barrel for another hornful. It was then that I saw my chance to end this. When he lifted the horn out and looked into it, all he saw was the hops; Rafn had reached the bottom of the barrel. "By all that's wrong in Miðgarð, the barrel's empty," he slurred, knocking the barrel over with a grunt. It rolled across the decking with the movement of the ship.

I stood up as Rafn looked through the supplies for another barrel. The beer suddenly hit me, but I was still able to walk. I staggered back up to the upper deck using the containers in the hold for support; my condition, combined with the movement of the ship, made walking difficult but not impossible.

It had stopped snowing and the wind seemed slightly milder than when we'd boarded Rafn's boat. I hoped that this was an indication that our voyage was close to an end. I think I missed the land—any land at all; I missed the greenery. I also craved stillness. The constant motion of the sea does take its toll on the body.

Taliriktug was sitting where I had left him, next to our cargo. He stared out across the water and didn't look at me when I approached. I assumed that he was mad at me for leaving him by himself. It didn't occur to me till later that Taliriktug may be missing his home and his people. I realize that at the moment I began to think of Taliriktug as property, all the things that made him human became less and less important: his feelings, his thoughts, his dignity. If I ignored his humanity, it was easier to treat him as if he wasn't human; I could also avoid complicating my feelings with the potentially crippling feelings of guilt.

I followed Taliriktug's line of sight and looked out to sea. The sky was darkening but the milder wind tempered the cold a little. For the first time I saw the distant shoreline of some unknown land; our route ran parallel with it.

Small pieces of drifting ice were all but nonexistent along our route, and we passed only a few of the large islands of ice. These drifted in front of dark and hazy landmasses in the distance.

The rowers' strokes became less and less frequent; the current and the wind now carried us. I sat back and rested my eyes from the bright sunlight. We drifted by a distant, snow-dotted shoreline; there were large patches of brown and the land seemed ready to burst into life. We passed pebbled beaches, tall trees, animals, and at times I glimpsed people. We were still too far away to see any detail, but they were unmistakably people.

Taliriktug nudged me on the shoulder and pointed in the direction of our destination. At the navigator's order to turn to the port side, the rowers' strokes became longer and longer. I could tell that we were moving out of the current and closer to what began as a hazy shoreline on the horizon. This quickly grew into a rocky, sun-washed and salt-bleached shore with green coniferous trees rising in the background. Despite the cool air, perspiration dripped down the rowers' foreheads.

The keel of the boat ground into the gravel bottom. It was a welcome sound. Eager to be not just on land, but land that was filled with life, I leapt out of the boat into a mixture of gravel, stones, and muddy water. I was able to keep the bottom of my robe dry by holding it up, but my shoes sank into the mud and were soaked with the frigid water.

Taliriktug threw my pack out to me as well as the chest containing the book, and the lance. The crew of Rafn's ship watched blankly, not one of them lifting a finger to assist us. I cradled the items in my arms and walked to shore with them, happy to finally be off that ship and away from its crew. Taliriktug followed behind me with the rest of the cargo.

We gladly stood abandoned on that shore as we watched the ship's sail catch the suðr wind and sail away from us. As the human voices receded into the distance, the natural sounds all around us slowly took over and I immediately felt alone once again.

Taliriktug looked at me in the same way that he had looked at me many times during our journey. I didn't need to ask him what he wanted.

"No, Taliriktug, I still need you to get me to Kjalarness. Once we are there, I will let you return to your land and your people."

Taliriktug's face sagged with dejection and then hardened with anger. I knew he saw me as evil. I felt as though I was looking at my own reflection.

I opened the chest and transferred the Book of Kells into the hide pack, trying to make my load a little less cumbersome. The suðr wind began picking up, and the waves hit the shore with much more force and urgency. I felt that I needed to move quickly or I'd miss something. I felt a constant pull from Kjalarness—spiritually based or otherwise. It was a gnawing feeling in the pit of my stomach. I knew that I had to get to that place.

We entered the woods of pine trees and birch, our feet sinking into the soft, mossy ground; it was like stepping onto a sea sponge. Water filled the depression around my foot with a squishing sound. I hardly noticed the millions of insects fighting for a taste of my blood; my mind was keenly focused on my destination.

The sky continued to darken and the wind steadily increased. The air thickened and felt heavier. There was a storm approaching. The surrounding woods quieted—the birds stopped chirping and there was a general cessation of noise until the rain tapped on the tree boughs and on our heads. Only the rumbling of distant thunder interrupted the rhythm of the beating rain.

The rain intensified to a torrential downpour that sometimes blew into our eyes and other times showered us with leaves, twigs, and pine needles, driven by the rising wind from the towering forest around us. The sky was turning black and I feared that, unless we took cover somewhere soon, we'd be caught in a catastrophic storm. In all of my years of travelling both on land and at sea, I had never seen a sky as threatening as this one. I feared that something was amiss, that it was supernatural—and that somehow I was at the centre of this rising storm.

I felt I'd gradually been changed by what had happened over the last day or two. I couldn't find a reason for it, but I somehow seemed lighter and unburdened by my situation. I had more energy than I'd had in years—in fact, I couldn't remember the last time I felt this good, if ever. I didn't want to stop, for fear of missing something—what, I didn't know. Taliriktug was falling farther and farther behind. I stopped several times so that he could catch up with me.

With a sudden crack, the sky split with a flash of light, and Valhalla released its oceans of water in one great burst. The wall of rain was so thick that I couldn't see in front of me, let alone keep my eyes open long enough to see where I was headed. And to make matters worse, as we ventured farther into the interior, the thickness of the brush, the weight of the packs, and the swarms of biting flies slowed us down. Doubt slowly entered my mind. I began to think that my decision to follow this map was foolish, a waste of time.

And then Taliriktug pointed to the top of a hill. I stumbled back in shock and awe. Atop the moss-covered hill stood a Christian cross. I now knew that the Culdee god must've ordained recent events and that coming here was my destiny. My life and the things that I'd done, either right or wrong, didn't matter to me anymore. The only thing that mattered was my life from now on.

We started up the hill, leaving footprints in the soggy moss, a symbol of the path of my new life. The torrent of rain lessened, but the wind continued to blow. Treetops bent like blades of grass, old and inflexible branches snapping with a deafening crack before crashing to the ground. I grabbed Taliriktug's wrist and pulled him up the hill with me, fighting the wind every inch of the way.

Suddenly I realized that the resistance was coming from Thor, and that he didn't want me to fulfil this destiny that I was rightly chosen to pursue, a destiny that would lead me away from him and move me closer to the Culdee faith. My course became clearer and clearer as I climbed higher and higher.

The cross rose majestically above me when I finally stood on the hilltop. I stopped and stared at it, realizing that I'd seen it before. This was a Celtic cross—the shape and design were unmistakable. Dionysius's group of religious monks should be near here. Perhaps this place marked the location of Culdees and acted as some kind of boundary marker. I was excited because I'd reached my destination, taken one step closer to my destiny. Nothing seemed to matter anymore except Kjalarness.

I walked around the cross and stopped in my tracks; there was a sound coming from the other side of the hill—voices, the words they spoke drowned by the rush of a river. I looked down the slope. Standing in the flowing water was a monk engaged in what looked like a baptism ritual. He yelled something that I couldn't understand.

The inductee looked to be a native female. The monk repeatedly pushed her head underwater, then reached into the current and pulled her up again, chanted some more, then pushed her underneath the current once more. All this happened while the rain blanketed the hillside and the river. I looked around the forest. Here and there amidst the foliage stood native men and women, watching the ritual bath with interest.

The lightning cracked the heavens with another flash of light, followed by a concussive boom that felt as if it penetrated my chest and punched my heart. I walked back to the cross and glanced ahead of me, noticing for the first time a rock with writing chiselled on it: *Here lies Thorvald, husband to Gudrid. He died as heroically as he lived.*

I'd reached the grave of Thorvald. Soon I would have the map in my possession. At least, I hoped the map was still in the hands of Thorvald, as I'd been told.

"Taliriktug, come here. We are going to dig," I said.

His face twisted with revulsion at what I was proposing, to dig up a dead body. Ignoring his expression, I tore a large branch from a nearby tree, stripped it of its leaves and branches, and attacked the mound of soft, rain-soaked earth. After a moment, Taliriktug joined me in digging.

Using the stick to loosen the earth and our hands to clear it away, we managed to make good progress in a short time. We had not dug too deep when my hands touched stone. I pushed away the dirt, trying to locate its edges, and discovered that it had a rectangular shape. We dug deeper on all sides and the rectangular slab began to take the shape of an oblong box. There was a seam just under the top of the box. I instructed Taliriktug to help me push the stone slab; it easily slid aside to reveal a body wrapped in a shroud.

Raindrops quickly dotted the cloth, revealing the outline of a decayed corpse. In the Viking tradition, his weapons were buried with him, but my eyes were on the object clutched in his hands, just visible through the paper-thin shroud. I tore through the gauze and saw a rolled piece of cloth in his skeletal hands. I tore it free and unrolled it. A map was sketched onto the translucent cloth. I rolled it back up again and placed it in my pocket.

I began the gory task of examining the body for anything else that might be of some use. Other than the weapons and the shield, which I didn't want to carry, I didn't see anything else of value. It took little time to recover the shallow grave.

I peeked over the side of the hill to see if the monks were still performing their ceremony. They had disappeared. We picked up our gear and walked down the other side of the hill toward the river. I had hoped to catch up with the monks to see where they were headed. I now believed that they were the Culdees.

The heavy rain had slowed to drizzle, for the moment not heavy enough to penetrate the overhanging boughs of a nearby pine tree. I sat under their protection to examine the maps further. I unrolled the map I'd taken from the grave and laid it beside Dionysius's copy. Both maps were of the same geographic area, presumably my current location, but the markings were different on each map. I noticed another strange thing about the map from the grave: it was drawn on the same type of cloth that the body was wrapped in, a translucent material. The only similarity that both maps possessed were five circles—one drawn on each corner and one in the centre.

I placed the translucent cloth map on top of my map and flattened it out as best I could. I lined up the circles in different configurations and turned the compound map till a solid line formed from two crosses that indicated útnorðr. That would make it from my current location. But the line was fragmented. I had no choice but to assume that there was something at the location where it stopped.

I rolled up the map. I had no choice but to make contact with the Culdees. Taliriktug and I could not do this alone. We were unfamiliar with this land and we needed allies to assist us. My only hope was to pose as a monk coming to join their colony.

* * *

Adam heard voices in the next chamber. He quickly closed the book and was about to put it back in the rock niche where he'd found it when he turned and saw a figure standing in the chamber's doorway.

"You find my tale interesting?" the figure said, reaching for a wall torch.

"So, you are the skald—you are Ari," Adam said slowly, not sure of the appropriate word to use.

The torch revealed that Ari's face and body had retained their youth and vigour. He chuckled. "I never thought of myself as a skald, but I guess I am. And who are you?"

"I am Adam of Bremen. I've traced you from information I obtained from the Iceland authorities. You were on a ship that was lost delivering the Book of Kells and the holy lance to Columba, in Ireland. I lost track of you until I came across an old Viking trader named Rafn, who said that you were left at Markland."

"Why are you here?"

"I am . . . a traveller who seeks out the Culdees—"

"I would like my book back," Ari said, extending his hand.

Adam closed the journal and returned the volume to its author. The cloth map that had fallen out earlier was still on his lap. He laid his palm over it. When Ari turned away from him to place the book back on the shelf, Adam casually slid the cloth map into an inside pocket of his habit. "You didn't elaborate in the book, but how is your stomach wound from the lance?"

"It hasn't given me any trouble since the day it happened," Ari replied.

"Ari, are you aware how much time has passed since the events that you so accurately recorded in the book?"

Ari stood and thought for several moments. Adam suspected that time on Markland passed from day to day without clear demarcation; the rising and the setting of the sun were insignificant events, one season changed to the next season, but both always began again.

"No, I do not know," Ari said at last.

"The ship you sailed on left Iceland over twenty years ago. Ari, you have not aged a day in twenty years."

The pompous grin momentarily disappeared from Ari's face, replaced by a look of epiphany. "Yes, I remember," he said thoughtfully. "But I didn't see a wound or blood, so I thought I had imagined the lance's tip penetrating my skin. It's difficult to remember things that happened so long ago. It feels like another lifetime."

"The lance has given you eternal life. A drop of the Lord's blood stained the tip and when it comes into contact with another's blood, it gives eternal life—so the story says."

"Of course," he said. "But you see, this is the reason that I've been spared. Come with me."

"What else do you remember?" Adam asked.

"I married Freydis Eiriksdÿttir," Ari said in a dazed voice, staring off into another time.

"Did you leave Vinland?"

"Yes, I returned to Grœnlandia with Thorstein Eiriksson, his wife Gudrid, and his sister Freydis. Once I became a member of Eirik's family by marriage, I was told of the treasure cave and the plan to open it. I returned to try to steal the treasure for myself."

Ari led Adam down a long, gently sloping natural corridor. They passed underground waterfalls and springs of fresh water. In time, Ari spoke. "As you noticed, we have created not only a monastic group, but a community. We've built on what the Culdees began. Our brothers, while maintaining their monastic life, are now allowed to take a wife and father children. The natives of this land are helping us to sustain ourselves and in so doing are securing our future in this new land."

"And who is the leader of the group?" Adam asked.

"I am the appointed one."

"Appointed by your peers?"

Ari stopped. There was an uncomfortable pause. Adam heard only the trickle of an underground stream.

"Appointed by God," Ari finally answered, not turning around to face Adam but instead leading the way over a makeshift bridge.

Adam recognized the self-appointment in that sentence; he'd heard it so many times before. Although Adam recognized that God did have his hand in the creation of religious leaders, ultimately their peers elected them. It was easy to confuse the two. "And whose authority do you answer to on earth?" he pressed.

"We answer to no authority. I am recognized as the one true authority."

Things became clearer to Adam. He had a good idea of what he was up against. Ari and the people that he led were no longer a religious order that was part of the Church. They were becoming their own independent community and Ari led them by using the holy relics and the Church's name as the basis of his power. Adam could not allow this to happen. Ari had usurped power from a communal entity, using objects that he kept for his own evil purpose.

"Ari, I am curious how the natives of this land feel about you and the Culdees living here."

"They have not shown any resistance that is capable of overwhelming my authority. In fact, they have willingly taken a totally subservient position. They are willing to live under our authority and by our laws." His voice deepened with enthusiasm. "The more natives we talk to, the more we learn of the vastness of this land. It is not an island as originally thought; its size rivals that of Europe. Just think of it, Adam—a new country, and it is learned clergy like us who will lead it."

Ari led Adam through lit catacombs that seemed to be used as accessways from the forest above. *This must be how the people of this land are getting around,* Adam thought. He'd found it strange that since landing on Markland, he hadn't seen many natives wandering the forest.

"Ari, where are you taking me?" Adam asked as he saw daylight filtering into the tunnel up ahead.

"I'm taking you to our main camp," he answered.

On top of his satisfaction at finding the person that he'd travelled so far to find, Adam felt both fear and exhilaration—

exhilaration that increased along with the light from the cave entrance.

They exited the catacombs and squinted in the noonday sun at the bustle of a thriving village. All around them, men and women worked on the land, wove baskets, or tended pots of steaming liquid suspended over fires. Children chased one another around Ari and Adam's feet. People momentarily stopped and looked at Adam, but soon returned to their duties.

It appeared to be a normal community but there was a strange and ordered dynamic to the people. If Adam didn't know better, he could've been looking at a European town. Adam knew that this was a result of Ari's control. He'd squeezed the natives' identity out of them and replaced it with his vision of a society.

Several Culdees, dressed in white robes and using their lances as walking sticks, exited the caverns in slow and measured steps. Their heads remained lowered in prayer as they passed Ari and Adam.

Ari turned to Adam. "Adam, why are you here?"

"I want to join the Culdees," Adam replied, ready with his answer.

"You will need to petition the council of the Servants of God."

"I understand," Adam said.

"In the meantime you may stay with us."

Kjalarness was not so much a place as a landmark. It was a marked grave atop a hill with a cross at the head of it and a jelling stone a few feet away, depicting to anyone who gazed upon it that an explorer and adventurer was buried at this place. Chiselled into the stone were illustrations celebrating the life and adventures of Thorvald Eiriksson—his position in the Eiriksson family line, his conquests on land and at sea, and, tucked into a corner of the stone, a map of Markland.

But the actual reason for his burial in Markland lay inside the grave of Thorvald: a map rolled up in his folded hands revealing the location of the cave of gold.

For Gudrid, coming back to this place conjured a stew of different emotions that threatened to boil over. The flame of her marriage to Thorvald still burned inside her to this day, although that life had been extinguished for both of them years ago.

Gudrid had ordered them to race here, before they lost the sun for the day, but now it was quickly disappearing behind the horizon. Tostig and Snorri took the lead up the hill, followed by Freydis and Gudrid and Jarlabanke. The two warrior escorts, Ingibjörg and Ásgeirr, remained in the rear, watching their backs.

When Tostig and Snorri reached the top of the hill they ran

to the grave, then stopped. Gudrid arrived behind them, Freydis at her elbow, her red face dripping with perspiration and the hem of her dress dragging on the ground, wet with mud. Her wheezing breath could be heard above the rustling leaves. The others followed immediately after. They all stopped when they saw Snorri and Tostig. Something wasn't right.

When Gudrid reached the grave, she saw what had made Tostig and Snorri pause. The body of Thorvald, her first husband, son of Eirik the Red, brother to Leif the Lucky, was gone.

The flat stone lid of Thorvald's sarcophagus had been lifted off and placed on the ground next to the hole. Puddles and debris were the only things left within. Tostig knelt down and investigated the grave. "This tomb has sat here like this for quite a long time."

"Is this the work of the landvættir?" Snorri asked, his nervousness clear in his voice.

"No, I don't think so. This looks like the work of something much more human." Tostig stood and looked toward the sky. "All is lost. Our return to Markland has been for nothing."

Tears trickled down Gudrid's cheeks. Her hopes of returning Thorvald's body to the place of his birth dissipated in the autumn wind. His body was gone and with it the map that would lead them to the meiðmarhellir, the treasure cave.

"By all that is unholy in Valhalla!" Freydis cursed.

"Curses will not solve our problems, Freydis," Gudrid snapped. "I will retreat and think of an enchantment to recite for a solution."

* * *

As Gudrid walked away from the rest of the group, leaving them to whisper about what this tragedy meant, Tostig took Freydis aside and began questioning her.

"Freydis, the position of the cave cannot be located without the second map. I need both the tracing that I am about to make from the jelling stone and the map that we placed within the tomb. Only a combination of these two tracings will give us a complete map of the cave."

"I know, I know," she answered, desperation in her voice. "We have only tomorrow, Sunnundœgr."

"What are we to do?"

"You are the best person we have, Tostig. If anyone can locate the cave, it is you."

"The maps do not work that way," Tostig said. He led Freydis to the jelling stone and knelt down by the map. "The individual maps don't contain any visible landmarks for a good reason," he said, pointing to what appeared to be random sets of lines and dots. "But once the maps are laid on top of each other, the lines and dots on Thorvald's map join up with the lines on the jelling stone map, outlining the landmarks as well as the path to the cave."

Freydis nodded. "Then whoever has the map knew of our previous trips to Markland and knew of the discovery of the cave. And there is only one person that I know of who is not with us today."

"Your husband, Ari," Tostig said, nodding. "If that's true, he may know the location of the cave!"

"At least we know that he doesn't know about the map stone. Or if he found the map stone, he still wouldn't be able to open it. Only the red moon tomorrow can open the entrance into the cave. And he won't be able to find the treasure in time before the cave seals itself up again; the interior map can only be illuminated by the sun on that day," Freydis said, satisfied that even though the group was at a disadvantage, they still had one advantage in getting the treasure, and that was to fight for it.

"Why didn't you make another copy of the map, both the one on the stone and the one that was buried with Thorvald?" Tostig asked, his voice tinged with frustration.

"It was a controversial decision, but we agreed that one copy leads to more copies and we couldn't risk the secret of the treasure getting out."

Gudrid returned to Freydis and Tostig. "Tostig, take a tracing of the jelling stone map, then roll the rock over the side of the hill into the river."

"Yes, Gudrid," he answered. He waved for Snorri to join him and as they walked back toward the jelling stone he yelled, "Jarlabanke, Ingibjörg, Ásgeirr, to me."

Tostig found a birch tree with a large piece of bark peeling off and tore it completely off. He peeled layer after layer until he was left with several sheets of the bark that were thin enough to make etchings.

* * *

Freydis and Gudrid watched the others for a moment, then Freydis turned to Gudrid. "Did you have a vision, Gudrid?"

"No. The land spirits were not revealing their knowledge. I did get one thing, but I think it was more of a memory. I had a vision of Ari. I know it is uncomfortable for you, Freydis, but we must talk about it."

"Yes, Gudrid. I think I am comfortable with it now."

"Unless we have both pieces of the map, we may not be able to find the map stone," Gudrid said.

"I know, I know," Freydis said, her voice tinged with frustration. "What are we going to do?"

"We are going to try to find the stone without the map," Gudrid said. "Tostig is an expert tracker. Our memories of this place are strong. Ari was not with us when we found the cave the first time. If he is involved, he will not have the exact location of the treasure cave. Also, he wasn't with us when we chiselled the map into the jelling stone. I'm betting that he didn't make a tracing of it. We will start here and look for milestones—places we camped, familiar rivers and rocks—places and objects that do not change much over time."

"But if we fail—"

"Then we fail. But if we muster our courage and our resolve, we will not fail—we must not fail."

Freydis squared her shoulders. "Yes, we are Norse. This is a small obstacle compared to our journey from Brattahlið."

As their conversation concluded, grunts and yells in the background drew their attention. Tostig and the others had managed to wedge a log underneath the boulder-size jelling stone and, using a smaller rock nearby, were pushing down on the log, using it as a lever.

After several attempts they managed to loosen the boulder from the soft ground. Once they'd lifted the boulder high enough, its weight took over. Ingibjörg threw her body against it and it rolled down the side of the hill and dropped into the rushing river. They were not sure of the rock's destruction, but it was certainly concealed underneath the surface of the foaming river.

"Well, that's done," Gudrid said. She looked at the sky. "We must go. The day is getting away from us."

She gathered the group around and quickly explained that the missing map did not mean that they were giving up the search for the treasure. It just meant that, rather than relying on a map to point the direction, they'd have to rely on their memories and on one another. " It is harder, but not impossible," she told them.

They got underway. Freydis, walking with Gudrid, resumed their conversation by asking, "Where are we headed?"

"I am going back to the place where we saw the Culdee Father."

Freydis lifted an eyebrow. "And once we arrive there?"

Gudrid sighed. "I don't know, Freydis. I'm making this up as I go along."

They chuckled and welcomed that brief respite from the last two days of tiresome travelling and disappointment. Although she was happy for his new life in Valhalla, Gudrid missed Thorvald; if he were here, he would know what to do. After all, it was he who discovered the cave.

"We must convince this group of people, whoever they are, that we are not a threat to them—that we are travellers and that we know nothing about the cave or the map," Gudrid said.

"And what about Adam? He may have already revealed who we are, and what he knows of our reason for being on Markland."

"Yes, I have considered that. But I do not think he would. If he was truthful when he told us his reason for seeking Ari, then he will have as much to lose by revealing his true intentions as we will," Gudrid said.

"Meaning that our secret must be his secret as well," Freydis said.

"Exactly. Besides, how threatening would a pregnant woman be to them?"

They both laughed again.

"If we appear to be non-threatening, then I believe we will be all right. In fact, we may earn their trust and they may assist us," Freydis suggested.

"I'm hoping that Adam has infiltrated the Culdees; that could be our way into their trust," Gudrid said.

"If he hasn't betrayed us," Freydis said, her tone ominous.

"We need to be on our guard for anything and everything," Gudrid decided.

* * *

Crouching in a row at the top of a rocky embankment, Gudrid, Freydis, Tostig, Snorri, Ingibjörg, Ásgeirr, and Jarlabanke peered at the clearing below, carefully scanning it for signs of occupancy. They saw only a cold hearth. But at the edge of the clearing, within a rocky outcropping protruding from the ground, Gudrid spied the entrance to a cave.

Gudrid could not explain why, but she felt that they were at the right location for an event. The feeling hovered just below the level of her consciousness; she didn't know what it was—premonition or merely gut feeling—but she knew that they needed to be here, right now.

About to give the go-ahead for the group to proceed to the clearing, Gudrid threw up her hand instead when she saw two figures exiting the hole in the ground. One was Adam. The other was Ari. She felt her hands curl into fists, hardly believing what she saw. It clearly looked as if Adam was voluntarily accompanying the traitor—as if Adam was in league with him.

She crawled back from the edge and sat with her back against the rock. Freydis joined her a moment later and returned Gudrid's shocked stare. Gudrid didn't know if Freydis's expression was due to Adam's betrayal or the shock of seeing her husband again.

"Are you all right, Freydis?" Gudrid asked, noting Freydis's pallid complexion.

"Yes, I think so. This was unexpected, Gudrid," she said after a moment. "I don't know how I feel."

Gudrid had been a member of Eirik's family for long enough to know the history of Freydis and Ari. Their love had begun with respect and passion and blossomed into something that neither of them could always control. But they had loved each other very much, and it looked as if Freydis still loved him.

Gudrid didn't know at which point their relationship began to deteriorate, but over time their passion slowly turned into anger, and then into physical violence initiated by both of them. She could remember the divorce agreement. Ari's announcement that he wanted to leave Grœnlandia was the last straw for Freydis who, in a fit of rage, yelled, "You are no longer my betrothed, no longer my husband. Ari Marsson, from this day forth, you are dead to me!" With that she'd torn off her hustrulinet and thrown it into the wind, which carried it over the shore. Caught by the ocean breeze, it floated out of sight. Even though there were enough witnesses to validate the divorce, Gudrid remembered that moment more than any other as the final act of their permanent separation.

Thank the Æsir that Ari immediately disappeared and that the feud between both their families was mild compared to most feuds during the separation of property.

Freydis's expression was reminiscent of that day. Her face displayed anger, hurt, and rage in turn as she traced her memories back to her life with Ari. Freydis was not a woman to be trifled with, but people forgot that she was a woman and she still had feelings, even though she kept them tightly contained. Freydis's strong exterior did not fool Gudrid.

"Gudrid, I thought Ari was in my past, but I don't know if he is," Freydis admitted. "Seeing him now, it almost feels as if I am back at that hurtful day. If I look up, I almost believe I'd see my hustrulinet still blowing in the wind toward the ocean."

Ingibjörg and Ásgeirr, who had not been present, listened to Freydis and Gudrid with eager interest; the others' glum expressions revealed that they too were reliving the events that they'd witnessed so long ago.

"If you prefer not to participate, the rest of us can take care of Ari and Adam," Gudrid offered.

"What will you do with Ari?" Freydis asked.

Gudrid didn't know how to reply. She had her own rage to handle.

Freydis saved her answering. "No, I am a part of this group," she said firmly. "I will stand and fight with you. If I hesitate when the time comes, then I do not deserve to be called your kin."

Gudrid didn't need to guess what Freydis meant by that comment. "Adam may have betrayed us," she said, not wanting to believe that Thorfinn was right about the untrustworthiness of the Christian. She'd sensed that he could be trusted. But there he was, talking to Ari. Moments like these confused her. Was what she saw influenced by what she felt, or was it the other way around?

"Is that what your sight is telling you?" Freydis asked.

"I can't be sure. But we've come too far. I'm not willing to risk our kin by taking a chance on someone that I hardly know." Gudrid looked from Freydis to the two warriors. "Ingibjörg?" she said, giving a command with the look in her eyes.

Ingibjörg pulled an arrow from her quiver and placed it ready in her bow. She was an experienced archer, and Gudrid was confident that she could hit Adam or Ari from their current location.

"Yes, but what if he is not in union with Ari?" Snorri asked. "What if Adam is infiltrating the Culdee camp, just as we are?"

"I've considered that," Gudrid said. She felt herself

becoming angry and distressed and she knew why. Her fear and loathing of Ari created false images in her head. She needed to sort through them; she needed to suppress her feelings toward Ari for the moment so she could see the truth based on the current circumstances, not the past. It could mean their very survival.

"Shoot Adam," Gudrid ordered without a moment's hesitation.

Ásgeirr slowly drew back her bow, took aim, and released the bowstring. Milliseconds later, Ari, perhaps hearing the displacement of air as the arrow sped toward its mark, jumped in front of its intended target. With a flesh-ripping impact, the arrow lodged in his back.

Adam turned as he heard Ari grunt, and noticed the bulge in his robe where the arrowhead protruded from his chest. Grimacing, Ari grabbed the arrowhead in his fist and pulled the arrow all the way through. He looked down at the rip in his robe.

Adam at first looked confused, as if he wasn't sure what had happened.

A bloodstain from the exit wound formed on the front of Ari's robe, but rather than growing as it soaked up more and more blood . . . it stopped. Instinctively, Ari's hand went to his chest and he took a few deep breaths. The colour slowly returned to his face.

"Ari?" Adam asked.

"I'm all right," he replied, raising his hand from his chest.

Gudrid had seen enough. She and the others made to retreat, but before they could, natives surrounded them. Freydis leapt to her feet, wildly swinging her sword in front of her; the blade cut air as natives jumped back out of its range.

* * *

As Ingibjörg armed her bow and scanned behind them for more natives, two of them dove from a nearby rock and took her down. Thrown onto her back, she released her clenched fingers and the arrow pierced the stomach of one of her attackers. She stared into the horrified face of the wounded native as he fell on top of her, and then white pain radiated from her chest as something penetrated her flesh, slid past ribs, and plunged into her heart. She looked down at the stone dagger clenched in the native's hand. Blood welled and flowed over the blade; it had ruptured an artery.

Her last corporeal thought was that the short, lean natives looked like children next to her people. She didn't feel the second dagger enter her chest. She didn't realize that her eyes didn't close. All she saw was a vortex opening in the centre of the sky and a bright light streaming through, dimming the light of day by comparison. The light's brilliance didn't hurt her eyes; its energy bathed her with soothing calm.

The sky darkened and the vortex spun larger and larger. Ingibjörg wasn't sure where they came from, but ravens appeared overhead. She thought they were coming from the centre of the spinning vortex, appearing out of the point of bright light. Then the ravens morphed into Valkyries mounted on the backs of wolves, swooping low over the battleground, competing for the dead. They rose again and disappeared into the hole in the sky.

Suddenly her body became light and she saw the ground receding. She looked overhead and saw a beautiful, smiling female carrying her by the back of her tunic. With her other hand, she reached into Ingibjörg's chest and pulled out the dagger. Ingibjörg waited for the piercing, burning pain, but she felt nothing other than the wind streaming through her hair and the warm light bathing her face. The female touched the wound; the gash closed and her skin absorbed the blood.

They were pulled into the horizon of the vortex and down a long tunnel, their velocity increasing every moment. Ingibjörg turned and looked through the tunnel opening at the world she'd known, watched it receding. She wasn't scared; her concerns for this battle were over. She looked at her kin with detached longing.

As she approached a single point of light at the far end of the tunnel, it grew larger but its intensity didn't increase. She suddenly realized where the spectral light originated. She felt like she was going home . . . to Valhalla.

"Enter Valhalla—the shining citadel."

She looked to her right. There stood Bragi, god of poetry.

"Your struggles have ended, Ingibjörg," Bragi announced. "When the death of my brother Baldur binds Loki, the battle of your death, the Ragnarök, will begin."

Trumpets blared in the distance, the wolf howled, and the gates opened.

"It is the living who are dead and the slain who are alive," Ingibjörg heard in the wind.

Inside the citadel, doors seemed to magically open at their approach—or did they transcend through them? Ingibjörg was not sure. Each chamber was a circular room within another circular room.

They reached the inner sanctuary. In the centre of the circular room a man sat on a throne atop a circular podium. He held a staff. At the approach of Ingibjörg and her Valkyrie escort, he straightened up and looked at them in anticipation. "Welcome, Ingibjörg of Miðgarð, I am Óðin," he said.

"I am honoured," she replied.

The Valkyrie gently placed Ingibjörg on the floor in front of the podium. She didn't know if the surface was solid or if it was like the surface of a pond in the early morning. A thin, white mist clung to its semi-reflective surface. She bowed her head in reverence to her god.

He was not what she'd expected; he looked more like a traveller in a hooded cloak than a god, a wanderer who forever traverses vast oceans to journey to new lands. It was not so out of the ordinary that her people looked like him, she thought; after all, part of Óðin was her, as he was part of all of her people.

"Your new life as a warrior in the Ragnarök begins," he said. "You will fight by my side along with tens of thousands more who, just like you, have earned their place in this glorious army."

Ingibjörg smiled as she inclined her head.

* * *

Crouched within the protection of the group surrounding her, Gudrid saw Ásgeirr lift his sword and thrust it into the back of Ingibjörg's killer, then kick the native off his dead mate. She looked up and saw the translucent and flowing bodies of the Valkyries hovering over the battle. They quickly moved between each person in the group with a whisper of air, waiting to kidnap the souls of the fallen to fight the approaching battle in Ásgarð.

One stopped and gently took Ingibjörg's hand. It pulled what Gudrid saw as her soul from her body and lifted her above the ground. For a second Ingibjörg hovered above the fighting, then turned and smiled at Gudrid. Gudrid couldn't help but return a tearful smile.

An image of her shackled wrists invaded Gudrid's thoughts again. She pieced together the fragments of what she felt and joined them with the images in her visions, and suddenly realized the purpose behind the natives' attack. It was her—the natives were attacking to take her. The others in the group must've known that on some unconscious level, which would explain their protective circle around her.

She couldn't be responsible for their deaths.

Pushing through the protective wall of her fellows, she ran toward Ari and Adam, standing on the periphery of the battle. "Ari," she yelled, "stop this—now!"

"And in return, what will you give me?" he asked, raising his hand to signal the native warriors to stop fighting.

"Gudrid, don't do it," Freydis begged.

Gudrid gave Freydis an apologetic glance. "Spare the lives of my people," she said, turning back to Ari, "and we will share our treasure with you. That is what you want, isn't it? That is why you came back here, isn't it?"

Adam looked on in silence. Gudrid stared at Ari, waiting for his answer. *Of course,* she thought as his behaviour began to make sense. For all of Adam's religious posturing, he'd been after the treasure all along, just as Ari and the rest of them were. Adam was willing to betray them all for it.

"I will agree on one condition," Ari said. "That you come with me, Gudrid."

"No, Gudrid, it is a trick!" Freydis urged in a low voice.

"I know it is," Gudrid replied. "But I see no other choice."

She looked around at the woods and saw more and more natives approaching them, moving slowly, as if stalking game. The longer she delayed, the more the safety of the entire band was threatened. She looked back at Ari. "I agree. Let them leave and I will stay with you."

Ari yelled something to the natives and waved his arm. They stepped back then parted, clearing a path.

Freydis gaped at Gudrid. Gudrid ignored her and walked toward Ari and an uncertain future, hands cradling her stomach as if they could protect her baby. Behind her, the Norse warriors put their weapons away and slowly picked up their gear. Gudrid was now at the mercy of Ari's plans.

"There is one last thing," Ari said to the others as they silently watched Gudrid's wrists being bound. "Give me the map."

Tostig slowly pulled the cloth map out of a tunic pocket and handed it to one of the nearby natives.

"Now, leave Markland and never return!" Ari commanded

and, with his army of natives, turned and disappeared into the forest, leaving the Norse warriors standing in disarray and defeat.

They buried Ingibjörg in Thorvald's grave. Jarlabanke was able to make an inky paste from berries and wrote *Ingibjörg* across the marker. They didn't have the time to boil her body down to bones to transport her remains back to Grœnlandia, but Markland seemed to be a place where life renewed itself. Ásgeirr hoped that it would be the case with his mate.

The meagre funeral service, a semicircle of comrades around a grave dug for someone else, would have to do. In the coming days they would all mourn in their own individual way, some with screaming swords and axes, others in silent reflection. And still others burying themselves in the situation of the moment and allowing new challenges to replace the recent loss, with the hope that time would and could heal them.

They silently turned and descended the hill in quiet resignation, not headed in any particular direction.

Freydis had to admit to herself that she was scared. Gudrid was alone with a man whom she knew was capable of anything. When they were together, she had often questioned his honesty, until the final straw at Markland. She didn't want to think of what he, in his anger, was capable of doing now.

"Freydis, we can't leave Gudrid in the hands of Ari," Snorri said.

"I know . . . I know!" she snapped. Even at the best of times she had a difficult time keeping her emotions under some semblance of control. Now she was in a far-off land, they were at the mercy of the approaching red moon, and her sister had been kidnapped. In this last, she felt that she'd not only failed Gudrid and Thorfinn, but the unborn child, as well. The worst part about it was that she didn't know what to do.

She looked at Ásgeirr. He appeared physically ill, and he walked silently with head bowed, avoiding everyone's eye. He had lost one of his oldest and greatest friends. The loss of Ingibjörg was a blow to the whole group, as well. If they were going to survive in this new world, they needed more people like Ingibjörg.

And yet she couldn't help but feel envious. Ingibjörg was now part of the celestial army of warriors fighting in Valhalla. *Perhaps our fight will be a fight that Ingibjörg will look on from the heavens,* she thought. *Perhaps we too will be judged worthy to fight in the heavenly battle at the end of all things.*

Tostig had also noticed Ásgeirr's sombre demeanour. He matched his pace to that of the younger man and said after a moment, "The death of a friend is a hard thing to deal with, especially when you're not given the time to properly grieve."

Ásgeirr looked at him with a blank stare, his eyes as inhuman and lifeless as two holes in a fleshy shell. Tostig had to look away.

"In a quiet moment, make time to grieve," Tostig urged.

"My grieving will be with a sword," Ásgeirr growled, "swinging at the neck of Ari. I do not care for my life anymore."

A native appeared ahead of them. They all stopped in their tracks. Ásgeirr unsheathed his sword, ready to strike, but Tostig grabbed his wrist.

"What are you doing?" Ásgeirr yelled.

"Allow him to speak," Tostig said.

Freydis studied the young native. There was something in his expression that suggested he was here to talk, not fight.

"I come with a message from A . . . dam," the native said, hesitating over the unfamiliar name. He held out his hand. When Freydis stepped forward, he gave her a piece of cloth.

She unfolded the cloth. On it was drawn a map. The others crowded around her. "This is the map we seek!" Tostig yelled in excitement.

Freydis looked at the native; he gazed nervously at the

unfamiliar faces staring back at him. She was relieved that Adam was still on their side, but she was curious to know how he'd been able to convince the native to deliver this to them. Why would he risk revealing his true intentions?

"Wait!" Freydis yelled as the native cautiously backed away. "Can you tell us about . . . our friend, Adam? Is he all right?"

"Who are you and where are your people?" Snorri interjected.

Without another word the native disappeared among the trees.

Instinctively, Freydis scanned the forest for signs of watchers; she felt uneasy in a frightfully uncontrolled sense, as if she was powerless to do anything. She only knew how to fight, and she couldn't do that.

Tostig was examining the map. He handled it as if it were the gold in the meiðmarhellir. Freydis turned back to the group still gathered around him. "How are we going to find the cave?" she said. "Ari has taken the other map."

Tostig grinned at her.

"You didn't give Ari the map?" she said, her voice tentative as she held her elation at bay.

"I did give Ari the etching that I made from the stone," Tostig replied, pausing for effect; the group hung on his every syllable. "But I made two etchings before we destroyed the jelling stone." He bent and pulled the second etching from his boot.

"Tostig, I could kiss you!" Freydis screamed, grabbing his cheeks in her dirty hands and squeezing them.

Freeing himself from Freydis's enthusiastic grip, Tostig knelt and tried as best he could to align the markings on the cloth with the ones on the birch bark copy that he'd made from the stone, to create one complete map. The registration marks were a little off.

"Try moving this line over to here," Snorri suggested, indicating the relevant point on the map with his finger.

"But then these lines will not match," Jarlabanke said, also pointing.

"By all that's unholy in Hel," Tostig pleaded, "be silent! I cannot think."

"Let's leave Tostig to his work," Freydis said.

They retreated in silence to watch Tostig from a few steps

away. Freydis's thoughts drifted back to Gudrid, alone and powerless in Ari's hands. She began imagining the worst again. Was all of this worth a few scribbles on a few pieces of cloth and paper that led to a chamber of riches, a chamber whose existence rested on the sole testimony of one person, given so long ago? She couldn't or didn't want to answer the question.

R

It was time.

Tostig had successfully pieced the two maps together. The resulting map had guided them to their present location, the next milestone in their journey: the map that would show them the way into the cave.

The engraving was partly obscured by decades of dirt and debris, but it was unmistakably the right place. The map was etched on the curved surface of a smooth stone outcrop, partially buried in the ground. As Tostig and Freydis knelt and brushed the map clear, Freydis ran her fingers along the intricately carved lines in the stone. Its chiselled routes and markers all looked familiar now. This was the land that she had travelled across for the last viknatal, and years earlier, with friends and kin who were no longer with them.

But now it was time to let the dead rest and to celebrate the glory of their memory with the treasures of the deep.

Freydis looked up, saw Snorri watching the sky, the bright yellow sun appearing and disappearing behind clouds that partially covered the azure heavens. It was Baldur's day to be honoured; it was he who would help the band to complete this segment of their journey. "Can you read the map, Tostig?" she asked, looking from the sun to the lines on the rock. She couldn't discern any features that could be shaped by its shadow into an enlightening configuration.

"Yes. But Freydis, I need to do one more thing." Tostig looked around, plucked a small, straight stick from the ground, and whittled away the bottom with his knife. Then he leaned forward and blew dirt from a small hole on the stone. He jammed the stick into the hole as far as it would go.

"We are approximately here," he said, tapping a spot on the rock, then closing his eyes briefly to recall the symbols and cryptograms of his map before indicating a point on an arc around the stick that Freydis now saw was divided into equal sections. "When the sun reaches here, it will be time."

"And when will that happen?"

He pointed at the sun in the sky, halfway between the horizon and its zenith. "Do you see where the sun is right now?" Freydis looked up and nodded. "It will not touch this scale until it has passed overhead."

"Oh," she said. "So we have time."

"Yes."

"How long will the cave stay open?" Snorri asked.

Tostig looked at him. "For as long as the red moon is in the sky. Once the moon sets, the cave will seal itself again."

Freydis felt another surge of uncertainty and wished that Gudrid was with them. She was not used to leading, and wondered if she could guide the band successfully in gathering as much treasure as they could within that time limit, once they were in the cave.

As well, there was something about this place that distracted Freydis, an attraction that went beyond the promise of wealth. She felt that this was Valhalla; this was as close to the heavens that her people could get on Miðgarð. She wasn't alone; she'd heard others in the group whispering that this was the Bifröst, the Rainbow Bridge guarded by Heimdall that connected her world to the top world, Ásgarð. If this was indeed the route to Ásgarð, then perhaps Heimdall would allow Freydis to return with the dead.

Suddenly Tostig threw up a warning hand. Freydis heard it too: rustling within the nearby bushes. It was too loud to be a small animal; it sounded like something much larger. The sound spread, until they heard rustling from the other side, then in front of them, and then behind. They were being surrounded. The group drew their weapons.

Seconds later, arrows nocked to bows emerged from the foliage, followed by the human hands that held them, and finally their native owners.

"Wait," Freydis said. "Do not attack." She was not sure why she gave that order, but in that moment she thought of Thorfinn and the future of Vinland. It was what he would've wanted. And she thought of the safety of her sister and the unborn child Gudrid carried. It was her responsibility to protect them both.

"Put your weapons down," Freydis ordered.

"But Freydis—"Ásgeirr protested.

"Trust me."

Ásgeirr didn't need to hear another word. His trust of Freydis had very few limits. The rest of the group followed suit. They put their weapons away and allowed the natives to lead them away to an unknown destination.

Freydis couldn't explain it, but she didn't feel like a captive. They were being escorted, not taken. The natives kept their distance and gently guided them through the forest without force or coercion.

The group entered a camp, and were surrounded by more and more natives, the deeper into the village they walked. They passed staring families and natives emerging from their tepees to look at the new arrivals. None of the natives approached them and none showed any aggression; they maintained a curious distance.

Freydis looked ahead and saw a group of monks waiting for them. *These must be the Culdees that Adam talked about,* she thought. As she got closer she noticed that one of them was not a Culdee in the sense of a common cultural background. He wore similar robes, but his features were those of a native.

"We are honoured by your presence," one of the Culdee monks said.

"Why have you brought us here?" Ásgeirr snapped back.

Freydis glared at him; his comment was out of turn and inappropriate, as well as potentially stupid. They were surrounded by at least a hundred native warriors carrying spears or daggers. The last thing she wanted to do was engage them in a fight.

"Everything will be revealed in due time," another monk said, disregarding Ásgeirr's aggressive stance. "Our goals are, after all, not too different."

"In what respect?" Freydis asked.

"We both want to stop Ari's tyranny. We know that he's captured one of your women, presumably to force you to do his bidding. He's used the sacred artifacts to give himself immortality and is using this to present himself as a god to those Culdees who are willing to follow him and to the natives of this land who are powerless against him."

"We're only concerned with the safety of our people. Can you help us get Gudrid safely returned to us?" Freydis asked.

"That has already begun," the monk replied. "We only ask that you continue with your quest to find the treasure cave."

"What cave?" Tostig quickly replied, his expression innocent.

"We are not concerned with the riches of the cave. We only seek to restore our community to its former monastic dignity."

For some reason Freydis noticed her breathing; it was possibly the first long breath she'd taken since entering the camp. "What is your name?" she asked.

"My name is Dionysius."

"Have you been watching us?" Ásgeirr asked, his tone accusing.

"Yes, but not in the way that you may think. It was not us who attacked you. We had to be sure that your motives were in line with our goals before we revealed ourselves to you," Dionysius answered.

"And now that you have," Freydis asked slowly, "are you sure you don't want some of the gold?"

Dionysius smiled. "No, as we told you, we don't. Our monastic order forbids it. And besides, what is the use of gold to us, with our current religious goals? We cannot exchange it for food or water. God and the land provide us with everything we need."

Freydis was reluctantly satisfied with their answer. From everything she had seen so far, they seemed to live by what they said. She felt that she had no other choice but to trust Dionysius's words. "So, we are free to go?" she asked.

"Yes, you are free to go," Dionysius answered. "But we encourage you to stay to take advantage of our hospitality."

Freydis was tempted by the offer. They were hungry and tired. It would mean a much-needed and deserved break. She looked around the settlement at the open, welcoming faces. They looked optimistic that the Norse would free them of Ari. It seemed that Ari was not seen as a messiah come to save the natives, but a tyrant who dominated and forced them to do his bidding at whatever cost to their community.

"Thank you for your offer, but we need to find our kin and to finish what we came here to do," Freydis answered.

"As you wish. We've heard that the tribes on Vinland are organizing for an attack on your settlement," Dionysius warned. "We will try to do what we can to quell their anger, but it may be too late."

Once they were out of sight of the settlement, Freydis stopped and turned to the others. "Tostig, do we have enough time to rescue Gudrid and still make it to the opening of the cave in time?"

Tostig looked upward, thinking. He shook his head. "No."

"Then we must secure the treasure before we can rescue our friend." She paused, realizing something. "We could use some of our treasure for ransom, to get Gudrid back."

"What of our kin on Vinland?" Ásgeirr asked.

"They will have to fight till we return. There is nothing we can do."

From the Norse line, Harald silently prayed to his God as he looked across the meadow at the approaching native army; he'd not seen an army of warriors this large since his childhood. They massed together into one ferocious beast, determined to drive the Norse from this land. This battle would determine the future of the Norse in Vinland.

Harald had kept his conversion to Christianity a secret. Vikings and seafaring Norse in general refused to convert, and Harald had felt that if he revealed his allegiance to this new God, Thorfinn would not have hired him for this journey; he wanted to share in the wealth so that he could build his church.

He wriggled his toes in his boot, felt his crucifix there, where he kept it concealed. His thoughts turned to the day of his baptism. It had taken place in Limingen. The priest and the rest of the clergy headed the procession, with Harald's father and mother in front of him and his wife and two daughters behind him.

The priest led the long line into the gentle surf at the river's mouth and stopped in knee-deep water. The clergy's robes floated with the ocean current. The priest instructed Harald to kneel before him. Beside him, a clergyman opened a prayer book with slow and deliberate movements and handed it to the priest, who read a short passage in an unknown language that Harald didn't understand, even when he could hear the voice above the wind and the surf.

Then the priest handed his staff and book to his attendants, laid his hands on the crown of Harald's head, and pushed him underneath the water. The priest continued his chant, the sound of the words resonating hollowly through the water and sinking into Harald as smoke permeates a room.

Harald was quickly running out of air. His focus moved from words that he neither heard nor understood to watching air bubbles escaping his mouth . . . was that a fish? He tried to take his attention off the lack of air in his lungs for fear that he'd lose all control and leap out of the water, requiring that the whole thing be performed again from the very beginning. He watched the reeds swaying in unison with the motion of the surf, dropped his eyes to the riverbed shimmering in the afternoon sun.

Instinctively his throat tightened as his brain told him that he needed to breathe; he felt that he'd suffocate in seconds. Then the hand that held his head beneath the water grabbed a hank of his hair and pulled him to the surface. He choked out air and salt water. But as quickly as it was pulled to the surface, his head was quickly pushed beneath the water again.

Before his head again submerged, he glimpsed a lone, hooded figure in grey robes walking down the pebbled beach. The image haunted Harald. In that single glance, he'd seen the figure stopping, saw wisps of hair as grey as the man's cloak flowing with the blowing wind, saw a craggy hand lift to wipe a tear from a lined cheek.

The shifting of those around him drew Harald back to the present. The Skræling army spread across the entire width of the peninsula, from one body of water to the other; hundreds of human heartbeats pumped lifeblood through their veins, energizing their muscles, pumping adrenaline through their bodies.

He looked right, then left. If faith had a human form, the sixty-five Norse men and women with him were it. The natives overwhelmingly outnumbered them. Unlike the Norse, though, fighting was not their way of life. Even Harald could tell they had no concept of strategy. This fight, like every other event in their lives, was a communal effort; the chiefs of the three tribes stood tall and proud to the right of their army, their ornate headdresses fluttering in the breeze, their ceremonial spears at their sides, witnesses to the bravery of their warriors.

Harald's arm quivered but he wasn't scared or cold; he didn't know why it trembled. He quickly realized that it was his kin, next to him, shaking with fear. He cringed as he heard his fellows drumming their swords against their wooden shields. Within their war cries he heard a hint of fear, fear that would, within the last moments before the attack, change to ferocity and then quickly to barbarism.

He felt almost claustrophobic with his kinsmen huddled together around him; he smelled their sweat and the strong stench of their breath. But once they engaged the enemy, Harald knew that they would spread out, swinging swords and axes at native chests and heads in wild abandon, not caring where the blade fell as long as it made contact.

He couldn't resolve his Christian beliefs with the killing he was about to commit. Did they deserve to die for protecting their homeland? Because they were not Christian, did that make them any less entitled to life? Shouldn't he, as a protector of the faith, devote himself to preserving life no matter what the circumstance?

Harald knew what was right and what was wrong. It was specific and clear in the Bible that he should not kill another person. Why was he about to commit this atrocity? He couldn't answer that in the context of his new belief. This was always as it had been with his people.

The horror of the Norse invasions from his youth flooded his memory; the field of natives disappeared and he found himself back on the shores of the North Atlantic.

Harald's father had believed that for him to be one of the greatest warrior leaders of his generation, he needed to be on the battlefield at an early age. He would've been thrown into the fight as soon as he could wield a sword, but his mother protested and so Harald's father had relented. Even for a boy of sixteen, the harsh reality of the Norse campaigns was too much for him to bear.

Harald, along with a hundred other warriors, had landed on the shores of Brittany fifteen years ago. Their chieftain wore his winged helmet, a symbol of his authority from the Vanir that he was chosen to lead the army of Norse; Harald still remembered how its shiny silver gleamed against the dreariness of the heavily overcast afternoon sky. If their leader's life were threatened in any way and his personal bodyguards were overtaken, his warriors would have to respond immediately to save his life. If he should be killed on the battlefield, it would affect the course of the battle.

At that time in his life, one battle seemed to merge into the next. Harald suffered severe memory loss that seemed to get worse and worse as the months of horrific victories escalated into years of never-ending slaughter. The fighting didn't seem to have a beginning or an end; the battle was constant, from the dawn when he hoped to see a day of peace, to the tragic night when, weary from battle, he returned to their battle camp. Two dœgur turned into one viknatal then into one mánuðir.

It was a continual prison of swinging hammers and axes shattering human bones, their razor sharp splinters stabbing outward through the skin. The sound of tearing flesh and the crack of splitting human skulls filled his ears and his mind. Human organs catapulted in all directions; rivers of blood covered the ground. His attack was unfocused and all too automatic, the chieftain once criticized; there was no thought behind each strike of the sword.

Red became Harald's most hated colour. The smell and look of cooking meat was sometimes too much to take. If the meat had any trace of red pigment in it, the suppressed trauma of those fighting years would resurface and he'd flash back to his many battles. In some cases his unconscious mind created battles based on whatever was happening in his life at that time, or any difficulty he was experiencing. And in some extreme cases, he either became violently ill or unknowingly struck out at people.

Harald, although brought up to fear very little, feared much, which was his reason to seek the sanctuary of the Church. This was not so much running *to* something as running *away*— from his father and a warrior life that he'd neither asked for nor wanted.

Even on the voyage here, the salt air penetrating his nostrils made him nauseous, resurrected the smell of rotting fish and a beach stained with the blood of his kin, conjured images of seagulls swarming for food, landing and pecking at the mangled bodies floating on bloody water . . . Bloody water . . . oceans of bloody water . . . It stained the rocks and his boots . . .

With the surf jumping from the ocean behind him like flames from a hearth, Harald looked toward a screaming fighter and saw the winged helmet of his chieftain. An arrow stuck out of his right side; a second arrow pierced the chieftain's armpit. His battle axe, raised above his head, seemed to freeze for a brief second. Then in slow motion, the axe fell with a whoosh—

In a second of reality, Harald saw that he'd hacked through the body of a young male native. He didn't have enough time to see the face before the body dropped facedown in front of him.

His sword was out, swinging at an attacking foe. His opponent's weapon was too big for the man's size, causing him to strike ineffectively. One of Harald's blows struck its target, more out of luck than skill. He hacked with his sword again, slicing his falling target across the chest, leaving a trail of splitting skin behind the tip of the blade as the man fell.

Another attacker struck Harald's shield. Harald thrust his blade out under his shield and struck the attacker's side. He was about to strike the fatal blow when he glanced past the man, saw that the Skræling chiefs, along with their bodyguards, had moved back to a safe distance where they could observe the battle in relative safety, and he realized that the ocean didn't exist, the sounds of the surf didn't exist. He was not on the shore of Brittany; he was on Vinland, and the two opposing masses had converged.

A young native boy lay on the ground next to the first youth he had felled, his bloody hands covering the wound that Harald had inflicted seconds earlier. The hurt in his face reminded Harald of his children, after falling while climbing a tree or fighting with a sibling. This was a boy sent out to fight before he could fully understand what he was fighting for. And now he never would.

Harald emotionally withdrew from the fighting, blocked the array of screams and shouts that rose in diseased harmony, and buried his humanity somewhere beneath the bloody surf . . .

Another Brit attacked, holding his sword as one would a spear and thrusting it at him . . .

The native didn't make it beyond the tip of Harald's sword.

He squinted at the sun's reflection, glinting hot and bright off of his blade. He thought he saw Óðin's handmaidens, the Valkyrie, flying over the battlefield, searching for those to be taken to Valhalla. He'd never seen a Valkyrie, but the flying beings had white bellies and black backs with orange beaks and webbed feet. They looked more bird than human; there was an aura around them that couldn't be explained. One seemed to hover overhead and looked into Harald's eyes as if looking into his soul, judging its worthiness to leave this existence and to forever live in Valhalla.

Harald felt the warm sensation of a spear piercing his chest; it was a strange sort of warmth, moving from the wound to his arms . . . then he felt nothing. And as quickly as his mind moved from battle to battle, he understood what had happened to him; he understood the reasons his father treated him the way he had and why he felt the way he did; he knew the intricate workings of his mind. In fact, he could now manifest whatever he wanted. He was no longer the victim but rather, the creator of his future.

He looked up and understood that these birds were not Valkyries.

"Harald, I am here," a voice whispered in his ear.

"I know; you've always been here. Why couldn't I hear you before?"

"Because of all those other voices in your head."

"I don't understand."

"I know, but you will. Do you see that female coming toward you?"

"Yes, I do."

"She will bring you to me. Just allow her to touch you."

"I will. Will it hurt?"

"It will be different, but it will not hurt."

"I feel . . . lighter."

"That is good. You are now ready to begin your journey to me."

"What is your name? Is it God?"

"No, my name is Óðin."

"Oh, I thought . . . because I was baptized . . . "

"We all inhabit the same realm of the human consciousness. Does it bother you that I am not the God you expected?"

"It might've bothered me before, but it doesn't bother me now."

"Good, because such things are part of human matters."

"Óðin, will my friends be well?"

"You already know the answer."

"Yes . . . you're right; I do."

Though Tostig was waiting for the red moon, its appearance was as magical as it was sudden. His eyes momentarily strayed from the night horizon when all he could see were distant stars. The rising moon had changed all of that in an instant. Its orange-red glow dressed it in a startling and terrifying gown of mystery. He had witnessed this event in the past, but never in a strange land and never in the open.

He awaited the appearance of a vein of some magical mineral that ran through the centre of the stone map; it joined Tostig's current position with the location of the cave door. The mineral glowed green when it was subjected to a heat source, but only once. As it cooled, the mineral's glow faded. Beyond that, despite his certainty when speaking with Freydis and Gudrid, Tostig couldn't figure out how the red moon could open a cave entrance. Local natives had told him only that the red moon warned of death to those willing to defile a holy city, a city reserved solely for the gods the builders had worshipped. Tostig took this to mean that the red moon would grant access to that city.

"Is it time?" Freydis asked.

Tostig looked at the map; the stick's shadow was a hairsbreadth away from the centre of the arc. "It's now or never," he said. He took the torch from Jarlabanke and pushed it against the rock map. Its flame flickered and jumped across the map's surface. When he removed the torch, the magical vein was there, glowing a dull, milky green.

He looked at the lines that ran from the top to the bottom of the map and found the exact location of the cave door; it was concealed in a rock wall above the river. He looked up; the moon, if not now, would soon be in position. He led the others to the rocky riverbank, and they carefully stepped down onto a ledge only wide enough to accommodate their feet. With their stomachs pressed up against the wall, the river raging below them, and their only light the guttering torch held high in Tostig's hand, they carefully shuffled along the length of the ledge, hands pressed against the wall for balance.

"Look!" Ásgeirr yelled.

Tostig followed his line of sight to the opposite side of the river, where the red moon was reflected off the rock face. *This doesn't make sense,* Tostig thought, looking at the reversed image of the moon. *The map clearly positioned the door . . .*

Suddenly the ground beneath them quaked and a part of the rock wall caved in. Opposite to what his senses were telling him and what was possible, Tostig and the others fell forward, through a doorway that had opened in the rock face on their side of the river, directly opposite the reflection.

"We only have hours at the most before we must leave," Tostig said as they picked themselves up off the cave floor, "or we'll be sealed in here forever."

"But the door is here on the cave floor, how can it close again?" Ásgeirr asked, indicating the stone slab.

"I don't know, but the warning was very clear: do not be in the cave once the red moon 'hides beneath the sky.'"

"But how will we know in which direction to head?" Freydis said, looking around.

"There!" Jarlabanke yelled, pointing at the red light of the moon beaming into a rocky corridor, where it struck a mirror-like mineral and focused into a thin band of refracted light.

They followed the light to the next marker and the next, each marker leading them along a path of refracted moonlight like a trail of breadcrumbs, and getting dimmer and dimmer the farther it was reflected into the tunnels. By the time the light had faded into nothing, they no longer needed it. They stood at the top of a staircase.

Tostig sniffed. The air held a familiar scent. He held his torch up toward the cave wall and saw a ledge with a trough chiselled into it. He followed it for as far as the torchlight allowed him to see; it looked like it encircled the entire chamber. He gently lowered his torch to the trough and the flame jumped from his torch to the substance within, racing around the wall of the great chamber in a whoosh of air. The cavern glowed with amber warmth.

They couldn't have imagined the sight that lay before their eyes. The beauty of a thousand sunsets couldn't rival it. Their reflections stared back at them from glowing walls of gold, polished to such brilliant shine that the buildings appeared to contain a light source of their own. Protected from the elements aboveground, there was nothing to tarnish their splendour and beauty.

No one spoke. Not one person could take a full breath. For one eternal second, reality didn't exist. There was nothing real, no thoughts to be thought, only *Gold*. It was as if the gold had siphoned their ability to think.

Tostig's eyes filled with tears that he couldn't stop, no matter how hard he tried. All of the stories of Valhalla and the afterlife didn't compare to the majestic glory of the rooftops, gold after gold after gold. One room of these monolithic structures contained the wealth of kings. Tostig blinked. It was simply too big and too overwhelming to be real.

"I could never have imagined this," Freydis whispered. "Are we dreaming?"

"I think we are the dream," Ásgeirr said, his voice drifting off to some unseen place.

"I wish Gudrid were here to see this."

"She is!" a voice yelled from behind them.

They turned to see two natives holding Gudrid by her arms. She looked exhausted but unharmed. Ari stood in front of them.

"Gudrid, have they hurt you?" Freydis yelled. "Is the baby all right?"

"The child will remain safe, as long as you cooperate," Ari interrupted. "It will join the rest of the order and be conditioned to lead."

* * *

Gudrid had been silently praying. "I can still feel the baby," she called to Freydis. Then, even though she was distraught, the beauty of the city drew her eyes away. She stared in wonder.

You were right, she silently said. *Thorvald, my love, you were right.* Then she swayed, caught herself as the earth shifted slightly.

* * *

Behind Freydis, Tostig whispered, "We are running out of time."

"What do you want from us, Ari?" Freydis said.

"I just want you out of the way."

With his words, an army of natives entered the chamber carrying large wicker baskets. Without hesitation, they bypassed the group and entered the city, scooping up anything of value and placing it in their baskets before moving on to the next item.

They collected gold plates and gold pitchers, jewellery set with precious gemstones, faceted goblets, and urns with intricate designs etched into their gold faces by expert craftsmen. There were helmets and bracers that glistened in the dim amber light, and statues that ranged in size from the length of an arm to life-size replicas gleaming on either side of building entrances.

The army of natives carried away more than their weight in gold-filled baskets, never stopping and never faltering. A steady stream of natives filed in and out of the cavern, undaunted by the trembling of the ground. They filed past a building face the height and width of the cavern, blinded by the wealth they carried in their arms. Engraved on a plaque next to the door in an ancient and a forgotten language was a warning to all those who sought out the beauty and the riches of the city: *Do not be fooled by its brilliance. For the weight of a man's heart is worth a thousand times its weight in riches.*

The ground spasmed again.

"Tostig, what is happening? Why is the ground shaking?" Freydis whispered.

Tostig dug the toe of his boot into the dirt floor of the cavern. "I can't say for sure, Freydis, but the ground looks like it is made of clay. For some reason it's shifting."

"What would make it do that?" she asked nervously.

"I don't know. Maybe the supporting ground underneath is giving way, being eroded like a river eventually does to its banks . . . Water, that must be it," Tostig realized. "Water from the river must have been diverted somehow, and it's flowing beneath us, carrying away the foundation of the cavern floor."

"We have to get out of here, and quickly," Freydis said. She turned to her husband. "Ari, your agreement with us was to share the gold, not to take it all for yourself. If you will not honour your agreement with Gudrid, then let us go. You have what you want—you have power, you have riches; you need nothing more."

Freydis knew better. She was all too familiar with greed and its exacting toll on the soul; there was always room for more, or so the perpetrator reasoned. Ari was no exception to that rule. Just like all the others, he would crave more and more. There was no "enough" because the more he acquired, the larger that dark hole grew inside of him.

"By all that is sacred," Freydis whispered. "This is just like our marriage."

The earth shifted again, but this time with a pronounced effect: one of the buildings at the other end of the cavern collapsed. Water bubbled up from the break in the ground and the building disappeared into the dark and watery hole.

A short native ran up to Ari. "Abba, we are being attacked," he said urgently.

* * *

These were the words that Gudrid had been waiting to hear; the words pressing on her ear had the sound of victory.

"Where is the rest of the camp?" Ari asked, his expression desperate.

"They've been cut off. The river's flow has shifted; it's spilling over its banks and flooding the forest between here and the camp."

"Of course," Ari said. "The moon has raised the level of the ocean tide and it's raising the height of the river."

He seemed to gain some satisfaction from figuring out what was happening. But Gudrid knew that Ari didn't suspect the full extent of what was happening. The gold and other riches in the cave had blinded him.

Still, Gudrid could sense fear and desperation in Ari's tone when he asked, "Who is attacking us and how many are here?"

"No more than twelve. Abba, it is the others."

There was a loud inhalation and then Gudrid felt the grasp of the natives loosen on her arm. *Ari is now showing his true colours,* she thought; *he is a coward.* She considered escape, but worried about injuring her baby. Her eyes drifted to Ásgeirr, who was staring at Ari in loathing, his rage growing visibly by the moment. Suddenly, in one movement partially concealed by the darkness of the cave, Ásgeirr had his bow in his hand and an arrow out of his quiver.

"Stop!" Gudrid yelled—too late. Ásgeirr's face registered surprise as blood streamed from a stone dagger sticking out of the back of his neck. His knees buckled and his body sank to the ground as if all the life was slowly being let out of it.

Tostig's hand went for his sword.

Gudrid whirled toward Ari. "Let them try to save him," she begged.

"It's too late," Ari announced for all to hear, as if to prove his control over the situation. "The dagger's tip is poisoned. He will not survive."

Gudrid hoped that he was lying, but that hope was slim. Ásgeirr flopped forward onto the ground, his falling body taking her heart with it. Not only did she see a fallen man, but fallen kin.

Gudrid worried that with Ingibjörg and Ásgeirr dead, their risk of failure tripled. She needed a solution and she needed it immediately. Her typical strategy was violence and fighting her way out of a situation, but that would only get more people killed. She needed a nonviolent solution.

"Ari," a familiar voice yelled from the tunnel, "we need to call reinforcements or retreat."

Gudrid turned to see Adam walking toward them. The black and white robe of the Culdee had replaced his walnut-coloured monk's robe. He held a lance similar to the ones that the Culdee monks carried. "Adam, you snake," she hissed. "By all that is right, you will pay for your betrayal with your life."

"Please, Gudrid. Don't utter threats that you are not prepared to act upon," Adam replied with a superior sneer. "Your mission is a failure. Soon Thorfinn's plans for permanent settlement will be a distant memory, crushed by the death of his people and his wife, along with his unborn child."

"No, Ari! This is too evil, even for you," Freydis begged.

"When death is no longer part of your life, killing becomes easy." Ari pulled a stone dagger from a sheath tied around the waist of one of his native guards. He raised his arm and punctured the skin at his wrist, then drew the dagger along his arm to his elbow. As the skin parted and blood flowed from the gash, the flesh bubbled and the opened skin rejoined. He replaced the knife and looked back to the group with satisfaction. "I cannot be destroyed," he yelled, raising his wrist high above his head and showing it to those present. The natives quickly bowed in reverence.

"You are wrong!" a voice answered from the dark. "For every state there is an opposite and opposing one." The owner of the voice moved into the light.

"Dionysius!" Ari gasped. "You died!"

Dionysius raised his arm to show a healed wound. "No; you made sure I did not, by cutting me with the holy lance. By now you've witnessed its power."

Dionysius raised his other hand, clutching a wad of pages. "But in the Book of Kells lies the secret to reverse its effects. You are not immortal Ari. None of us are."

In one swift and fluid motion, Adam lifted the lance he was carrying and thrust it into Ari's back. Unlike the demonstration with the dagger, this time he writhed in pain. A small spot of blood appeared on Ari's robe and grew larger and larger. His gasps became louder and louder as the pain gripped him and the air leaked from his lungs.

Adam pulled the lance out, taking a piece of the blood-soaked robe with it. Ari crumpled to the ground.

Dionysius strode forward and stood over him. "The lance can also take away what it gives. You are not meant to have eternal life; no one is." He grabbed the tip of the lance that Adam held and scratched his hand with it, drawing blood. "Not even me."

The cavern shook with a tremor so violent, it ripped a boulder-sized section from the roof; the rock crashed through the cavern floor, leaving a gaping chasm. Water bubbled up, creeping toward the tunnel where the monks and Gudrid's group were gathered.

The natives dropped the gold they were carrying and ran to the cavern entrance. Some fell through cracks in the ground that opened beneath their feet; others were pinned by the rocks falling from the roof. Gudrid's captives let her go and ran for their lives.

Freydis and the others ran up to Gudrid; Adam joined them and they too headed out of the cavern.

"Adam!" Dionysius shouted. "Throw the lance into the cave. No one should possess it."

Adam stopped and snapped off the wooden shaft; he looked at the spearhead in his hand as if tempted to disregard Dionysius and keep it. Then he drew back his arm and threw the spearhead into chamber, to be buried with the rest of the subterranean city.

They turned and ran.

One by one they stepped out onto the crumbling ledge, their only means of escape to the solid ground of the forest above. The rushing river roared below them, hollowing out the rock face and pulling out dirt. Large boulders splashed down into the rushing river to be instantly consumed by the rapids below. Soon the ledge would be impassable.

A broad section of the ledge fell away before Tostig, in the lead. They were trapped.

"What are we to do?" Tostig yelled. "We'll be swept away by the river if we stay here."

Gudrid looked down at the river; falling in would mean certain death. Even if they survived the fall from the crumbling ledge, they could very well be dashed against boulders, or crushed by boulders falling on top of them.

"I am so glad that you are still one of us, Adam of Bremen," Gudrid yelled. "I will go to my death knowing that I will one day see you in Valhalla!"

"Or heaven." Adam smiled. "But it will not happen today."

Six ropes dropped from the cliff above. Whether they came down from Valhalla, heaven, or the forest above was not important. The only important thing was that each one of them grabbed onto a rope and held on tight. One by one, they were pulled from the disintegrating ledge and the rushing river to the safety of the mossy ground above.

"This is Taliriktug," Dionysius said when he'd been pulled up and helped to his feet by a squat native with a round face. He slapped the man's shoulder and smiled his gratitude, then looked at Gudrid and the others and warned, "We're still not safe. The network of caves beneath our feet is collapsing."

They ran through the forest without looking back or thinking; they ran on instinct over ground that shuddered and quaked as it collapsed all around them, sometimes buckling under their feet like a thin layer of ice on a frozen lake. Gudrid couldn't describe the sensation. It didn't split so much as give way. Then she was pitching forward, falling inexorably toward a gap widening before her.

The root system of a nearby tree broke her fall; she fell hard, but not hard enough to hurt herself. She gasped her relief, clutching a root, then opened her mouth in silent horror as the roots also began to sink.

"Gudrid!" Snorri, the closest to Gudrid yelled, leaping toward her. He fell short, and could only watch helplessly as she fell through the forest floor.

The others, alerted by Snorri's shout, stopped and turned back.

The roots supporting Gudrid cracked and groaned, about to give way at any moment; she tried to find a firmer purchase but her questing fingers slipped over the wet and slimy surface. Snorri reached down into the hole and grabbed Gudrid's wrist. "Don't let go of me!" she screamed.

"I won't, but you will have to help me pull you up," he said. "Can you give me your other hand?"

The others arrived to help; Jarlabanke and Tostig held onto Snorri's body and Freydis reached into the hole to grab Gudrid's other wrist.

Below her dangling feet, the ground crumbled away as water bubbled through growing gaps, then heaved and disappeared into the rushing underground river. "Oh no!" Gudrid yelled, looking over her left shoulder.

"Gudrid, what is it!" Freydis screamed.

"Let go of me!"

"What? No!"

"Let go of my wrists!"

Gudrid managed to wrestle free of Freydis's grip, but Snorri hung on, the strength of his grip cutting off her circulation. "Gudrid, we're trying to save your life. What are you doing?" he pleaded.

"Please Snorri, trust me." Her tone was frantic. "I know what I'm doing!"

Snorri looked at Freydis in disbelief.

"If you don't drop me I will be killed," Gudrid begged. Snorri, without another thought, released her.

* * *

Snorri watched helplessly as Gudrid splashed into the black water below. Seconds later a wave of incredible force and height moved past the hole, followed by a smaller surge that heaved over the edges of the hole, then subsided.

Snorri jumped up and took off his weapons and shed any clothing that would slow a swimmer down, then jumped into the hole. Black, murky water and silence engulfed him. The frigid water numbed his fingers and within moments the slightest rubbing of his clothing stung his skin.

His mind focused on one goal: find Gudrid. What a loss to the future of his people if he failed, Snorri thought. But where to look? If Gudrid were anywhere, she would be as deep as possible to avoid the surface current, in a place where she wouldn't be dragged away from the hole. Once the wave passed, the water should rise high enough for them to reach the hole, and return to solid ground. Silently congratulating Gudrid for her ingenuity, Snorri kicked wildly, pushing himself deeper and deeper into the water.

There was only one problem with this plan: there was no guarantee that they would find the hole again.

He glanced upward. The setting red moon provided a surrealistic doorway through the murky water. He relaxed, but only for a moment as he felt the tug of the current. Finding the hole might not be the problem; keeping themselves from being swept away from it would be. Once they surfaced, they'd have to use the underside of the rocky ground to stabilize themselves and keep from being swept away by the rushing river.

* * *

On the surface, the others watched the hole for any signs of Gudrid or Snorri, hoping that their wait didn't turn into a vigil for their two companions.

One of the natives approached with a torch. Freydis grabbed the light and leaned over the hole, hoping to see movement under the water or to provide a beacon for their friends to follow back to safety. She saw nothing.

She was about to lose her sister and friend, Freydis thought. She knew that, the more time that passed, the closer Gudrid would come to death . . . and the next thought was too horrific to think of, even with her warrior mentality—the death of her unborn child.

In desperation, Freydis reached into the hole and waved her arm back and forth in the water. She touched something—a garment, then flesh—an arm. Wrapping her fingers around the limb, she reached in with her other hand, risking being pulled in. Seeing this, Jarlabanke grabbed her legs, anchoring her.

Heaving with all her strength, Freydis pulled. A hand broke the surface of the water.

"Help me!" she yelled.

The others reached in and grabbed whatever their hands encountered. Snorri surfaced—still breathing, but nearly unconscious. His long, ginger curls were plastered around his face. Even with everyone's help, Snorri was heavy. They heaved again.

"Gu . . . drid," he whispered.

Freydis let go of his arm and reached beneath the water once again. She followed Snorri's arm to another wrist, held tight in his grasp. *Gudrid,* she thought, and pulled.

As the others dragged Snorri away from the opening, Dionysius plunged his arms into the water beside Freydis's and wrapped them around Gudrid's chest, lifting her by her armpits. The gathered natives reached out as she burst from the water and swung her legs around onto the ground.

"Gently," Freydis urged, "she is with child."

They placed her on a soft bed of moss near Snorri. No one moved for several moments. They stood over her and stared, saying nothing. Her shallow breaths were almost unnoticeable. Her body was in shock, but she was alive. She sputtered, then coughed up water in heaving gouts, inhaling loudly before releasing another loud explosion of saliva and water.

Freydis helped her sit up. Gudrid's head flopped forward. Her eyes slowly opened and she looked around at their faces, half-concealed by the night and shadows. She smiled. Then her smile faltered. "Snorri," she whispered. "Snorri saved me."

"Yes, Gudrid. He is right here," Freydis whispered in her ear.

* * *

Gudrid looked around and saw Snorri lying several feet from her, his matted hair stuck to his face. He was looking at her. When he met her gaze he slowly moved, trying to rise up on one elbow, but he collapsed back onto the ground.

With Freydis's help, Gudrid managed to pull herself closer to Snorri. "My friend," she said, hoping he could hear her. "I knew that my child's name would be Snorri, and now I know why." Snorri's mouth managed to curve in a smile, and his breathing calmed.

"We're still not safe," Dionysius said.

As if the ground had heard his warning, another quake shook them to their feet. Gudrid staggered over the mossy ground, hoping that her next step would not be the one that plunged her back into the subterranean river.

Once they were a safe distance from the destruction, the group paused and looked back. The ground had an almost fluid quality to it, shifting and bending like the World Serpent's back. Rocks millions of years old rose, then slowly sank back into the ground as the surface collapsed. The forest exploded in ear-shattering geysers of rocks, water, and plants. The heaving ground was like a giant's chest, rising and then exhaling with an inhuman roar, sending rock and plumes of water high into the air.

The cliff over the river was unrecognizable, permanently altered by the quaking and shuddering. Without a substrata to support the ground, what the raging river did not take, the earth swallowed whole.

"The treasure is lost forever," Gudrid said.

"Perhaps, but I think it's still there . . . somewhere," Snorri replied.

"My people," Taliriktug said, "on Vinland will attack your people."

"How do you know this?" Gudrid asked, thinking of Thorfinn.

"We've watched your people's comings and goings for many years now, on Vinland and here on Markland. Your presence is a threat to our way of life—to both the Culdees and the people of this land."

"He's telling the truth," Freydis said.

"But the Culdee presence is a threat to your people as well," Tostig said.

"Yes, but while you threaten to conquer . . . as it may look on the surface, the Fathers of the Lord's people and this land's people co-exist. We accept each other and live harmoniously. We've left the basest part of our religion behind. There are new rules here . . . to survive, our way of life must change."

Adam looked surprised. "I wasn't expecting this admission," he admitted when Gudrid gave him a quizzical look, "but I am not surprised that it would come to this. In a land where the Irish monks were so hopelessly outnumbered, they were not in the position to force their beliefs onto a larger and unwilling body. And from what I know of the Culdees, why would they?"

Dionysius nodded. "The act of suffering defines and exemplifies our love for our doctrine. A display of force would permanently change that delicate relationship and irreparably destroy any hope of redemption." He rested a hand on the squat native's shoulder. "Taliriktug's people are leading the attack against your people. We were under the impression that your intent was conquest, and that an attack was our only option, rather than risk more of your people landing on Vinland and overrunning the natives of this land."

"Is it too late to stop the attack?" Gudrid said.

"It may be possible," Taliriktug said, though he sounded uncertain. "Once warriors have risen to madness, it is difficult to break off the attack."

"We have to try. Our people will not survive. There are too many of you," Gudrid said.

"Yes, you are correct," Taliriktug agreed. "But it was not us who started this. We are concerned only with our people and protecting our lands. You think that we look on you as gods; we do not. We have our own gods. We know that you are flesh and blood like us."

For the first time in all the years she had travelled back and forth to Vinland and Markland, Gudrid knew that Taliriktug was right. Her people were the strangers and they had taken it upon themselves to pursue this course without regard for the peoples affected. The natives extended their hospitality as far as their code of ethics allowed, but once crossed, it was difficult to re-ignite their trust. Now she understood Thorfinn's principle to peacefully coexist with the natives. Coexistence secured the future of both peoples. There had been too much conquest and destruction for too long. That destruction needed to be performed in a framework of creation, as well.

In nature, destruction and creation existed in a union where destruction created abundance. This lesson was all around them, Gudrid realized, but in the midst of human events, it was ignored, or mistaken for weakness, just as the natives were often seen as an inferior people that needed to be tamed, conquered, shaped into something useful.

Thorfinn was right, she thought; as the land thrived, so did the people inhabiting it.

"It will be us who will end this," Taliriktug added. He headed for the river. The others closely followed.

Adam scrambled in behind Gudrid as the natives launched their boats into the river. Taliriktug and Jarlabanke also climbed into their boat and grabbed paddles.

"Gudrid, it was never my intention to betray you or the group," Adam said as Taliriktug and Jarlabanke began paddling the boat downriver.

"Yes, I know."

"I had ventured upon Dionysius, a monk from Helluland, who took me to Taliriktug and his people and the few Culdees who were against Ari and his plan for domination of this land; I originally thought that I was walking into Ari's camp." Adam's voice dropped. "I learned that Ari's plans of domination extended as far as our homeland, and possibly the known world."

Gudrid watched Taliriktug expertly move his paddle in and out of the water.

"Dionysius told me of Ari's power-hungry plan to take control of the Culdees. When some revolted, they were banned from the group, and he ordered the allied natives to hunt them down and kill them. But Ari underestimated the love that their cohabitants had for the Culdees. They joined the rebel monks and formed an opposing force that planned to one day fight Ari and destroy him."

"Until we came along," Gudrid said.

"Yes. When they saw us, they realized that I would be the perfect one to infiltrate the Culdee camp and find the Book of Kells and the holy lance. I was unknown to Ari and the rest of the Culdees. Together, we devised a plan to infiltrate Ari's camp, gain his trust, and set the stage for an attack. We knew that the final battleground would not be in the woods of Markland, but under the forest, in the treasure cave. There Ari would be at his most vulnerable."

Gudrid could see the wisdom of the plan. Ari would be drawn to the treasure and his greed for the gold would blind him to all else. His only known adversary would be their group of six people—hardly a threat to him. And with Adam seemingly on his side, his authority would be all the more substantial. "His overconfidence was his downfall," Gudrid said. "I see how Dionysius and you used it to your advantage."

They'd reached the mouth of the river. Taliriktug didn't show any signs of tiring. He kept up the same pace as he paddled over the ocean waves.

* * *

Taliriktug listened to the two Europeans talking as he moved the boat through the water. In the twenty years he had been on Markland, he had become much more knowledgeable in their ways. In his mind they'd transformed from gods to friends, as was the case with Dionysius, and hated enemies, like Ari—Ari, whose machinations split the tribes into two opposing factions.

He didn't want to make it generally known among the immediate group, but he feared that those wanting vengeance for the death of Ari might soon join the battle they were speeding to stop. He needed to end the fighting before it escalated into something that would kill most of the tribes of these lands. He didn't care about the Norse. In fact, any alliance with them was convenient for the moment, but would eventually live out its usefulness.

* * *

Ahead of them in the open water, Gudrid saw a flotilla of small boats waiting for their group to join them. It appeared that Dionysius and Taliriktug were not taking any chances; they'd made sure reinforcements stood ready to assist their lead party, if needed.

The mass of boats parted and allowed Dionysius's and Taliriktug's boats to glide past them to take the lead. Then the natives took up their paddles and began struggling against the strong ocean current. The group slowly shaped itself into a triangular formation, just like flying geese. Those in the rearmost boats had the important job of keeping a watchful eye on the rear, in case they were attacked from behind.

Gudrid focused on the distant line of land ahead, washed by glowing sunlight under a white-dotted sky. *Thorfinn is under that same beautiful sky,* she thought, *fighting for life and glory. And fighting for a child that he does not yet know exists.*

She feared her world changing. For the first time in her life she feared the absence of the world that she knew, and most of all, she feared for the life of her third husband and the future of herself and her unborn son within her. She had survived the previous losses but she didn't know if she could or wanted to try to endure another loss in her life.

Our son, she thought. She allowed her emotions to absorb that word. She knew that the human being growing inside of her would be a boy, her son. Her visions were very powerful and very clear. She saw the face and the blonde hair of the child, as if she could reach out and stroke it. She knew that it was her son. She smiled and for a second was able to forget that on the other side of this body of water, her Thorfinn was fighting for his life, and for the lives of his people and their future.

"How long will it take us to get back to Vinland?" Gudrid asked.

"Hard to say, but we will be there soon. The ocean is pushing us farther and farther down the coast," Taliriktug answered.

Gudrid paused, afraid to ask her second question. She pushed her fears aside and asked anyway. "Will we get back to Vinland in time? I mean, in time to stop the attack by your people?"

Taliriktug did not have to answer; his look spoke to her. Anything he said would only be verbal confirmation of the truth—nothing more.

"It is too late. I know my people have already attacked."

It was not the answer that she wanted to hear. Always, in the human mind, there is some hope drifting below the surface of consciousness that things are different than how our fears shape them to be. But she knew that Taliriktug spoke the truth.

Live in the present, she told herself. She knew that Thorfinn wanted to believe in the past and to allow that to dictate his future, whether it was the immediate or the long-term future. Gudrid allowed the past to influence her but never to dictate the present or replace the future. The future would come whether she feared it or not, so why not look at it as positive, and at present events as how things should unfold?

Her ability to *see* was a gift that allowed her to accept the future. She wished that all of her people could have the same sight. They'd discover that what they really feared was the fear of not knowing rather than what may or may not happen. Destiny was the means to the end, not the end itself.

The shoreline slowly grew, from a vista that was easily managed by the human eye to one overfilling the human senses. Moving dots littered the surface of the land like ants moving grains of sand. She instinctively extended her hand to clasp Freydis's, then remembered that her sister was in the other canoe. With no one to comfort her, she relied on herself and her sight for comfort.

Her ability to *see* had always allowed Gudrid to avert danger and harm before it affected her or those closest to her. She needed to reaffirm her abilities, and most importantly, reaffirm her faith in those abilities.

Thorfinn will be fine, she thought. *He has good and loyal people with him. They will fight to the death protecting his dream and the dream of a new land for our people.*

Thorfinn had the superior firepower. Weapons of metal, crafted to fight men with armour-protected chests. His men were skilled warriors who had trained for years and fought many times; they were more than capable of protecting themselves from any aggressor.

But the reality of the situation between the Norse and the natives was that it was like a pack of wolves attacking a bear. For all the skill and firepower of the Norse, they lacked the intimate harmony of the natives. They were much more communal than her kin was; neither economics nor status separated these people from each other. There were neither slaves nor masters, merchants or landowners; all were connected on a fundamental level. She understood because she too was connected on this same level. But unlike her people, the natives formed a network of intuitive connections.

They reached the rocky shoreline. In the not too far-off distance, she heard the cries of battle, the sound of metal shattering thin spears into splinters.

* * *

A Norseman of indomitable stature and strength wrestled with three native attackers—one on his back and two others attacking from the front, jabbing at him with stone daggers. Although their stone blades did not penetrate too far into him, trickles of blood coalesced to run down the back of his neck in a wide swath, and down his forehead into his eyes. The wolves' teeth bit many times into their enemy.

His attackers were intentionally weakening the Norseman, similar to riding a buffalo and striking it repeatedly until they could easily strike the finishing blow. On a larger scale, this was the strategy of the entire native army: to weaken the Norse and then conquer them or chase them off. All were expendable for this common goal.

Another Norseman watched as his kin fell under the natives' onslaught, their struggling bodies disappearing in the tall grass of the meadow. He took some comfort from knowing that his final resting place would be among these long blades of trampled and battle-worn meadow grass.

His quiver had emptied out quickly. There were so many natives that he couldn't miss, no matter how badly he aimed. They didn't employ any means of protection, shield or otherwise, so he'd had a fifty-fifty chance of inflicting either a superficial or lethal wound.

They were killing and being killed for trees; he couldn't believe it—trees! Gold and other precious metals were worth killing for, but trees were just trees.

Two natives ran toward him with their spears raised, ready to attack. Their eyes pierced into his soul, ripping through his flesh as if they could reach in and tear it out of his chest. He absentmindedly reached into his quiver—empty. He pulled out his sword, ready to strike.

His body leaned to the right, partly deliberate, partly an unconscious reaction. He simultaneously swung his weapon. The point cut a bloody line across the throat of the first native and lopped the head off of the second one. Blood spurted from a severed artery as the headless corpse toppled at his feet, spraying blood over his legs and shoes.

The other one had enough life left in him to hurl his spear, point-blank. The Norseman reached for the shield at his side—too late. The spear pierced his leather armour and lodged between his ribs. With his waning strength, he thrust his sword into the native's stomach, then pulled it out.

In the corner of his eye, he saw another native attempting to sneak up on him. Using the momentum created in pulling his sword from the fallen native, he swung the edge of the sword into this new foe.

He looked down at the spearhead lodged in his ribcage. Blood stained its base and soaked his tunic. He pressed his hand against the wound, managing to slow the blood flow only a little. Desperately, he looked around for help from one of his kin; no one was near. They were all busy defending their own lives.

The final blow had been struck; he fell to his knees, and his attackers swarmed over him, thrusting their daggers in and pulling them out, ripping out the last of his life.

ᚾ

One by one the canoes beached on the Vinland shore and they leaped over the sides to the rocky shoreline. Gudrid's eyes immediately lifted to the raging battle. She heard the war cries of her people and the crack of metal splitting wooden spears. Metal and wood clattered in harmony as the Norse fought as one unified fighting force.

The battle was not going to well for them. The inferior firepower of the natives was not a factor in this fight. It was raw manpower that mattered, and that was something that her people did not have on their side.

In the minutes that she stood on that shore, slowly gazing from left to right, she knew that battle tactics were not going to save her people. Retreat or truce were their only options left for survival. She looked at Taliriktug in desperation. "Can you do anything?"

Gudrid guessed that Ari's rise as a self-proclaimed leader had split the tribes of this land into opposing factions; tribes that were once friends and allies were now blood enemies; families fought against families in bloody retribution for crimes committed against one another and their kin.

Gudrid glanced at Taliriktug. She was slowly beginning to understand the effect that her people had on the native society, an effect that would last for hundreds of years to come. One non-native in this land was a curiosity, something for the community to look at in wonder. Ten were enough to upset the balance of power and their communal and pastoral existence. One hundred or even two hundred threatened the existence of the entire native civilization.

Even though it was much more temperate than Grœnlandia, life in this land was harsh enough. The growing season was too short to rely on crops so the natives moved where the food went, following the herds and living on its rocky shores for fish, even sometimes going without the traditional food if the year was not a good one. But they still survived.

Then strangers started coming, beginning with the robed Culdees who initially refused their daughters as gifts and had nothing to trade because their god did not allow them to possess anything. But they lived in peace with the natives, took what they needed from the land without over-harvesting its resources, so they were welcomed as kindred.

But then her people, the Norse, came and took everything without giving back. They remained strangers, which was confusing and in opposition to the way the natives lived. They went too far, until the patience and kindness of the natives was stretched so far that war seemed the only recourse, something that they'd managed to avoid for time out of mind.

* * *

Taliriktug scanned the battlefield, searching for the chiefs or even their Firsts, commanding the tribes, of which Taliriktug counted several. Minor differences in their war paint, their clothing, even the colour of the feathers they wore in their hair, identified the warriors' tribes.

"I do not see the chiefs," he said after a moment.

He climbed onto a rock and looked beyond the sweat-covered Norse splattered in the blood of his people. Standing on a rocky outcrop at the far edge of the battlefield were three men in elaborate headdresses. Their stance and posture exuded tribal nobility. "I think I see them, Gudrid," he said, pointing. "Standing on those rocks."

"We must go to them. We must tell them that they have to stop."

"Gudrid," Freydis interrupted, "you are staying with me, in safety. I will not allow you to endanger your life again."

"I will not be told to choose between my husband and my child," Gudrid snapped.

"There is nothing you can do, Gudrid. You will be killed," Freydis insisted.

Gudrid turned to the man of heroic stature behind her. "Snorri, can you see Thorfinn?"

Snorri lifted his chin and scanned the battlefield. "No, Gudrid, I can't. I'm sorry."

Gudrid seethed silently. She didn't know what that meant. Was Thorfinn at some safe location? Was he lying in the tall grass of the meadow, bleeding? She couldn't deal with questions that she couldn't answer right now. She held her stomach and prayed to the first god that entered her consciousness. As usual, it was Óðin, the wanderer with whom she had felt a kinship since her childhood. *Please,* she silently said, *you've taken two husbands away from me. I cannot bear to have my son brought up a stranger to his father. Could you not exclude him from fighting the final battle . . . for now?*

The battle became a veil that was pulled aside, and she saw, yes, a field occupied by fighting natives and Norsemen, but also a clear pathway between the point where she stood and where the chiefs stood; she need only take the first step onto that path across the battlefield.

Gudrid dropped her pack to the ground and stepped onto the path.

"Gudrid, what are you doing?" Freydis screamed. "It's too dangerous." She grabbed her arm.

Gudrid managed to wriggle free of Freydis's caring clutch. However much Freydis feared, she had to trust Gudrid's ability to see things that others could not.

Freydis didn't attempt to grab her again.

As Gudrid walked into the battle, her presence did not go unnoticed by the Norse. She knew of their unspoken duty to protect the non-warriors on the voyage at all costs, especially her, Thorfinn's wife. Some warriors glared at her, questioning her sanity in this matter, but they couldn't deny the bravery that she exhibited. She walked into the fighting at a steady pace; her sword remained in its sheath, at her side.

"Gudrid, go back," Brönfóldr pleaded while hitting an attacking native with his shield. "It is too dangerous! You will be killed!"

Gudrid's focused movement across the battlefield was

distracting, to say the least. All the Norse warriors knew who she was and the importance of protecting her. Seeing their opponents' reaction to this single female moving across the battlefield, the natives sensed her importance, and concentrated their efforts on getting to her.

Gudrid heard her heart pounding in her eardrums and the beating of her unborn baby's heart echoing it. The salty Vinland wind blew across her face. But anything else around her was lost in the ether. It was strange, seeing mouths opened in screams that were not heard, wooden shields hitting bodies in silence. *Is this what it is like to die?* she wondered.

The fighting around her changed into a waking dream; the warriors became translucent, and watching the battle was like watching a reflection in a pool of water. She saw the action in front of her as well as what was happening beyond, below the surface.

On the other side of the battlefield, Thorfinn and his senior warriors protected the structures of Leif's settlement from natives trying to set the grass roofs on fire with a continuous stream of flaming arrows. Thorfinn and his men held them as far back as possible, trying to push them farther back, beyond the range of the arrows. They were fortunate; the third line protecting the Norse settlement quickly extinguished the arrows that did hit their targets. The other arrows were either blown off course by the ocean wind or guttered out in mid-air.

"I am not a warrior," Thorfinn kept repeating to himself. "I'm a man of commerce. I do not want to do this." His anger went into the swing of his broadsword, which struck a native on the back, nearly cleaving him in two.

They will set the entire meadow on fire, Gudrid thought; *don't they see what they are doing?* They risked not only the land that they relied on for growing food and foraging wild berries, but the animals they hunted that the land sustained— not to mention their own lives.

Gudrid didn't fully discount the idea; it was a plan that she tried desperately to get out of her head. To set the entire meadow ablaze was a destructive and evil thing to do, a tactic that, unfortunately, was popular among her people; they called it blazing. When Norse armies gave up fighting, knowing that they could not win the battle, they would set the land ablaze, preventing the enemy from either gaining a stronghold or pursuing the fleeing Norse army. The act was stupid, óvitr for two reasons she could think of. It didn't guarantee victory—the battle could be easily fought somewhere else—and it was uncontrollable; a warlord could wipe out his own army as well as the enemy, not to mention the land that he was attempting to conquer. Warrior trust could easily falter and be permanently lost with such a desperate battle decision.

Thorfinn was defending everything that he had worked so hard for over the last year—the homes of his friends that they'd rebuilt, and the excavated land where the permanent fort would one day stand. Blazing would be the furthest thing from Thorfinn's mind.

* * *

Thorfinn quickly examined his troops. They were brave to defend what they had worked so hard for in the last year; he was very proud of them. But as he looked into the heart of the fighting, something was not right. He couldn't quite understand why, but there was a calm where there should've been tension; the imbalance was not threatening, but bothersome, especially when his people were intently engaged in battle.

Then . . . he saw the source of his unease.

Someone was walking through the centre of the battle, surrounded by fighting Norse and natives. She moved like an apparition across the meadow, as easily as an eagle would fly though the air. At first he thought it was a being from Valhalla. Then the figure walked out from behind the layers of battling men, and he saw Gudrid calmly walking toward him . . . smiling.

Thorfinn's initial shock switched to reflexive action. He jumped, bashing a native in the head and shoulders with his shield to knock him out of the way, leapt over another whose body had dropped moments earlier, and hit another with the flat side of his broadsword.

"Gudrid," Thorfinn yelled as he stomped over the bodies of two more natives; his sword flailed in front of him, propelling him closer to Gudrid.

Anger intermittently interrupted his desperation, mingled with worry and fear; his mind raced from one emotion to another. What was she thinking, putting herself in jeopardy like that? Where were those who had promised to protect her: Tostig, Snorri, Ingibjörg, Ásgeirr, and Freydis, who were supposed to be her friends?

But in his milliseconds of reason, Thorfinn noticed that, as

Gudrid walked toward them, the fighters immediately in front of and alongside her opened a narrow pathway through the sea of thrusting and swinging swords. As they hacked off limbs, as blood shot and sprayed in all directions, as spun flails struck the soft, tanned faces of the natives, Gudrid walked by unscathed.

Thorfinn plowed through the front line of the flank he and his men fought to maintain. He wasn't a warrior so he didn't think in warrior terms; his instincts told him that in a way the threat was not the natives, but him and his people. Like every other community, including the Norse community, this one had rules and protocols that needed to be followed; they had ignored them, and they were now paying the consequences.

Thorfinn now saw the arrogance of believing that he could create a community, a country, and even an economic empire on the tip of this peninsula. He saw the effect of that human failing right before his eyes.

He looked above Gudrid, and gasped. A native warrior had climbed over two men fighting behind her in close combat, a sharp-edged rock tensely clutched in his fist. He was bearing down on his intended target—Gudrid. Thorfinn knew that he couldn't reach her in time, and his fighters, so severely outnumbered, were already struggling to keep the fighting away from Gudrid.

With a quick hand signal, Thorfinn instructed Gudrid to move out of the way. Then he hurled his broadsword, desperately hoping that his aim was as good as he thought. The sword twirled through the air and struck his target in the side of the head, hard enough to knock the native off balance; he toppled to the ground and lay there motionless, stunned and bleeding from a gash on the side of his head.

Gudrid was picking herself up off the ground, careful not to get in the way of any of the fighters. Thorfinn ran forward and grabbed her around the waist and picked her up. Cradling her in his arms, he carried her away from the centre of the fighting.

"Gudrid, my love, it's so wonderful to see you," Thorfinn puffed. He frowned. "Have you gained some weight? You seem a little heavier."

"Yes, I have, and it's your doing, Thorfinn," she said, smiling.

"Do you mean . . . ?"

"Yes, our child."

Thorfinn felt another surge of adrenaline pulse through his body. His heart pounded, but this time with joy rather than anger, courage rather than fear. But as with all impulsive emotions it began to subside and the reality of caring for and being responsible for a helpless human life damped the initial euphoria.

Thorfinn set Gudrid down behind a clump of bushes in a copse of trees that offered some protection from spears and arrows and any native attacks that broke through Thorfinn and his men. Then he returned to the fighting.

* * *

Gudrid watched Thorfinn leave. Her thoughts shifted from worrying about him to hoping that Taliriktug had safely made his way to the chiefs and convinced them to end the battle for the sake of everyone.

She thought that maybe she could use her powers to influence the chiefs. If they listened to what she had to say, then perhaps they could come to an accommodation—the Norse would leave Vinland in exchange for sparing their lives. There were too many native warriors for the Norse to overcome in battle. If both sides could not live in peaceful co-existence, then eventually the fighting would wear her people down to the point that their existence was threatened.

Life on Vinland was over for Thorfinn and her. She would not return to this land again. She could see far enough into the future to sense that much.

She looked out through the clump of bushes toward the rock where the chiefs stood. From her vantage point she couldn't see their faces, but their headdresses could not be missed; they towered at least another fótr above the chiefs' heads.

She knew that she'd be all right, walking behind Thorfinn and the others. The natives could not harm her. Her dreams and waking dreams had shown her surrounded by fighting, and she'd known that even though she was a part of the fighting, she remained separate and safe from its effects. This had to be that battle. Whether the outcome was good or bad for her or the Norse, she knew that things were unfolding the way they should.

"Gudrid!" a female voice yelled behind her.

Gudrid wasn't sure if she heard her friend's voice over the battle happening nearby, or if she merely sensed her presence. She looked behind her and saw Freydis running toward her, holding her shield up over her head to protect her from the arrows that were being fired at her. She even dispatched a native or two running across her path with a quick swing of her axe.

"Gudrid, I am here, to stand by your side," she announced when she stopped, panting, before Gudrid.

Gudrid didn't know what to say. Freydis's gesture was an honourable one, but she didn't think that she needed the protection. Gudrid's visions of this day revealed that this was her path; she wasn't sure why, but she was confident that it would be revealed to her sometime soon. "Freydis, you are my greatest friend, my sister and my protector. But this is something that I must do alone."

Freydis started protesting, but Gudrid raised her hand to quiet her. "I know you are concerned and fear for my life and my baby's life. We have seen too much death, you and I, but please believe me—just as I safely walked across the battlefield, I will safely return."

She gave Freydis a brief hug. Then she stepped out into the meadow. She didn't look back.

The battle had not reached this far. The stalks of wild wheat were upright and bowing from side to side in the wind. Showing no fear, with her head raised high, Gudrid walked toward the rock where the chiefs of the three tribes stood, overseeing their warriors.

Neither their sight nor their posture wavered. The numbers they commanded gave them confidence. As Gudrid approached these men of power, she knew that they would not find a single female threatening. At the opportune time she would disarm herself and approach them with open arms.

As Gudrid drew closer, she could see some of the features of these warrior leaders. They were slender and tall, even without their headdresses. Their chins jutted proudly. Tattoos lined their foreheads, and the hair on the front half of their heads had been shaved, enhancing their wide skulls. She wondered if these cosmetic enhancements enforced the illusion of larger heads and therefore smarter leaders. They did seem majestic and powerful as they observed the force that threatened their life in Vinland.

Three warrior guards near the chiefs noticed Gudrid and raised their spears. She stopped and raised her hands in front of her chest, then slowly moved her hands down her abdomen to her sheathed sword. Slowly, she pulled it out and dropped it on the ground. With her hands raised in front of her, she walked closer to the triad of leaders.

One of the leaders shouted what sounded like an order to the guards; they backed away immediately and lowered their spears. Gudrid took it as a sign that she was allowed to approach. She stared up into their faces as she did, never taking her eyes off them.

The chiefs stared at her in astonishment. Then one of them slowly opened his arms and his expression changed from aggression to acceptance. He began talking in the language of his people.

"I can't understand . . . I-I don't . . . " She gave up in frustration.

"I can help," Taliriktug said from behind her.

"Taliriktug, I am so glad to see you!" Gudrid exclaimed. If the warrior guards did not trust Gudrid, she knew that they'd trust her now, with the arrival of Taliriktug. She stepped to one side so Taliriktug could stand beside her, then watched as he spoke to the chiefs.

* * *

Taliriktug turned to the chiefs and bowed.

"How do you know this woman?" the Beothuk chief, Wabanip, demanded.

"This woman saved us from the villain, Ari," Taliriktug replied.

"This woman is our tribeswoman, Yakima" Wabanip retorted. "We saw her die in childbirth two seasons ago, right before our eyes; our medicines could not heal her."

"With all due respect, Chief Wabanip, this is Gudrid, wife of the Norse leader who arrived here on a large ship."

Gudrid touched his arm. Taliriktug turned to her and relayed their conversation so far.

"Tell him that I did see a woman at our settlement," said Gudrid. "In the longhouse I had a vision: a woman in a kirtle, with a band around her head, appeared. Her hair was brown, her face pale, and her eyes like those of the chief's people. I asked her to sit down and we tried to communicate, but there was a loud crash, and she disappeared. I looked out the door but I didn't see her; a commotion distracted me—one of Thorfinn's men had killed a native who tried to steal weapons."

Taliriktug took several minutes to translate Gudrid's story. As he did, the chiefs' expressions changed from intrigue to surprise and then to understanding.

"I see this as an omen. This brave woman has risked her life and the life of her child to save her people. We must call off the war," Wabanip said to the Micmac and Wendat chiefs. Both leaders nodded in agreement.

Taliriktug turned to Gudrid. "They will call off the fighting."

Wabanip nodded to one of the guards, who picked up a horn and set it to his lips. His cheeks puffed out as he blew into its wooden mouthpiece.

Over the sounds of the battle—the clash of weapons and the cries of the injured and the wails of the dying—the horn bellowed, to the top of the sky and back again. Gudrid covered her ears. And again—another loud boom reverberated over the battlefield.

As quickly as the Micmacs, Wendats, and Beothuks had begun their attack, they retreated. Some of the Norse tried to continue their attack against the retreating natives, but they were either too injured or too battle weary to be effective. The native warriors melted into the woods, leaving their dead and wounded on the battlefield. The Norse who were still mobile dropped to their knees, shoulders sagging in exhausted relief.

The three chiefs turned and climbed down the rock without looking at or acknowledging Gudrid or Taliriktug. Then Wabanip stopped and turned back to them. "You may stay till your child is born," he said. "Then you must leave our land forever. Tell your people that they must never return."

He turned and walked after the other chiefs.

* * *

Gudrid nodded numbly when Taliriktug relayed this ultimatum to her, then she turned and looked back at Thorfinn. He was approaching her, not really angry, but she noticed that he didn't look too pleased with her for leaving the protection of the bushes.

He reached out and pulled her into a hug. "I thought I asked you to stay behind me, Gudrid. I believe one day you will cause me to drop dead from fright," he said.

Freydis joined them, followed by Tostig and Snorri. Gudrid acknowledged them with a nod, then turned back to Thorfinn. "We cannot stay here, Thorfinn. The chiefs will allow us to remain here only until Snorri is born."

"Snorri?" Thorfinn said, lifting an eyebrow.

"Yes." Gudrid's hand fell to her stomach. "It will be a boy, and his name will be Snorri. After the man who saved my life."

All eyes turned to Snorri Thorbrandsson, who looked back with a sheepish look on his face. Thorfinn approached him in such haste that Snorri stumbled back a few steps, confusing his advance as aggression.

"You are from this day forth my kin," Thorfinn announced. "Wherever you are, know that you will always have a home at Brattahlið."

"And a sister," Gudrid added.

"And a sister." Freydis echoed.

"My son." Thorfinn was grinning, his tone musing. "I'm going to have a son." Then he turned to his navigator and said briskly, "Tostig, how soon can you build a ship that will take us home?"

"With the crew and all hands helping, I could have a ship built in two tvö misseri."

Thorfinn nodded. "As soon as we get back to the settlement, begin organizing the people and the resources."

Gudrid touched Thorfinn on the shoulder; when he looked at her, she tried to read his expression. Under his mask of confidence, she saw disappointment and dejection. She understood why. This voyage had been an expensive venture for him. To return only with the meagre resources that he'd managed to harvest from Vinland was a loss that he would have to bear over time. The embarrassment of returning to his own people unsuccessful—at least in his eyes—was a blow to his ego. And her announcement of a baby must've added to his worries. She knew it would take a while for Thorfinn to get through it. But she was confident that he'd recover; he was energetic and strong. They would both get through it together.

"I didn't get a chance to ask you," Thorfinn said as they led their people back to the settlement, "was your Markland mission a success?"

She thought about it, mulling over in her mind whether she would reveal the details of that trip to him or wait for another time. Her near-death experience and their discovery of the treasure cave . . . Thorfinn knew and respected her previous life. His question went as far as his concern for Gudrid's safety.

She smiled. "That will be a tale best told later," she said.

She didn't mind his methods. This was how couples

communicated in areas that were sensitive; it was like taking a pot of boiled water off the hearth. Carelessness could spill the cauldron, causing pain. And when accidents did happen, burns healed . . . some sooner than others.

When they arrived at the settlement, men were still dousing the smoking roofs with buckets of seawater. They were happy to see the fighters returning, and especially Gudrid and the rest of the Markland group.

"This is a triumphant day," Andor yelled from his perch. "We are victorious in battle."

Gudrid didn't have the heart to tell them how the battle had been resolved. They'd hear of the events that took place in the last few hours soon enough.

"Gunnor, Anniken, when you put those fires out, come down here," Tostig yelled.

Tostig looked happy to be back in their temporary home. Gudrid met his eye. "Will you miss this?" she asked.

"This?" Tostig swept his arm out, encompassing the settlement in the gesture. "I was happy navigating the *Mimir*."

Gudrid knew better. Tostig, like everyone else, had nothing. For all the work that they had done, there would be no sharing in the riches and the resources of the voyage. He hadn't come on the trip merely for the glory of travelling on the back of the great Serpent, or to share in adventure; he'd come for one thing, and one thing only—for the money.

"You are different now, Tostig," Gudrid said. Like all of them, he'd be going home a different person. He'd earned Thorfinn's trust, and his mates respected his authority. There would be no whispers and snickers from the crew when the diminutive Tostig stepped up to the knarr's bearing-dial on the trip home.

Tostig shrugged. "Such is life. You never step in the same river twice."

Gudrid looked at Thorfinn. "We're going home."

Thorfinn nodded, eyes on the shoreline. Gudrid followed his gaze, watched the surf advance and recede at what seemed like a snail's crawl, much like the hopes and expectations of Thorfinn and the crew. Standing next to him with her hand on her stomach, Gudrid prayed to the gods that they would leave Vinland unharmed.

Gudrid put her arm around Thorfinn's waist. "I wanted to make sure you are all right."

"I'll be all right. I was just thinking about all we had lost."

"Lost?" Gudrid questioned. "We've traversed an ocean, we've seen a new land, and we've encountered new peoples. What have we lost? We have gained, my love."

Thorfinn hugged her to his broad chest. The wind caught the tall grass and set it dancing. "Perhaps you are right. If we came to Vinland for more than conquest and wealth, then we have been successful. Now that this new land is known, perhaps more people will seek it out. And this endeavour will not be lost."

GLOSSARY

Angakkuq: wise one

Ásgarð: home of the gods and Valhalla.

Baldur: Norse god of light = so handsome, wise, and bright that light shone from him.

dagsigling = a day's sailing

dœgr (dægurs): defined in the ancient Icelandic work on chronometry called Rímbegla as "In the day there are two 'dœgr;' in the 'dœgr' twelve hours.

fótr: foot (measurement)

Histoplasma capsulatum/ histoplasmosis: a respiratory disease with symptoms like those of influenza that is caused by a fungus (Histoplasma capsulatum) and is marked by benign involvement of lymph nodes of the trachea and bronchi or by severe progressive generalized involvement of the lymph nodes and tissues (as of the liver or spleen) rich in macrophages

Hustrulinet: a universal Scandinavian symbol of the wife. Sometimes worn as a headband.

iViking: the term "**i viking**" means to go raiding; this means that you are *going* to raid a specific place, most common on land or ships.

Kjalarness: The place name where Thorvald was buried.

landvættir: land spirits

Ljüs-álfr: Light Elf

Mánuðir: month

Maungarpok: "come in"

meiðmarhellir: treasure cave

Miðgarð: Middle world inhabited by men.

misseri: actually a composite with an etymology corresponding directly to "half-year."

norðr: north

Óvitr: ignorant

Qallunaat-Aaari: non-Inuit

Quyanaghhalek tagilusi: thank you

ragna-rokkr: "the twilight of the gods"

suðr: south

Sunnundœgr: Sunday

Túnlengd: "Homefield-long," the length of an enclosed homefield. A short distance.

tvö misseri: two semesters (instead of "one year").

umiak: Inuit boat

viknatal: week—literally, counting of weeks

Wodnesdæg: Woden's Day—Wednesday